'With feisty heroines and rich period details,
Jensen is one of the best historical writers around.'
The Bookseller on *Sigrun's Secret*

'Written with economy and verve,
it's terrifically exciting stuff.'
Amanda Craig, The Times on *The Girl in the Mask*

'Any girl in her early teens is going to love this.'
The Bookbag on *The Lady in the Tower*

'Lose yourself in an enchanting world.'
Bliss magazine on *The Girl in the Mask*

'Jensen's storytelling is enthralling.'
The Scotsman on *Sigrun's Secret*

'I loved this so much . . . utterly wonderful.'
Waterstones bookseller on *The Lady in the Tower*

'I was left with a real sense of having been there
myself, and can offer no higher praise than that.'
Philip Ardagh, The Guardian on *Between Two Seas*

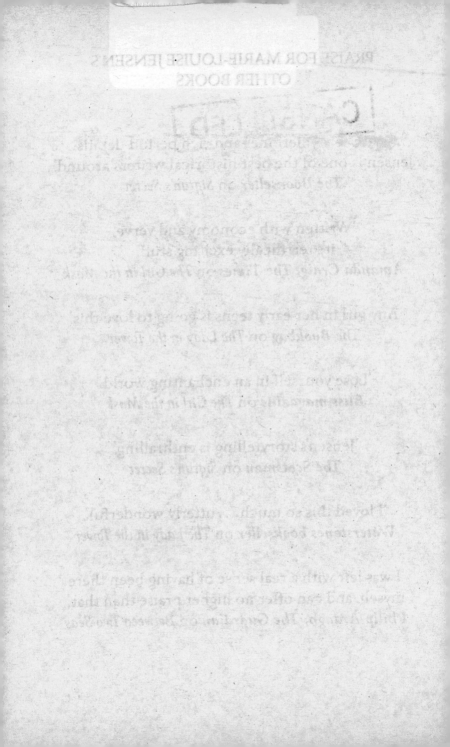

Smuggler's Kiss

Smuggler's Kiss

MARIE-LOUISE JENSEN

OXFORD
UNIVERSITY PRESS

OXFORD
UNIVERSITY PRESS

Great Clarendon Street, Oxford OX2 6DP

Oxford University Press is a department of the University of Oxford.
It furthers the University's objective of excellence in research, scholarship,
and education by publishing worldwide in

Oxford New York

Auckland Cape Town Dar es Salaam Hong Kong Karachi
Kuala Lumpur Madrid Melbourne Mexico City Nairobi
New Delhi Shanghai Taipei Toronto

With offices in

Argentina Austria Brazil Chile Czech Republic France Greece
Guatemala Hungary Italy Japan Poland Portugal Singapore
South Korea Switzerland Thailand Turkey Ukraine Vietnam

Oxford is a registered trade mark of Oxford University Press
in the UK and in certain other countries

British Library Cataloguing in Publication Data

Data available

ISBN: 978-0-19-279280-8

1 3 5 7 9 10 8 6 4 2

Printed in Great Britain
Paper used in the production of this book is a natural,
recyclable product made from wood grown in sustainable forests.
The manufacturing process conforms to the environmental
regulations of the country of origin.

For Ann

A Smuggler's Song

If you wake at midnight, and hear a horse's feet,
Don't go drawing back the blind, or looking in the street.
Them that asks no questions, isn't told a lie.
Watch the wall, my darling, while the Gentlemen go by!
  Five and twenty ponies,
  Trotting through the dark—
  Brandy for the Parson,
  'Baccy for the Clerk,
  Laces for a lady, letters for a spy,
And watch the wall, my darling, while the Gentlemen
 go by!

Running round the woodlump if you chance to find
Little barrels, roped and tarred, all full of brandy-wine,
Don't you shout to come and look, nor use 'em for
 your play,
Put the brushwood back again—and they'll be gone
 next day!

If you see the stable-door setting open wide;
If you see a tired horse lying down inside;
If your mother mends a coat cut about and tore,
If the lining's wet and warm—don't you ask no more!

If you meet King George's men, dressed in blue and red,
You be careful what you say, and mindful what is said.
If they call you 'pretty maid', and chuck you 'neath
    the chin,
Don't you tell where no one is, nor yet where no
    one's been!

Knocks and footsteps round the house—whistles
    after dark—
You've no call for running out till the house-dogs bark.
Trusty's here and *Pincher's* here, and see how dumb
    they lie—
They don't fret to follow when the Gentlemen go by!

If you do as you've been told, 'likely there's a chance,
You'll be give a dainty doll, all the way from France,
With a cap of Valenciennes, and a velvet hood—
A present from the Gentlemen, along o' being good!
    Five and twenty ponies,
    Trotting through the dark—
    Brandy for the Parson,
    'Baccy for the Clerk.
Them that asks no questions isn't told a lie—
Watch the wall, my darling, while the Gentlemen go by!

Rudyard Kipling

CHAPTER ONE

✴

I stood motionless in the darkness, looking out to sea. Dark waves with arching white crests were breaking on the shore before me. The water tore back from the shingle after each wave with a fierce rattle before crashing back onto it. It was like a hungry beast trying to devour the beach. To my left, a short way out in the bay, a black stone archway towered over the waves.

It was a chill, autumnal night. An onshore wind blew my long white veil straight back from my head. It tugged and fluttered to fly free. My white lace petticoats and my pink silk skirts flapped frantically around me. The sharp shingle bit into my silk-stockinged feet. I ignored it all and stared hopelessly into the darkness. Despair swept over me; hot tears poured down my cheeks. I let them fall unchecked.

I'd done what I'd had to do to rescue my family. I'd played my part. They were safe. But I couldn't face the life that was my end of the bargain. I'd thought I could bear it. But what I'd discovered today had changed all that. I now knew I'd been wrong.

Still weeping, I sank down onto the cold shingle, casting aside the pink shoes that I'd been clutching tightly in my left hand. Without any clear intention, I began to scoop up handfuls of damp shingle. I took the hem of my petticoats in my hand to form an apron and began to fill it with stones. My tears continued to run down my cheeks, cooling swiftly in the sharp wind. My petticoats grew heavier and heavier on my lap. At last I swiped the tears from my eyes with gritty hands and struggled unsteadily to my feet. I clutched the heavily-laden petticoats to me. Blackness as impenetrable as the night filled my heart and obscured all my thoughts except the need for flight.

'No one can deny me the right to escape,' I whispered to myself. The wind tore the words from my lips and flung them away. What I was about to do was wrong by every law of man and God, but I couldn't see a choice. There was no other way out of my predicament. Shaking with fear, but determined, I stepped deliberately forward. One, two, three steps before the first wave washed over my feet. I was shocked by the cold, but didn't allow it to deter me. I walked on, half sliding down the steeply-shelving shingle bank. I was calm now; focused. My breathing was unsteady, but I walked on, ignoring the pain in my feet, the icy chill, somehow keeping my balance on the steep slope, despite the powerful tug and swirl of the sea around my legs.

My shimmering brocade-silk gown grew heavy about me and I fought to hold on to the heavy load of shingle I carried in my petticoats. It kept me steady, my feet on the bottom. Without it, the waves would have picked me up and tossed me about. I walked on, gasping as the waves smacked me in the face, until at last I was completely submerged. The water was dark and still around me; the rattle and swish of the waves muffled.

It was frightening and lonely under the water. I held my breath as long as possible, staring into the murky gloom as though it mattered whether I could see anything. How ridiculous, I thought. Death is always lonely, and it doesn't matter that my eyes are darkening. Soon my suffering will be over.

My air was running out. My lungs were crying out to breathe. I fought the urge, forcing myself to stay quite still. But my body, young, healthy, full of life-force and potential, was screaming at me. *Don't do this*, it shrieked. *I want to live!*

My body battled my determination to drown. My instinct to breathe was so powerful, it overruled every other consideration. It freed the petticoat from my numb, unresisting hands, allowing the stones to rush away to the sea bed. Without them, I rose up like a cork and bobbed on the surface of the storm-tossed sea.

The first breath of air was the sweetest, most beautiful thing I'd ever known. A noisy, inelegant gasp of sheer desperation. The second was half salt water, causing me to choke and sag back under the surface. My gown and petticoats were sodden now, the air gone from them. Their weight was dragging me down.

What a reversal. I now fought the downward pull, thrashing frantically in the water, to keep afloat, to keep breathing that sweet air. Nothing could be more important than that. But I was no swimmer. I'd never learned how. And so it was a battle I swiftly began to lose. It was bitterly ironic that now I no longer wanted to die, I couldn't save myself.

I was already swallowing salt water and sinking below the surface when something caught in my hair and tore

3

at it. If I'd had breath to cry out, I'd have done so. If my arms hadn't been weighed down by the weight of my brocade silk sleeves, I'd have tried to pull free. As it was, I just gritted my teeth and endured the pain, still fighting my losing battle to stay above the waves.

Except that now it was no longer a battle. Somehow I was able to breathe. Something was dragging me backwards. I fought against it, terrified. Stories of sea monsters, sirens, and wicked mermaids rushed over me.

'Hold still, yer fool, we're tryin' to help!' shouted a rough voice in my ear. Then my back banged into something hard, and I was scraped upwards and tumbled into a crowded wooden rowing boat.

At first I could take in nothing, think nothing. Every part of me hurt. I was coughing, spluttering, and choking up sea water. Someone held my head firmly over the edge of the boat while my body rejected all the water I'd swallowed. When the paroxysm was over, I hung on the side of the boat, noisily gasping the fresh air into my lungs.

'Quiet now!' ordered a voice behind me. I struggled round in my heavy, sodden gown to see who'd spoken. I could make out little in the darkness, but he looked like a fisherman. He was wearing a smock and a coarse petticoat over his breeches and his face was strangely blackened. Only his eyes gleamed.

'I nearly drowned!' I told him indignantly, my voice hoarse. 'I can't help it.'

Speaking made me cough again, a hacking, gagging fit. The man grabbed me and clamped his hand over my mouth. I thought I was going to suffocate and squeaked my protest.

4

'Stow it or we'll 'ave to knock you on the 'ead,' he ordered fiercely.

I tugged uselessly at his hand, but made no more noise, drawing the air I desperately needed through my nose only. I was angry and confused. What was a rowing boat doing out in the bay after dark? And what on earth did it matter what noise I made out here?

The rowing boat bobbed up and down in the swell while the wind chilled my wet garments. None of the men in the boat were actually rowing, just sitting quite still, oars at the ready. All had the same blackened faces. They seemed to be waiting for something. It was very strange. I wondered if perhaps they were fishing, and this was how it was done. How would I know?

One of the men gave a hand signal; the others went to work with the oars. The small boat stopped bobbing idly and shot forward. We headed along the coast, the swell making me giddy as it pitched us about. We reached the furthest end of the beach as far as I could make out. Dark cliffs were looming over us. We turned about and headed straight for the shore. A breaker picked us up and shot us forward in a roar of foam and spray. I moaned with fear. The hand, which had relaxed a little, tightened over my mouth again.

Then the water dropped away beneath us and we crunched onto the shingle. Three men leapt out and heaved the boat out of the churning waves.

Everyone looked around, staring blindly into the darkness. I could feel the tension in the man who was holding me. At last there was a slight movement in the shadows. One of the men growled: 'Cousin Jacky's arrived.'

'He's hearty welcome,' was the response, and a dark-lantern was unshuttered to our right. A collective sigh of relief rose up. I was abruptly released and collapsed in a heap in the bottom of the boat, breathing heavily. I thought about climbing out of the boat and running away, but when I tried to get up, I found my legs were completely tangled up in the heavy, soaking layers of my petticoats. I couldn't move.

By the light of the single lantern, the men in the boat shipped their oars and started hauling heavy, roped barrels out of the boat and passing them to the men ashore. It was all done with practised speed, efficiency, and almost no speech.

'More boatloads on the way, but the Philistines is lurkin',' growled the man who'd been holding me.

'We'll give 'em a little distraction,' responded a man on shore, barrels slung over his shoulder. 'Over beyond the door. Make 'em think we've warned you off. Meanwhile we'll get clear by way of Scratchy Bottom.' Their words meant nothing to me. They might as well have been speaking Latin. 'What you got there?' he asked, pointing to me. 'Mermaid?'

'Maybe,' said the man who'd been holding on to me. 'Jacob just fished her out the sea. Can we leave her with you?'

The man looked appalled. 'We can't have no dainty wench screeching and holding us up!' he whispered fiercely. 'The place is crawling with Philistines!'

'You deal with her,' said another man on the shore in a hoarse whisper.

Then men were all around the boat, pushing her out into the waves once more. She lifted, climbing the crest

6

of a wave and dropping down the far side of it. The wind was bitterly cold. I started to shiver uncontrollably in the bottom of the boat as the men pulled on the oars. Water slopped about, drenching me each time the boat tilted. If I'd expected any sympathy, I'd have been disappointed. None of them so much as spared me a glance.

Facing the stern of the boat, my eyes adjusted gradually. I watched the shore draw steadily further away. Across to my right, high up, I saw golden flames shoot up suddenly, licking the darkness. Somewhere below the fire, a shot was fired and voices came faintly to us.

'That's the decoy,' called a man in the prow. 'Signal the other boats they're safe to go ashore.'

I turned and watched as another man lifted a lantern aloft and sent a beam of light out to sea. Once, twice, thrice it flashed and then he covered it again. 'What's going on?' I asked. 'Where are you taking me?'

'You'll see soon enough.'

I pulled my knees in to my body and wrapped my dripping arms around them, in a vain attempt to stop the violent shudders of cold that were passing through me. It crossed my mind that I had indeed drowned in the sea, and was now being ferried to hell for my crime. But I soon dismissed this. I was bitterly, bone-chillingly cold, and ravenously hungry besides. My throat was raw with coughing. I was certain that a dead person would feel none of these things.

Other rowing boats passed us silently in the darkness. At last a dark shape loomed above us, and the men shipped their oars, fending off against the towering side of a wooden ship. Above me in the gloom I could make

7

out the white lettering that bore the name of the ship: *The Invisible*. It sounded like a ghost ship. I shivered.

A rope was thrown down to us and made fast. A barrel was lowered from above. 'Hold hard!' my captor called up. 'A mermaid to come aboard!' The men around me guffawed. I bit my lip. As far as I was concerned, I was in the middle of a tragedy and all they could do was laugh.

Faces were hanging over the side of the ship now, staring down at me through the darkness. A rope ladder unravelled, and was caught deftly by one of the men in the boat.

'Up you go,' said the captor. I stared at it. The ladder dangled precariously, swaying to and fro against the slimy side of the great wooden ship. It was a very long way to the top.

'I can't!' I objected. My voice shook. 'I can't climb up that thing!' I was out on the sea in the dark, surrounded by rough men. I ought to have been terrified. But the whole scene seemed unreal; dreamlike.

'Course she can't climb it,' said my captor, slapping his forehead and pulling a face. 'Mermaids ain't got no legs, 'ave they, lads?'

There was more muffled laughter. Another head leaned over the rail far above us. 'What's this racket?' he demanded in a low voice that was vibrant with anger. 'Haven't we got the Preventers after us? You should be keeping silence.'

The largest man in the boat stood up, broad shouldered and bearded, swaying easily with the rocking motion of the boat and said quietly: 'Pass her here then. I'll take her up.'

'No, please, I . . . ' I began. The fear I should have felt before rushed over me now as I was picked up, tipped upside down, and slung over the giant's shoulders. I shrieked with terror as he swung himself onto the bottom rung of the ladder.

Someone grabbed my hair and twisted it. 'Silence from you!' he hissed in my ear. 'Or you get knocked on the head and dropped back in the sea. And don't think I don't mean it!'

''Old on, pretty mermaid,' added the man who was carrying me. 'Me hands'll be on the ladder, so it's up to you to cling fast.'

And then he swung himself up and out of the boat, climbing with astonishing agility up the swaying ladder. I clutched at his coat with the last of my strength, terrified he would drop me.

CHAPTER TWO

✳

I was dumped unceremoniously on the wooden deck and crouched there, terrified. Three pairs of eyes were watching me, while the other men lowered cargo down to the rowing boat. The giant of a man who had carried me up the ladder was still looking at me, stroking his beard thoughtfully, as was the fierce-eyed man who had hushed us from the ship's rail. Besides those two, a much younger man, scarcely more than a youth, was regarding me suspiciously. He was small-er and slighter than the other two. For a moment, I thought he was a gentleman. He was dressed like one, in breeches, a white shirt, and a waistcoat. However, as he turned away briefly to check on the men low-ering the barrels, I saw I must be mistaken. He wore his own fair hair caught back in a ponytail in the nape of his neck. No gentleman would be seen in public without a wig.

'What's this then, Jacob?' barked the man in charge, his voice as fierce as his eyes.

'A mermaid, we reckon, skipper,' responded the giant. 'We found her in the surf. Me and Kit hauled her out.'

'More fools you,' snapped the skipper. 'You should have left well alone. She'll bring trouble on us.'

'But she were drownin', skipper,' objected Jacob. 'We couldn't leave 'er.'

'She can't be a mermaid then, can she?' The fair young man had a cultured voice, quite different to the others around him, which confirmed my first impression of him. 'Mermaids don't drown.'

'I don't have time for this nonsense,' cried the skipper. 'You take charge of her, Jacob, or she'll have to go back over the side. You've five minutes then I need you back to work.' He turned abruptly away and joined the men at the rail.

I turned my eyes apprehensively on the man called Jacob, my heart hammering in my chest. 'Please,' I whispered, my voice shaking. 'Don't . . . '

The giant chuckled, a rich, reassuring sound. 'Don't you worry. Come along of me now!'

He held out his hand and pulled me to my feet. I tried to follow him across the rocking deck. After only a few unsteady steps, my chilled, shaking legs tangled in wet fabric and gave way under me. Seeing this, Jacob scooped me up in his arms and carried me in through a doorway into a tiny cabin. It was lit only by an oil lamp, burning faintly, suspended from the ceiling. He pushed the door shut behind us, and abruptly the noise of the wind and waves vanished. My ragged breathing sounded harsh and loud in the comparative silence. The only other sound was the soft creaking of timbers around us as the ship rolled in the swell.

'You need to get out of them wet clothes afore you gets sick,' said Jacob, lowering me onto the floor, his voice startlingly loud in the confined space. A new danger reared its ugly head. I backed away into the wall, still shivering violently, wrapping my arms tightly about me.

Jacob chuckled again, and stepped past me. 'Don't take that the wrong way,' he said. 'You're safe with me.' He pulled a rough wooden chest out from under the bottom bunk, opened it up and started rummaging through it. 'We've got no ladies' togs aboard, o' course,' he muttered, pulling various items from the sea chest. 'I reckon this'll have to do. Here you are!' He held out a pile of clothing to me. When I didn't take it, he put it on the floor next to me. 'Get dry,' he ordered me. 'Get wrapped up and warm. I got to go now, but I'll be back.'

He left the cabin, letting in a blast of wind and noise. I shuddered again. I was so cold. I reached out one shaking hand and touched the bunk next to me. The wood felt solid enough. So did the walls and the wooden lid of the chest too. I rested my fingertips on the garments Jacob had left for me. They were coarse and yielding to the touch.

I wasn't in a dream then. Nor did this seem to be a ghost ship. Everything was too substantial. Shudders of cold racked me again and I twisted round, trying to reach the hooks on the back of my gown.

I don't know how much later it was that a sharp rap sounded on the cabin door. When I made no reply, the door opened and the fair young man blew in from the deck, letting the door bang shut behind him. He stood and stared down at me.

'What the devil are you doing lying on the floor and still in that wet gown?' he demanded.

I tried to speak, but the lassitude that had stolen over me was too strong. I'd stopped shivering and got warm at last. What was this young man doing disturbing me? I just lay there, letting my eyes sink shut again.

Footsteps made their way to me. I forced my heavy eyelids open again when I felt my hand taken. The young man was on one knee beside me, a frown on his face. 'You stupid girl, you're half frozen! Do you *want* to die of an inflammation of the lung?'

I tried to tell him that I didn't care; I just wanted to be left in peace. All that came out of my mouth was a sleepy mumble. To my annoyance, he took hold of my arm and began rubbing it briskly. I tried to ignore him, and recapture the stillness. 'Rouse yourself, girl!' he ordered me loudly, shaking me. 'You'll die if you lie here like this!'

'Warm . . . now . . . ' I mumbled.

'You're no such thing! That's death speaking. Your lips are blue!'

Hadn't I been *trying* to die earlier? I could barely remember any more. I couldn't think what I wanted. But not this dreadful, painful awakening. Anything but this.

The young man pulled me upright, shook me and chafed at my hands. They tingled and burned unpleasantly, waking me up thoroughly. I began to cry, softly at first and then noisily, as a sense of unfairness and of misery swept over me. I was shivering and cold again.

'For pity's sake, stop crying! Why didn't you get out of these wet clothes as Gentle Jacob told you?' demanded the sharp, insistent voice.

'I can't . . . reach the . . . hooks,' I managed to reply, my voice slurred.

13

'Don't be so stupid! How do you usually undress?' he demanded, his voice impatient.

'I *don't*!' I cried; properly, uncomfortably awake now, my indignation as great as his. My hands and feet were burning. 'My *maid* undresses me . . . of course!'

We stared at one another, and for a moment he looked so thunderous, I thought he was going to slap me. But instead he turned me roughly away from him and began unfastening my gown.

'This is the one and only time I'll be your lady's maid, you spoiled brat,' he snapped. As soon as the hooks were unfastened, he went to the door. Pausing there, he spoke once more: 'Get dried and changed and be quick about it, for I'll be back in a few moments to see you've obeyed me.'

'I can't!' I sobbed. 'My fingers . . . so numb . . . they won't . . . work!'

He stood there, staring at me with a heavy frown. At last, with a sigh of exasperation, he returned to my side. 'There's no woman on board,' he told me, 'and the men are all busy. You'll have to make do with me.'

As he spoke, he hauled me to my feet where I swayed dizzily. 'You can't . . . ' I muttered, with a half-hearted attempt to push him away. 'Not decent.'

'Do you care most about decency or survival?' he demanded. I gave up. I had no strength to fight him in any case. He peeled the wet fabric away from my chilled body and dropped it on the floor of the cabin. The lace petticoats followed, layer by soggy layer. When he reached the hoop he gave an impatient exclamation. 'What is this?' he demanded.

'My hoop?' I asked groggily.

14

'Good Lord. How the devil do you take it off?'

I fumbled numbly at the buckles and tapes. My fingers were so chilled and unresponsive to my commands that he soon pushed my hands aside and took over the task. I stood before him in my shift, and numb as I was, unreal as all this felt, I blushed deeply. 'Don't . . . ' I murmured, ashamed, wrapping my arms around myself, anxious lest he intended to remove this last protective layer.

'I have no intention of stripping you naked,' he said mockingly. 'Trust me; it would be no pleasure at all.' He picked up the blanket Jacob had laid out and threw it around my shoulders, rubbing my arms through it so that the coarse wool chafed my skin.

'That hurts,' I protested.

'That's because the blood's beginning to circulate again,' he told me. 'I'm going to turn away now. Can you strip off that wet shift by yourself and put on these clothes instead?'

I nodded miserably and as he turned his back, I struggled to do as he said with clumsy hands. The shirt was rough, but clean and dry. It reached to my knees. I wrapped the blanket over the top. 'I'm done,' I said at last. My voice was very faint.

'What about the breeches?' the man asked, seeing them still lying on the bunk.

'They are for men.'

'Of course they are. What did you expect? Only men sail on this ship.'

'I didn't ask to be here,' I retorted weakly.

'Are you saying you wanted to be left to drown? That's what would have happened.'

I turned my face away and felt a hot tear steal down my cheek. My former misery overwhelmed me again. Very slowly I nodded.

'You should be ashamed of yourself,' he told me fiercely. 'People bear far greater troubles than you and don't give up.'

'You know nothing of my troubles,' I told him disdainfully. I was starting to feel stronger.

In reply, the man held the breeches up before me. 'Put your legs in here, and then hold them up to your hips, pull this flap between your legs to the waistband and button them *here* in front and *here* at the side. Do you understand?'

I looked away, colouring painfully with embarrassment.

'I'm going to find you some stockings. I knew you'd be work and trouble! They should never have brought you on board.'

He left the cabin, banging the door. Reluctantly, I buttoned the breeches on, fumbling with the unfamiliar fastenings. Even alone as I was, I blushed furiously at the indecency of putting on a man's garment. One that had been worn before, what's more. No girl should be called on to do such a thing. Once so scandalously clothed, I sat down on the lower bunk, my legs too weak to bear my weight for long.

When the man returned, he had woollen stockings in his hand. He knelt beside me and rolled them onto my legs. 'What's your name?' I asked him.

'I'm Nick to you,' he replied brusquely. 'The less you know, the better for us.' He fastened the first stocking below the knee with a garter. Gentlemen wore silk and fastened them above the knee. I felt insulted at being dressed as a working man, but didn't dare say so. The fabric was rough and scratchy, but I didn't dare complain about that either.

'You're rude and unpleasant,' I told him instead. 'What have I done? I didn't ask to be brought here.'

'I'm helping you, aren't I?' was the only answer I got. 'There you are, your *lady*ship,' he said with withering sarcasm as he tied the second garter. I turned my face away and bit my lip. Tears were close to the surface again, but they didn't cause my tormentor to relent. He simply got up and left.

I curled up in a ball on the rough bunk, wrapping the coarse blanket around me. My throat was aching from the salt water and my eyes were stinging. I felt lonelier and more miserable than ever in my life before and heartily wished I'd drowned.

The next thing I knew, my head was being lifted and a soft pillow slipped under it. I couldn't open my eyes properly, but saw a blurred glimpse of Gentle Jacob through my lashes, his face no longer blackened. A heavy, warm cover was laid over me and the world darkened.

CHAPTER THREE

✳

I dreamed of a door in a dark corridor. Something hideous was concealed behind it. As it began to slowly swing open, I ran forward, heart beating with dread, and slammed it shut again. At once, I awoke to find bright sunlight in my face. I shielded my eyes with one hand, and made out three dark shapes standing looking down at me. I sat up groggily and yawned. Every part of me ached.

'Where am I?' I muttered, rubbing my eyes.

'Halfway to France,' was the reply.

'*What?*' I demanded, thunderstruck. The events of the day before came rushing back to me: the near drowning and the men on the ship. 'But I don't want to go to France!'

'Got somewhere important you need to be?' demanded the fair young man. When I was silent he added: 'You don't have any say in the matter,' in a satisfied voice.

'Leave be, Will,' chided Gentle Jacob. 'There's no call for hard words.' He was leaning his massive shoulders against the door frame, watching me.

So the young man's name was Will. I glanced at him and saw him scowling at Jacob. 'Nick,' he said crossly. 'Or better still, no names at all.'

'What does it matter?' I asked, puzzled.

The skipper leaned back against the wall, his eyes on me. 'We need to get a few things straight,' he said. 'First things first. Who are you and what were you doing in the sea last night?'

'I'm . . .' I remembered my dream, and shame and pain choked my words in my throat before I could utter them. Did I want these men to know my story? They would no doubt consider it their duty to hand me back. I was desperate to avoid being sent back to the situation I'd fled. I sat silently, my sleep-drenched mind battling to think straight and to come up with a tale that would make them help me.

'Yes?' prompted the skipper. All three men were watching me. All looked interested, but only Jacob looked kindly.

'My name is Isabelle,' I said. I turned away, unable to tell them the truth.

'And?' asked the skipper.

'I'm an orphan,' I said after a long pause. 'So lonely and unhappy that I no longer wanted to live.'

Jacob looked sympathetic, the skipper frowned, and Will rolled his eyes. I glared at him and he shook his head, a scornful sneer curling his lips.

'Where are you from?' asked the skipper. 'I know most people living along this coast.'

'I'm not from around here. And I'm of age,' I said.

Will snorted disbelievingly. 'Twenty-one?' he demanded. 'You liar!'

The blood rushed to my face. I knew I looked older than I really was, but clearly not six years older. 'It's the truth,' I tried to insist.

'That gown you were wearing last night,' said Will. 'It looks costly enough to be a bride gown. Am I right?'

I shook my head, vehemently, my lips tightly pressed together. I saw Will look down at my left hand. I experienced a moment's panic and looked down at it myself, ready to whip it out of sight. But the fingers were bare.

'You've run away, then? Did you leave a note with anyone, saying what you planned to do?' the skipper asked.

'I . . . no . . . '

'Any sign of where you'd gone?'

I cast my mind back, wondering where his questions were going. 'I don't think so,' I said.

'Your shoes?' asked Will. 'What did you do with your shoes?'

'I . . . must have left them lying on the beach.'

The three exchanged glances. 'There won't be any hue and cry,' said the skipper. 'They'll assume she's drowned.'

'Aye,' agreed Jacob with a slow nod. 'It's likely safe enough.'

'But she's some rich man's daughter!' exclaimed Will. 'Just look at the clothing she was wearing. It cost more than most people earn in a lifetime. There'll be a hue and cry, trust me.'

'Not if they think she drowned. No point.'

There was a long silence. I wondered if they were planning to drop me over the side out at sea if there was no one to miss me. Fear caught at my throat. In the bright light of day, dying was no longer an attractive proposition. I wanted to live. I was just opening my mouth to tell the truth, when the skipper spoke again.

'We got a problem, see,' he said. 'It isn't so easy just to let you go.' He turned and looked around at the other two. 'What we going to do with her?'

There was a hideous silence, during which I started to feel sick. 'She'll not harm us,' said Jacob.

'You don't know that,' said Will swiftly. 'We can't possibly trust her. She's already lying to us. Can't you tell? How do we know she won't turn King's Evidence the moment her feet are on shore?'

'King's Evidence?' I asked swiftly. 'You're doing something contrary to the law?' Will sent me a fierce look and the skipper scowled. My suspicions were confirmed. I considered the possibilities and my eyes widened with surprise. Admittedly my knowledge of the sea was limited, but there were only two possibilities that I knew of: privateering without a licence or smuggling. And given the sneaking around in the dark, last night . . . I caught my breath as everything I'd seen so far clicked into place. 'You're *smugglers*?'

It all made perfect sense. I'd heard of smuggling, of course. Everyone had. Not having lived on the coast, I knew almost nothing of the way smugglers worked. But I could guess enough to make sense of barrels being unloaded at the dead of night. I also knew that I was in far greater danger than I'd realized. Smugglers were cutthroat rascals who defrauded the king of his revenues. They were a desperate lot, by all accounts, and thought nothing of violence and murder.

'That ain't what we call ourselves.' Gentle Jacob's voice rumbled deep in his chest. 'We're Gentlemen o' the Night.'

'I prefer free-traders,' replied the skipper.

'For God's sake!' The words burst angrily from Will. 'Stop confiding in her! She'll be our undoing!' His fists were clenched tightly at his sides.

'She knows it anyways, Will,' sighed the skipper. He shook his head reproachfully at me. 'Wisdom, my girl, is learning when to speak out and when to keep quiet.'

There was a knock at the cabin door. The skipper went to answer it. After a low-voiced exchange, he returned to us.

'The men want their say,' he said. He looked back at me, unease in his face. 'This ain't the Royal Navy,' he said. 'On board this ship, every man is equal and we all have a say in decisions that affect us.'

'Every man,' I said. 'What about a woman?'

'That will depend on the vote. 'Tis a pity. I can see ways you could be useful to us.' He looked at me, frowning, for a moment and then pulled a scarf from his jacket. 'You'll have to be blindfold until the vote is taken,' he said.

I submitted and then was led out of the cabin. My legs shook.

I could smell the fresh air and feel the warm sun on me, but could see nothing at all. It was disconcerting.

'Listen to me now, my friends,' the skipper began. 'We have a grave matter on our hands. As you know, Jacob and Kit was moved by impulse last night to rescue a mermaid.'

There were chuckles as he said this, but they swiftly died.

'I'll say nothing of the rights and wrongs of what they done. We all has moments when the Lord moves us to mercy and maybe it's right we should listen to those.'

'Aye, but this girl here could compromise all of us!' exclaimed a voice. 'We got our safety to consider.'

Every story I'd ever heard about ruthless smugglers crowded into my mind. They would cheerfully kill me to keep my mouth shut, I knew. Will would, I felt sure; he seemed to positively hate me. All my dependence was on Gentle Jacob living up to his name and speaking for me. Or perhaps the skipper, who thought I might be useful. How could I be useful to a smuggler gang? I dreaded to imagine what he might be thinking of.

'The case is this,' said a new voice. 'She knows what we does. She's seen some of us and our ship. She's a witness. We're all men who depend on secrecy for our work.'

'We hear you, Hard-Head Bill,' said the skipper. 'Does any other man have aught to say on this subject? Slippery Sam?'

'We all knows what we does with informers,' Sam said in a loud, uncouth voice. 'Jacob never ought to done what he done last night. Saving girls is not a job for them as needs to stay secret. Many of us got families what depend on us and we can't take no risks.'

My heart beat fast with fear. Would they all be so pitiless?

'Sly Pete!' called the skipper.

'You needn't think these are the men's real names,' hissed Will's voice in my ear. 'They know better than that and protect themselves well.'

I nodded. 'I wouldn't tell . . . ' I said. A disbelieving snort was my only reply.

23

'Free trading carries the risk of prison with it,' said Sly Pete. 'We know that. Murder, though, that's another matter. I've no hankering for the rope's end, nor to be gibbeted at the crossroads neither. I say we find a way of being rid of her what doesn't involve killing.'

'Noted,' said the skipper. 'Next? Boney Ben?'

I heard muttered laughs. 'It won't be murder,' he said. 'Nothing'll be proved ever. Jacob took her out of the sea. Putting her back won't be no different to if he never had. And a corpse don't tell no tales.'

At first I listened in a calm, detached way to these rough men discussing my fate. Then the realization dawned on me that this was *me* they were speaking of. I was on trial for my life. This was no court with legal gentlemen in wigs and a trained judge, however. And I had no defence. Only a rabble of unwashed criminals baying for my blood.

'The sea had claimed her!' shouted yet another voice. 'If we cheat the sea of its dues, it'll take another. We all know it's the truth.'

'That's superstition!' shouted another man.

'Don't interrupt,' the skipper said. 'you'll get your turn, Kit.'

I started at his name, because he must be the man who'd helped Jacob pull me from the water last night. I wished I could see him.

'But you can't leave a girl to drown. It ain't Christian!' shouted Kit, despite the captain's warning.

After many views had been expressed, the skipper said, 'I guess we should vote then.' His voice was tight.

'Wait!' I cried, indignantly, trapped and blind behind the black scarf. 'Don't I get to speak?'

The captain hesitated, and then pulled me forward.

'Make it brief.'

'I didn't ask to be rescued last night,' I began uncertainly. 'I was trying to end my life, though I knew that was wrong.' I paused and bit my lip, realizing my confession could make them ask me *why* I should attempt such a thing. That was the last thing I wanted. I rushed back into speech hoping to cover up my slip: 'But things look very different in the morning light. I was deeply mistaken to despair. I owe you all a great debt for rescuing me.

'I swear to each one of you that if you let me go now, I will never betray you. I'll forget I ever saw a single one of you. I'll swear it on the Bible. Please. Let me go!'

I heard only low mutters in response. I had a bad feeling about the outcome of a vote. Slowly I sank to the deck, shaking so much I could no longer stand. They were going to kill me. I was going to die. And for someone who had been eager to embrace death just a few hours before, I was ridiculously terrified. I bit my trembling thumb until I tasted blood. I was so absorbed in the horror of what was happening to me, I scarcely heard that Gentle Jacob had started speaking.

'I be thinking of the hidey hole at Studland,' he said calmly. 'No one ain't seen that ghost for a while. I heard tell the Philistines have been sniffing round it. And even the children ain't scared to go play there no more.'

'Stick to the point, Jacob,' interjected Will impatiently.

'I'm gettin' there,' replied Jacob, unperturbed. 'I was just thinking it was time someone saw that ghost again. You know the one, my friends. The young *bride*, what wrings her hands and wails in the grounds at night in a *beautiful gown.*'

There was a silence and then a muttering. 'You mean you'd trust her to play the ghost? To *help* us?'

'One of us can wear that gown and do just as good a job, and safer to boot,' snarled an angry voice.

'You perhaps, Generous Joe?' asked Jacob mildly. 'Fine slender bride you'd make with that belly.'

The other men guffawed with laughter and the tense atmosphere eased a fraction. 'All I'm saying is, there don't have to be no killin',' continued Jacob. 'There's other ways of keeping her mouth shut.'

'Accomplices spill no beans,' agreed another man in a low growl.

'And there's other ways a woman could be useful to us,' Jacob added. 'The financer's been wanting to bring some lace across I heard. Skipper's got some ideas about that.'

I heard Will sigh beside me. 'I doubt this is a good decision,' he muttered. 'But you have a point about the lace. And I'm certainly not for killing anyone.'

'And there was us thinking you was the old hand at that,' someone sneered. Will was silent.

'Enough o' that, Hard-Head Bill,' said the skipper sharply. 'A vote then. All those in favour of giving Isabelle a chance to prove herself useful—with Jacob and Will to take charge of her.'

There was a long silence. My heart hammered and I longed to tear off my blindfold.

'Right,' said the skipper at last. 'That's more than half. That's settled then; Isabelle, you stay.'

Relief flared in me, leaving me trembling. I left off chewing my maltreated thumb. Jacob pulled me to my feet and pulled the scarf from my eyes.

The sunlight was brilliant and I screwed up my eyes against it. When they had adjusted, the sight made me gasp. We were surrounded by sea, deep blue and sparkling brightly in the sunshine. The waves were crested white in places, and the ship carved a path through them, dipping and rising as she went. The autumn sun was warm against my skin and the sea air salty and fresh. I'd never been to sea before; had never imagined such beauty. It was a wonderful morning to be alive. A deeply poignant thought.

I became aware of the curious stares of the men. Most watched me with interest, a few looked openly hostile. Others were already dispersing about the ship. There were an astonishing number of them; the crew must have been some thirty men in all. I wondered how they were all accommodated on this ship. It did not seem to be especially large. Almost all of the men were uncouth and dirty. They looked a low bunch of ruffians to me. I was relieved I'd not seen sooner the kind of scum that were deciding my fate.

'Right then, men,' said the skipper loudly. 'The coast is in sight. Let's make ready.'

I was weak with relief; so relieved, in fact, that the prospect of collaborating with a crew of common criminals didn't horrify me as much as it perhaps ought to have done. I just covered my face with my hands and fought the tears that wanted to surface.

They left me a few minutes in peace as men bustled around me calling out about 'reefing', 'winding', 'hauling sail', and 'dropping sail'. Then Jacob touched me lightly on the shoulder.

I dropped my hands and looked up at him. 'Come and get a bite to eat,' he said. 'That'll put some heart in you.'

He shambled ahead of me to the galley, a tall giant in shabby, patched clothing. I could smell the crisp, rich scents of bacon and coffee and realized I was starving. When Jacob brought me out a mug of bitter black coffee and a hunk of bread and bacon, I fell on it gratefully.

'That's right. Eat up!' said Jacob in a satisfied voice. 'So thin and pale you are. You need fresh air and good food, I reckon.'

I refrained from telling him that fresh air was highly injurious to a lady's complexion, for I sensed he was trying to be kind, uncouth and common though he was. And he had saved my life. He'd done it in a roundabout way, as though he scarcely knew what he was doing. I couldn't make up my mind whether he had some native cunning or whether he really was simple and had made a lucky suggestion.

The coffee tasted fiery, and I guessed it had been laced with some unfamiliar liquor. Something nudged at my ankle and I looked down to see a black-and-white cat winding itself around my leg, meowing. I threw it a scrap of rind which it swallowed greedily.

'I've never been at sea before,' I told Jacob. He was standing next to me, arms folded. He looked about him with a contented smile.

'It's a grand life,' he said simply. 'You're going to love it.'

I didn't answer him, having a mouthful of bacon and not being sure what to say. Was I really going to stay aboard this ship with all these dreadful men?

'It was the best I could do, see,' said Jacob unexpectedly. 'If I'd have pleaded to let you go, they'd likely have put you to bed in the sea. But you remind me . . . Well, to tell you the truth, you remind me of the daughter I lost to the scarlet fever. I wanted to protect you. I hope you can make the best of it.'

I was startled. He *had* known what he was doing. I hadn't imagined he could harbour so much intelligence inside such a rough exterior. The mention of his daughter stirred a little unexpected pity in me.

'But how long are you expecting to keep me here?' I asked, my voice sharp to mask the sudden confusion of my thoughts. 'The rest of my life?'

Jacob grinned, a slow, cheerful grin. 'We're just keeping you and us safe. And how long you stay'll depend, won't it? On how well you win their trust an' liking. You ain't home and dry yet.'

He got up on the words and went back to work on the sails. I watched him. Win the trust of cut-throats and criminals? Of rough, working men who thwarted the law and cheated the king? My mind struggled with the concept. In my world, the working class treated me with obsequious respect. They did my bidding and performed tasks for me. They did not question my right to be superior to them, nor did they question my word. And I certainly didn't have to consider their feelings or what they thought of me.

But now I was being asked to gain their liking, and to work to get their trust. I'd never worked in my life. That was something the lower orders did. And to try hard to please *them*! It was outrageous. Such illiterate, uneducated oafs! I scorned the thought.

At once, however, I remembered how many of them would like to have put an end to my life, and this swiftly sobered me. I was completely trapped here with no prospect of escape and nowhere to go if I could get away. I had no choice, for now, but to play this game on their terms.

CHAPTER FOUR

✳

The French port was bustling with craft of all descriptions moving about under sail or oar. I watched interestedly from the deck as we manoeuvred through them all to moor up at the busy quay. The crew made the ship fast. Will did his fair share of work along with the roughest of the men and I wondered at it. Despite being wigless, plainly dressed, and aboard a ship full of criminals, it was clear to me he was gently born. Did he have no pride at all?

The men were divided into three groups: those who were to have shore leave, the few who were to stay aboard, and those who were to conduct 'the business'. No one paid any attention at all to me until Will was stepping across the gangplank with a dark-haired, older man with a shapeless figure, who answered to the name of Numbers Ben. The skipper turned to me and asked abruptly: 'You speak French?'

'Of course,' I replied haughtily. To question my ability was to question my class and my education.

'Go with them then, and maybe you can make yourself useful,' he said, calling Will back.

Will scowled at me. 'I can't possibly take her. She'll run off!' he objected.

'I can't go in such clothes,' I cried equally aghast but for different reasons, looking down at my apparel with revulsion. 'It would be shameful.'

'Very well then,' said the skipper. 'No one here's got time to guard her. Jacob, lock her in the cabin.'

'No!' I cried outraged. 'I won't be locked in.'

'Come with me,' said Jacob, taking a step to the cabin.

'I won't,' I repeated, stamping my foot. I glared at them all, daring them to treat me so badly. Will and his companion shrugged and left the ship, walking off along the quay. Jacob made one more attempt to reason with me, and when I refused to budge, picked me up and tossed me over his shoulder. For a moment, I was too shocked to make a sound. When I had gathered my wits, I began to pound my fists against his back and shriek. 'Put me down, you great looby! How dare you manhandle me! I'll scream! I'll tell the authorities you're keeping me against my will!'

Jacob carried me to the cabin and dumped me down on the floor. I scrambled to my feet, still furious. 'I won't be locked in here,' I yelled, feeling my temper burn inside me.

Jacob simply grinned sympathetically, winked and went out, locking the door behind him. I could feel the familiar screams of fury and frustration building in my throat. My family would have read the signs; they would have known better than to thwart me.

I kicked out at a chair, sending it crashing onto the cabin floor. My eyes misted over, burning hot, and then I let out my first scream of pure rage. I picked up the chair and threw it across the cabin. It knocked the oil lamp from the ceiling, smashing it down onto the floor with a clang and a shatter of breaking glass. I screamed again.

The door behind me flew open with a bang and I whipped round, fists raised, ready to lash out at whoever it was. It took a moment for my rage-filled, heated vision to take in the sight of a rough man with a scarred face and a front tooth missing. I screamed and flew at him, determined to tear his face with my nails.

The man caught my wrists in unbelievably powerful hands and twisted them until I gasped and dropped to my knees. Then he let me go and dealt me one ringing slap across the cheek. 'I've heard enough of your child-ish tantrums,' he ordered. 'You be silent now.'

'You can't make me,' I gasped, still defiant, although my head was spinning from the blow. To prove it, I be-gan to scream again.

The man crouched down opposite me and looked into my eyes. There was a cold anger in his own eyes that made me quail, and I stopped mid-scream and froze as he drew a long sheath knife from his belt. 'In case you're wondering, I'm the one known as Hard-Head Bill,' he said menacingly.

My heart hammered in terror. I was certain he was going to kill me there and then. He grasped a handful of my waist-length hair with one powerful hand, twisting it. Then he reached up his knife and sliced hard across it. I whimpered in shock as my beautiful golden hair show-ered over the cabin floor among the fragments of broken glass.

Bill raised the knife again and threatened me with it. 'I'll remind you, I was one of them as wanted you dead,'

33

he said slowly and deliberately. 'I ain't changed my mind. I'm in charge of this ship for the rest of the day. So you'll shut it, or you'll feel the edge of this knife.'

Bill clearly didn't doubt that I'd comply with his order, for he got up and left, turning the key behind him. I crouched on the floor in silence, aware of the pounding of my heart and the trembling of my limbs. I'd never, in the course of my short life, come up against anyone who had cowed my will and forced my obedience. But I wasn't inclined to try him any further. I believed his threat. I got up, trembling with shock and indignation.

My right knee was cut and bleeding, and I dabbed at it with a cloth I found by the washstand. My hands shook pitifully. I touched my hair, hardly able to believe what the brute had done to me. Half of it was still long and half now only reached to my shoulder.

I stayed silent and furious but too frightened to object, as the long hours of the day passed. I heard the men come and go, goods being loaded aboard and at last the crew cast off and sailed out to sea once more. My first visit to France had passed with no more sight of Cherbourg than the view of the quay.

I was hungry, thirsty, and very bored when the key eventually rattled in the lock, and the cabin door swung open. I lay quite still on the bunk where I'd passed the last few hours. 'Get up,' ordered a voice. I deliberately turned away to face the wall. These men were brutes. They needn't think they could just order me about like a servant.

I shouldn't have been surprised to be dragged backwards out of the bunk by two firm hands under my arms. I landed in an undignified heap with a shriek of indignation. 'How *dare* you . . . ' I began, but Will laughed harshly.

'You ought to be learning by now that we're not your servants. You are now the most junior crew member on board,' he said. 'That means you do as you're told. Get used to it and stop bleating like the spoiled brat you are.'

'I'm *not* spoiled,' I retorted.

'Ha!' said Will, folding his arms, his mouth set in an uncompromising line. He stared at me in silence for a moment, and then added: 'You're a particularly spoiled, indulged, arrogant rich girl, and you have a great deal to learn if you want to live long on board this ship.'

He waited to see if I would reply. I was furious at his brutal appraisal, but sought to retain my dignity with a chilling silence, fixing my gaze on a point to the left of him.

'Good,' Will said. He picked up a broom from just outside the door and handed it to me. 'First, you are going to clean up the mess you've made.' I glared at him, while he waited. I had no intention of demeaning myself. 'I would get on with it if I were you,' he advised unsympathetically. 'For there'll be no food for you until it's done.'

'You won't dare to starve me!' I retorted angrily.

Will raised his brows and looked at me in incredulous silence. I knew that he was right; there were many men on board who'd be more than happy to let me starve. Furiously, I snatched up the brush and carelessly swept the glass into a pile. Then I picked it up, piece by piece, taking care not to cut myself, and threw it into the bin Will offered me. 'You've missed a bit,' Will pointed out.

His eyes were glinting now, I suspected with amusement. I picked up the chunk of glass and threw it in with the other broken pieces.

'Satisfied?' I demanded.

He shrugged. 'It's your cabin, and your feet that will get cut if you leave shards lying about,' he said cheerfully. 'You should be thankful to *have* a private cabin. Two men have had to give up that privilege to accommodate you, you know.'

I shrugged. 'Well, I could hardly sleep with the rest of you, could I?' I pointed out ungratefully. 'And I didn't ask to be here.'

Will sighed. 'Follow me,' he said. 'I've another task for you.'

I rolled my eyes and got unwillingly to my feet to accompany him. The sun was setting in a blaze of reds and pinks in the west, as I emerged onto the deck. I paused, looking about me in some awe. It was a truly stunning view. I caught hurriedly at the door as the ship pitched. There was no land in sight; only a rolling green swell as far as I could see in every direction. There was a definite chill in the air and I shivered a little after the relative warmth of the small cabin.

Once I'd got my balance, Will led me to a bucket and a heap of crumpled fabric lying in the prow of the ship by the foremost mast. I recognized my gown. 'What?' I asked, looking up at Will. 'It's ruined.'

'Wash it,' he ordered.

My jaw dropped. 'Me?' I gasped. 'Me, wash my own gown? That's servants' work.'

'I told you, you were spoiled,' he said curtly.

'It's not a matter of being spoiled,' I objected. 'That's insulting. I'm not a washerwoman.'

'You are now,' Will said with a grin. 'You're anything I say.' It was obvious he was enjoying himself. I clenched my teeth together and looked hopelessly out at the endless sea.

'It needs rinsing,' he said. 'To get the salt water out. Otherwise as you say, it will be ruined.'

'I don't care,' I snapped at him. 'I don't want it; I have no use for it and I'll never wear it again.'

'Wrong on two counts,' said Will with a grin. 'We have a very fine use for it and for you. And you'll be wearing it tomorrow night.'

I lifted my hands in a gesture of surrender. 'Very well, but explain.'

'Wash the gown first,' Will said. He retreated to the side of the ship, leaning against the rail at his ease, watching me. His smugness annoyed me.

I looked down at the tangled heap of gown reluctantly, then sighed, bent and picked it up. Or at least, I tried. I was amazed at how heavy the gown was now that it was drenched through; at the reams of fabric that it consisted of, all of which trailed onto the deck, sodden and dripping with sea water. It smelled of sea water too. I tried unsuccessfully to stuff it into the bucket, but the more I pushed, the bigger and more unwieldy the gown seemed to become. I shoved hard, and water squirted up and drenched the sleeves of my shirt.

'You might want to roll up your sleeves,' said Will politely, and then turned away to hide his laughter. I could see his shoulders shaking. Angry that he hadn't warned me sooner, I yanked at my soggy shirt sleeves. Clearly, I was the evening's entertainment. Will wasn't the only one watching my humiliation, nor was he the only one openly enjoying it.

Being the source of so much amusement made me determined to spoil the men's fun by completing my task successfully. I fought with the gown and the water, dipping and squeezing the train and the bodice. I unpeeled the sodden petticoats and washed each one separately; that way, they were less of a challenge than the gown itself. Finally, I rinsed the veil. I only found out after I'd torn the hem just how delicate the lace was when it was wet.

At last I stood, wet through and panting with exertion, the whole pile of fabric rinsed. Will nodded nonchalantly towards the lowest rigging. 'You can spread it out to dry there,' he said, as though I hadn't done enough work for one day. 'There are pegs in the bag tied to the lowest rope.'

I was out of breath, my arms were aching and I was really hungry, but I wasn't going to tell him so. Instead, I did as he said, pegging out my hated garments on the ropes. It wasn't as easy a task as I'd expected, as they bunched and dragged on the ropes, threatening to tear again.

But at last it was done, after a fashion. I sighed and dropped my weary arms to my sides. Will surveyed my handiwork.

'Clumsy and untidy,' he said blightingly. 'If you were a servant, you'd be sacked.'

'But I am not,' I said. 'Nor do I have any expectation of becoming one.'

He regarded me enigmatically, as though about to speak, but then shrugged. 'You've earned your dinner now,' he said. 'And then we'll talk.'

Over a bowl of savoury stew with dumplings, I listened to what he had to say. 'I've been put in command of this action,' he told me. 'And that includes being in charge of you tomorrow. I don't relish it, but you may as well make yourself useful.'

'What action is this?' I asked.

'We're going to an empty house,' Will told me. 'Everyone knows it's haunted; that's why it's deserted and useful to our landing team as a hiding place. But, most inconveniently, the ghost hasn't shown itself for several years now. People are starting to venture into the grounds again. People that include the local customs men. We've even heard rumours a buyer was looking at it; a buyer who is not a friend to the Gentlemen. We need to set that to rights.'

I looked at him suspiciously, half-remembering Jacob's speech the other night. 'Just how shall we do that?' I asked. 'Find the ghost and persuade it to show itself?'

'Don't be stupid, Isabelle. There is no ghost. You and I do not believe in such apparitions. But many of the country folk do, and so we will give them a ghost.'

It was the first time he'd acknowledged his own background. I wanted to question him, to ask about how he had ended up with a crew of smugglers, but his expression was forbidding, so I refrained.

'Don't tell me,' I said instead, with a slight shiver. I wasn't quite sure that I agreed with him about not believing in ghosts, although I wasn't going to admit it. 'The ghost was a girl who died in mysterious circumstances. And I am to be she.'

'You have a certain quickness of understanding,' Will conceded. 'It makes up a little—a very little!—for your grave faults.'

'I don't admit that I have any faults.'

'Of course you don't. I doubt very much you even recognize them. It's what makes you so unbearable,' retorted Will indifferently.

I was silenced. There was no doubt he meant what he said. Will was the only man aboard this ship who shared anything with me—background, education, class. And he hated me. I felt shame and humiliation creep into my cheeks and turned away to hide it.

'Nice haircut, by the way,' remarked Will.

I put my hand up to touch my ragged hair and thought how much I hated him back.

CHAPTER FIVE

✷

The evening was moonless and overcast with rain misting in the autumn air. It was a complete contrast to the bright, sunny day that had preceded it. I shivered a little as I crouched in the damp rowing boat that was taking me and Will to the beach. I could make out the waves breaking on the sand ahead of us. Behind us *The Invisible* loomed, awaiting the return of the boat. I was looking forward to setting both feet on dry land again and had some secret hope of making an escape.

Will shifted restlessly beside me. In his hands was a sack containing my gown, a length of chain, some rope, and a flask of liquid courage.

The previous night, having sailed westwards up the channel, we'd lain off a dark and rocky stretch of coast. Two crew members had gone ashore to spread tales of ghosts ready for our escapade. They hoped to whip up an audience for the haunting.

The boat lifted in the waves and then dropped, crunching gently onto sand. Will jumped out into the foam and hauled the boat a little further in. He turned to me. 'Come on,' he said impatiently.

I stood up gingerly, clinging to the edge of the boat, waiting to be helped. Will stood back without offering. Hard-Head Bill was holding the oars and ignoring me.

Feeling aggrieved, I struggled to get one leg over the edge of the boat, but then pulled it back as a wave washed under it.

'Dear Lord, give me patience,' exclaimed Will rolling his eyes.

'A gentleman would assist a lady,' I said crossly.

'You aren't a lady any more. I've told you that already. You're a crew member and need to learn to behave like one. Now get out of that boat!'

I struggled out over the side, crying out as the waves washed over my feet, and stumbled up the beach onto the dry sand. Will pushed the boat back out, and then stomped off, leaving me to follow him as best I might. My borrowed, ill-fitting boots were soggy now.

We were on a narrow, sandy beach. Low sandstone cliffs ran along the back of it with trees growing at their foot. Out to sea to our left I could see some bright white cliffs and beyond them, white rocks rising out of the sea.

'Are they not bringing the brandy ashore here then?' I called to Will who was still striding ahead of me. He whipped round and pressed a hand over my mouth.

'Keep your voice down, you stupid girl!' he muttered angrily. He cast an uneasy glance around him. 'Don't you understand?' he hissed in my ear. 'The rumours of ghosts will have brought the Preventives over here. Which is what we want. Meanwhile the men will run the goods elsewhere in safety tonight. But we don't want them to hear talk of . . . for the love of God, Isabelle, if you have to talk about the goods at all, you say Cousin Jacky.'

I nodded obediently and he released me. 'You are a liability,' he muttered. I shrugged. I really didn't care.

'What are Preventives anyway?' I asked.

'That's our name for Revenue officers.'

'I thought you called them Philistines?'

'Preventives, Preventers, Philistines or just damned interfering scoundrels. They are all in the service of His Majesty's Customs or Excise.'

'Oh,' I said, digesting this. 'So we are a diversion tonight?' I asked.

'Something like that.'

We climbed a path off the beach up a sloping green hill. From the top, I could see a vast area of scrub, low trees, and water to our right. 'What is this godforsaken place?' I asked. 'And who is there to see or care about a ghost here?'

Will paused and glanced back at me. 'That is Studland Heath,' he said shortly. 'Its very remoteness is useful to the Gentlemen. But it's the village we're heading to now.'

As we approached the houses, the short day was fading. Smoke was rising from a couple of cottages and a few lights twinkled in the deepening dusk.

Will vaulted over a gate into a meadow with cows in. I paused and fumbled at the gate, unsure how to open it and reluctant to enter a field of cows at all.

'Just climb over it,' sighed Will. 'Can you at least try to bestir yourself? A lame snail could make swifter progress.'

His words stung me. 'You're unreasonable. No one told me I'd be climbing gates into fields full of beasts.'

43

'And no one said you wouldn't be. Give me patience! I'd rather have anyone else for a companion but you.'

'I'd rather walk with Hard-Head Bill than with you,' I retorted with a scowl. 'Is it the black hair that makes you so bad-tempered?'

Will put his hand up to his hair. He had either dyed it or he was wearing a convincing wig, I wasn't sure which. His eyebrows too had been darkened and there was a mole on his nose that had not been there before. He was wearing the rough smock and waistcoat of a farmer. I would barely have recognized him. I wondered why he had disguised himself. Perhaps it had something to do with the haunting.

'Just hurry, will you?' he ordered. 'Or the building will be haunted by the body of a girl in breeches and not a bride at all.'

Ignoring his threat, I followed him in silence past a small village church built of grey stone and up a lane to a tumbledown old house. It was clearly abandoned. Weeds ran riot in the neglected garden and there were gaping holes where windows had once been. It looked like a face with empty eyes, staring at me in the dusk.

Will forced open a creaking, broken door into what must have once been the kitchen. Pieces of broken furniture lay scattered about. The room was dirty and smelled of mice.

Will abstracted my gown from the sack he'd been carrying and threw it to me. 'Time to transform yourself,' he whispered. I caught it and glared at him. 'Don't worry, I'm going,' he taunted. 'I've had a bellyful of being your maid!'

He left and I began to pull the gown out of the sack, dreading the task ahead. I struggled out of the repulsive breeches I'd been wearing for the past few days and into the bride gown. Patches of it were still damp and it clung clammily to my skin. Putting it on once more, this time alone in the dirt and squalor of a ruin, raised all sorts of strange emotions in me. I remembered how I'd felt last time. Not overjoyed precisely. But excited, hopeful. And now? I was helping to protect a gang of thugs engaged in an illegal trade. My fortunes had fallen below what I could have believed possible.

I'd tied on my hoops and my petticoats as best I could and donned my gown before Will appeared. I looked over my shoulder at him, half afraid to ask him to hook up my gown behind. Luckily, he stepped up behind me without a word and began to fasten it. When it was done, I turned and found he was offering me a small bag. 'What is it?' I asked.

'Chalk, to whiten your face. At the moment, you look to be in excellent health. We need you to look dead.'

I accorded his joke a small smile. Tentatively, I dipped my fingers in the chalk and smeared the dust onto my face. It felt slightly greasy and unpleasant. Will shook the bag a little. 'We don't have all night,' he said.

I took a handful and rubbed it all over my face, working it into the skin, rubbing it down across the portion of my chest that was exposed too. I even rubbed it over my hands and forearms.

Will looked at me critically. He produced another small bag and dipped finger and thumb into it. 'Soot,' he explained in answer to my puzzled look. 'To make you look really scary if they get up close.'

With a few deft touches of his thumb, he smoothed the soot under my eyes. He was gentle for the first time since I'd met him, and the action brought unwanted tears to my eyes. I blinked them away, reminding myself he hated me. His touch might be gentle but it certainly wasn't tender. He stepped back and looked critically at me again. 'Good. You'll do now. Do you have the veil?'

Veil in place, arranged over my tumbled, cut-about hair that most definitely did not resemble a bride, I clumped outside after Will. 'No one who catches a glimpse of these boots will believe I'm a genuine ghost for one instant,' I muttered. 'Or at least not a ghost with the slightest fashion sense.'

Will chuckled. It was the first time I'd heard him laugh in a way that wasn't mocking. 'They're hidden by the gown and the long grass,' he said after watching me walk. 'If you're really concerned about it, you could take them off. A barefoot bride would be quite poignant, you know.'

I remembered walking into the sea just a few nights ago, all hope gone, my shoes left behind me on the beach, and swallowed hard. 'No, I thank you,' I retorted, trying to shake off the powerful memory. 'It's freezing cold, the grass is wet and probably full of slugs.'

Will merely shrugged. 'As you wish. We're probably going to have a few locals on their way to the local tavern looking over the wall there,' he pointed to a gap in an overgrown wall. 'You need to appear from the outhouse over there,' he pointed to the doorway we'd emerged from, 'and flit along the lawn here. You can flit, can't you?'

46

'Being a ghost isn't something I've a vast deal of experience of,' I told him acidly.

'Clearly you never had a governess you needed to get rid of,' Will responded.

'I didn't need to play the ghost.'

'I bet you didn't. Frightened her off without dressing up at all, I should think.'

'I find I can dispense with your observations on my character,' I told him, provoked to anger. 'You don't know me.'

'I don't need to and I don't want to.'

'That's entirely reciprocated, I assure you. I'd be very pleased if I never set eyes on you again. Now are we going to play this ghost or are we going to stand here bickering all night like children?' I demanded.

Will's eyes glittered in the darkness as he stood facing me. He was breathing heavily and I realized he was as angry as I was. I just wasn't sure why.

'How do I even know I can trust you with this?' he asked at last. 'How do I know that you won't deliberately sabotage this whole thing to expose us?'

I didn't reply at first. I couldn't deny that the thought had crossed my mind. I summoned up a wan smile. 'Can you imagine the scene?' I asked as lightly as I could. 'A ghost chasing some terrified local farmers, begging for help?'

Will continued to regard me steadily with those hostile, glittering eyes until my own dropped, half-ashamed of what my plans had been. 'This isn't a game. We hold many lives in our hands.'

'Criminals,' I said defiantly.

'Wrong. Men who are trying to survive and support their families in difficult times.'

I shrugged. 'Men are only poor if they are lazy or knaves,' I retorted. 'Everyone knows that. There's always honest work to be done.'

Will's fists clenched. 'You're spouting the convenient platitudes of your class,' he hissed. 'Abominable! These are phrases you've heard from the wealthy and privileged. You know nothing of work or wages. You do not have the slightest idea of what it entails to support a family on a few shillings a week.'

I stared at him in silence. I felt sure of my views. I'd heard such things said a hundred times, at dinners and at balls by men and women who knew the world: the poor deserve to be poor. They are poor because they're lazy and ignorant and can't be helped. No one had ever challenged this within my hearing. And yet somehow I didn't feel comfortable saying these things out loud to this angry young man. Instead, I challenged him on safer ground: 'What do you mean, *my* class? You are gently born, don't deny it!'

'I won't deny that I was born to as much privilege as you, perhaps more,' said Will. 'But since then, I've seen things that have made me . . . ' His voice tailed off as we both heard the unmistakable sound of footsteps and voices in the distance.

'They're coming. Can I trust you to do this?'

'This, but nothing more,' I told him. 'I'll make you no promises beyond the next half hour.'

'Very well. Get ready now. And you'd better hope neither of the real ghosts turns up tonight.'

48

'There's more than one?' I asked, feeling an icy finger of fear stroke my back.

'Oh, did no one tell you?' asked Will, cheerful once more. 'Not only is there a murdered bride who can't rest, but a headless spectre is said to stalk the grounds.'

I knew that I shouldn't ask. The less I knew the better. But I couldn't help myself. 'A headless spectre . . . ?' My voice trembled.

Will stepped closer, his face lit up with a ghoulish pleasure. 'He creeps up behind you, just as you think you've escaped him. He grabs you and tries to tear your head off. No one knows if he is seeking revenge or a head to replace the one he has lost.'

I shuddered and couldn't forbear a quick glance over my shoulder. 'You're making that up,' I said as bravely as I could. 'A ghost can't grab anyone.'

'Are you quite sure about that?' asked Will, in a hollow voice.

I shivered from a mixture of cold and nerves.

'I'm leaving you now,' said Will, reaching up to straighten my veil. 'This is going to be so much fun.'

'How can you say so?' I whispered indignantly, but he was gone, all but invisible in his dark clothing, running across the lawn, crouching low. I gripped my hands together to stop them shaking as I heard the crunch of footsteps and the sound of voices approaching. There was something altogether chilling about this tumble-down ruin and overgrown garden. It was the perfect setting for a haunting; eerie and other-worldly.

Somewhere nearby, a strange, unearthly wailing rose up. Ice cold shivers ran down my back at the sound. I stood frozen with fear listening to it. Slowly, it faded into silence, to be replaced, after a pause, by the slow clank of dragging chains. I shuddered with terror. I'd come here to pretend to be a ghost and the real ghost was so angry she'd come to haunt me. Perhaps she was offended and angry at my impersonation. I could feel myself sweating with terror at the very thought she could appear before me at any moment.

On the other side of the overgrown lawn, I caught sight of a slight movement. It took a moment for my fear-frozen brain to take in that it was by no means an apparition. Concealed behind some trees, shielded from view of the road, Will was beckoning me out into the open, his white hands showing up in the faint starlight. Had he not heard the appalling sounds? He couldn't be so lost to fear as to be calmly ignoring them, surely?

I realized what must be the truth and relief coursed through me. *Will* was making those dreadful sounds. Had he not brought a chain with us? He probably hadn't warned me because he'd wanted to frighten me.

The loud, confident voices I'd been able to hear from the road only moments ago were silenced. I needed to show myself to set the seal on their fear.

With an effort, I unfroze my limbs and began to step forward in response to Will's repeated beckoning. Slowly, falteringly, I stepped out across the ragged lawn, the damp of the evening quickly soaking through the hem of my petticoats. I tried to walk slowly, smoothly, as though gliding. A breeze blew over me, fluttering my veil.

There was a cry of terror from the road. Another. The pounding of feet and whimpers of fear. I turned my head cautiously towards the wall, to see the backs of a number of men fleeing up the road. I continued my glide across the garden until I reached Will. He was leaning against a tree, laughing. 'That was just too easy!' he said, not bothering to keep his voice down. 'We went to so much trouble to get them here and they barely stayed to look at you!'

I couldn't share his laughter. I was still trembling with fear. 'Why didn't you tell me you were going to make those awful noises?' I demanded.

'What noises?' asked Will, suddenly serious again. 'I didn't hear any noises.'

My stomach gave a sick lurch and I stared at him. 'The wailing . . . the chains . . . ' I stuttered. 'They were . . . ' I stopped as a sound came to my ears. It was voices and the sound of horses' hooves approaching. Will heard it too, and grabbed my hand, dragging me behind a tree. From where we were standing, we could see up the road, and could make out several men approaching on horseback. One of the horses was pale grey and his coat reflected the starlight.

'What luck,' whispered Will. 'These are the Revenue officers and two soldiers.'

'*Luck*?' I gasped. 'Are you completely mad?'

Will ignored me. 'This is exactly what we hoped for! They must believe there's a run on here. Oh, we can have some sport now. You must do your walk again.'

'No, please,' I begged, feeling sick with fear at the thought of the real ghosts and deceiving the king's men. 'We'll be caught! The ghost . . . '

'Nonsense!'

'I can't,' I protested desperately. I was faint with fear. The soldiers were drawing closer; I could hear the squeak of leather now and the snorting of the horses. 'The escape route is behind me. How do I get away after?'

'Just walk straight towards them. They won't stand their ground. And if they do, I won't let them near you. You must trust me. Go!'

I stood rigid and shaking behind a tree while Will disappeared into the darkness. Again the eerie wail drifted across the garden, rising to an unearthly shriek. I shuddered with horror. I knew I should move, but I couldn't. It had been madness to agree to come here. I couldn't go through with this.

A low shivering moan right behind me drove me from the shelter of the tree out into the open. My heart was hammering so hard I could hardly breathe and my legs were shaking. Then I heard a shout right in front of me and looked towards the wall. There were four mounted men. Two were backing off, crying out with fear at the sight of me, their horses skittish with nerves. The third looked restless, but the fourth sat quite still, staring at me.

I had no choice now but to play my part. Perhaps if they didn't run away, I could reach them and throw myself upon their mercy. I placed little reliance on Will's promise to keep them away from me. I took a gliding step forward, reaching out my hands towards them. Another wail began behind me and I stepped forward a little faster.

Two of the horsemen yelled in terror and fled. The third tried to hold his ground, but as I approached, turned tail and urged his horse after the others with a frantic clattering of shod hooves on gravel. The fourth, however, slid down from his horse and stepped over the broken wall towards me. I stopped, facing him uncertainly.

A low moaning sounded to my left. The riding officer glanced briefly towards the sound, but then looked back at me. There was, I sensed, more curiosity and speculation in his aspect than fear or horror.

'Please,' I spoke in a low voice. 'Help me.'

The sound of my voice gave him pause. I couldn't see his expression in the darkness, but he stopped dead, staring at me. Forgetting my face was painted, I put my veil back and took another step forward. The man took one look at me and turned and fled. Before he'd taken more than a few steps, he tripped and fell flat on his face, sprawling in the long grass. I didn't see what had happened. It was as though an invisible hand had reached out of the grass and grabbed his ankles.

He scrambled to his feet with a desperate cry and ran as fast as he could to the wall. He jumped onto his horse which began to canter after its fellows before his master was properly on his back.

I bit my trembling lip and turned away. My chance for rescue was gone. I looked for Will in the dark garden, but there was no sign of him. Only empty silence and shadows. My courage failed me at the thought of walking deeper into these haunted grounds. On impulse, I turned and crossed the damp lawn. I would follow the road and find help. I wouldn't stay to be part of this a moment longer.

I gathered my petticoats in my hands and climbed the fallen section of the wall, jumping down into the road.

I had scarcely taken two steps when a shadow sprang from the darkness and grabbed me, holding me fast and clamping a hand over my mouth. My heart lurched with fear. The ghostliness of the midnight garden and the tricks I'd been involved in had weakened my mind to such an extent that for a few appalling moments I was convinced I was in the grip of the headless spectre. He was about to tear my head from my body. I trembled helplessly, unable to move. 'Trying to escape?' Will whispered in my ear.

CHAPTER SIX

✦

'Get a *move* on, will you?' demanded Will, as I paused for breath by a stone wall.

'Please,' I begged him. 'I can't walk so far without a rest.' We had climbed some high downs where the night chill and the wind had whipped through every layer of clothing. We'd descended the far side into farmland. By then it felt as though I'd walked across most of England.

'We've walked no distance at all!' Will exclaimed impatiently. 'Listen to me. We need to get to a safe house by dawn. I have business to conduct on the way. If we don't hurry, we won't make it.'

'I don't care,' I cried. 'I'm exhausted, I ache all over, my feet hurt and I want to sleep.'

By way of reply, Will took hold of my hand and dragged me onwards. I stumbled after him for a while, careless how I placed my feet. It didn't take long before I caught my foot in a rabbit hole or some such thing, and fell, dragging my hand out of Will's. I lay on the grass, too tired to care that it was cold and damp.

'Get up!' Will cried.

'I can't take another step,' I told him, my face muffled in the grass.

Will kicked at a rock in the dark and swore with frustration. Then he sat down heavily on the ground and sank his head in his hands. I didn't move.

'What did I do to get landed with you?' he groaned.

I didn't reply, simply relishing resting my aching limbs. Sleep was engulfing me and I barely noticed when Will got up and walked away. When he shook my shoulder some time later, it dragged me back from a deep sleep to unwelcome reality.

'Isabelle. There's an abandoned cottage just half a mile away. If you can walk that far, I can get a fire going.'

I shivered in the chill darkness, and dragged myself unwillingly to a sitting position. 'Must I?' I leant my weight on one hand and then snatched my hand back with a cry of pain.

'Gorse,' said Will briefly. 'Come on, we can't stay here.'

I struggled up and stumbled after him. It seemed a very long way until at last we reached a tumbledown hovel that smelled of mould and sheep. I entered it with some distaste, wrinkling my nose. 'Are you serious? You want me to sleep here?'

Will struck a light and lit a candle stub that he pulled out of his pocket, standing it on a stone ledge. By its wavering light, I could see an empty room with an earthen floor. The sack containing my bride gown had been dropped beside the empty fireplace. 'Pillow for you,' he said pointing at it.

He disappeared outside, while I lay down and tried to get comfortable. The floor was cold and uneven. I wondered, not for the first time, if the life I had left behind me would have been as bad as I'd imagined.

It couldn't have been worse than I was going through now, surely?

But once Will returned with an armful of brushwood and kindled it, I started to feel better. He pulled a leather pouch out of the sack, and from it he took some bread, cheese and a flask. I hadn't realized how hungry I was. It was hours since our last meal on board *The Invisible*.

The food tasted good, and the flask contained a fiery liquid that made me cough and splutter but sent a warming fire right out into my fingers and toes. 'Is this brandy?' I asked, passing it back to him. He took a swig and grinned.

'It is indeed,' he said, holding up the flask in the firelight. 'This is our friend, Cousin Jacky.'

I remembered that first night when I'd been pulled out of the sea, the men in the boat saying 'Cousin Jacky's arrived' and I hadn't been able to work out who he was. 'Why do you call it that?'

'No idea, but it's a fine name for a fine drink. Taken in moderation, of course.'

I wriggled on the ground, a stone sticking into me and then winced as my boots rubbed against my sore feet. I reached forward and unlaced the boots, easing them off my feet with a gasp of pain. I peeled off one stocking and found that the heel and the side of the foot had blistered and then bled.

'Ouch,' remarked Will, not unkindly. 'Why didn't you say?'

'I tried,' I retorted. 'Listening isn't your strong point.'

'There's far too much to listen to,' said Will. 'You never stop complaining. How am I supposed to know when it's something serious?'

'It's always serious,' I replied, peeling off the other stocking and finding the right foot in no better state. 'You take me to a hideous haunted mansion in the dead of night and make me play at hide and seek in the dark with law officers and frighten me half to death. And you shriek and howl and then pretend it wasn't really you to frighten me even more!' Will laughed without remorse. 'How *did* you make that officer fall over by the way?' I asked him.

'A trip line. I'd tied a rope across the lawn earlier and jerked it tight as he reached it.'

'Oh. Well. Not content with all that you drag me for miles and miles across the roughest ground in borrowed boots and never so much as open a gate or lift a bramble out of the way for me!'

Will laughed again. 'You do expect a great deal, don't you? Remember, you're not a lady any longer. And that was a short walk,' he added.

'I've never walked that far in my life.'

'You aren't serious?' he asked, lifting his brows.

I shrugged. 'What are carriages and sedan chairs for, if not to avoid walking?'

'But you ride, surely?'

'Not if I can help it.'

Will shook his head in wonder. 'You must be the laziest person I've ever met,' he remarked. 'Do you take no exercise at all?'

I thought for a moment. 'Dancing,' I said with a nod. 'I enjoy dancing.'

'Well, that'll be useful to you in your new life,' said Will with heavy sarcasm.

'Are you really going to keep me prisoner?' I asked. 'You dislike me. You wouldn't miss me if I went. Why don't you just let me go?'

'You know why.'

'Yes, but I swear I won't tell. Not a word. I'll say I lost my memory.'

'You're very keen to run off all of a sudden. I thought you were tired. And had nowhere to go?'

I turned my head away, sudden tears starting to my eyes. I was so very tired. And it was true that I had nowhere to go. I couldn't go back. Unthinkable!

I was shocked out of my thoughts by Will taking my wrist and tying a rope around it. He tied the other end to his own wrist, and lay down beside me. 'Best get some rest,' he said. 'We can sleep two hours at most then we must move on. We have a much longer walk ahead of us.'

I turned away from him, humiliated that he felt it necessary to tie me up. I stared into the soft glow of the small fire. It was warming me through slowly, and despite the pain in my feet and my aching limbs, sleep was washing over me.

The door loomed before me in my dreams as it always did. It was dark and ominous. As I stared at it, it slowly began to swing open towards me. I dreaded what lay behind it. I covered my eyes and screamed.

'Hush, Isabelle,' said a voice in my ear. A hand was on my arm, warm and reassuring. 'It's just a bad dream.'

I opened my eyes to darkness, broken only by the dim glow of embers in the crumbling hearth. I remembered it was Will beside me, speaking to me. He knew nothing.

It was not only a dream. It was grimly, horribly real. I lay feeling wretched until sleep granted me another brief respite.

I awoke to Will shaking me once more, one hand pressed over my mouth. I jumped and struggled, but he hushed and then released me. Sunlight was streaming in through the window and doorway of the hovel and through a hole in the roof. The fire had burned itself to a pile of cold ash. I sat up and yawned, still tired and groggy after such a short sleep.

'There's someone coming,' Will whispered. 'Can you climb out of the back window and hide there?'

I saw that he'd already untied the rope that had bound me, so I started to pull on my stockings. 'No time,' he whispered, throwing the sack out of the window, and returning for my boots and stockings and disposing of them the same way. When I came to the sill, he caught me around the waist and swung me up onto it. I looked down with distaste, for it looked like a midden under the window. I wasn't jumping down into that.

The voices approached the cottage from the front and Will gave me a sharp push. With a cry of shock, I tumbled down into the heap of rotted straw, manure, and rubbish. Will coughed loudly to cover my cry and leaned on the sill. I scrambled to my feet, repulsed by the matter I was standing in, muck all over my feet and borrowed breeches. I was about to tell Will off when I heard him speaking. 'Good mornin' to you!' he said loudly, speaking like a working man. 'A fine day!'

I heard the rumble of a reply, but not the words. I retrieved the sack and my boots and hobbled out of the midden. Under the shelter of the cottage wall, I crouched down, trying to scrape the sludge off my feet onto some grass, feeling sick.

'Got lost, I did,' I heard Will tell the strangers. 'Darkness fell, so I took shelter here, like.'

'Be off with you . . . no vagabonds here . . . ' I heard the strangers say. They sounded angry.

'Ah well, no offence intended,' said Will cheerfully. The sound of retreating footsteps reached my ears. I wondered if it was just Will that had gone or if it was the others too. I crouched still and as silently as possible against the wall of the cottage. I didn't know what to do. Should I follow Will or should I stay put?

It seemed an age before Will appeared behind the cottage. He came from a different direction, sliding unobtrusively around the tumbledown sheep pen that backed onto the hovel. When he saw me still crouching uncomfortably by the wall, manure drying on my bare feet, he grinned.

'That was most unlucky,' he said jerking his head in the direction of the strangers. 'My, your ladyship, you look more elegant every time I see you.'

'Go to hell,' I swore at him. 'You tipped me into a midden, and I'll swear you did it on purpose,' I said. 'There was no need for me to hide.'

'Oh, wasn't there, though?' said Will with a chuckle. 'You should see yourself.'

I put my hand to my ragged hair, wondering if he was taunting me with that. 'Not just your hair,' he said shaking his head. 'You're part girl, part boy, and part ghost. Do you think a tale like that wouldn't get about? The last thing we need! You need to wash. And we should do something about your hair.'

I'd completely forgotten what a sight I must look. The thought brought a blush to my cheeks and tears to my eyes. Last winter I'd been the toast of London society and in the summer I'd been the reigning beauty of Bath. Now I must look like a mixture of vagabond and clown.

We found a small stream that trickled down from a sheep-nibbled hillside, sparkling in the morning sunshine, and there I bathed the sticky mess of chalk and ash from my face and soaked the manure from my feet.

Will took my chin in his hand, scrutinizing my face. I pulled away resentfully. 'I was just checking for you,' he said. 'There's still . . . wait . . . ' He dipped his right hand in the stream and scrubbed at my cheekbone. I turned away as soon as he was done. 'Just trying to help,' he said. I ignored him. 'Spoiled beauty,' Will taunted me.

I turned to face him. 'Firstly, you've done nothing so far that convinces me you've any kindness in you,' I told him fiercely. 'I don't need to be spoiled to consider you've treated me abominably from the start. And secondly, I don't want you touching me in any way. You disgust me.'

Will grinned. 'Of course I do,' he said, in a voice that suggested he thought the opposite. I glared at him, and he smirked back. I longed to slap him, but that would be unladylike. 'Put your stockings and shoes back on,' he said at last, and turned away.

As I pulled the scratchy fabric over my blistered feet, I found my eyes blurring with tears. This was all so unfair.

How had I fallen into such a nightmare? I followed Will without further complaint. We crossed fields and sheltered in a small wood for a time. I dozed off again and when I awoke, the brightness had faded from the sky.

'Come on,' Will said when he saw I was awake once more. 'We've a long way to go yet.'

I got up, my body stiff and sore from the unaccustomed exercise and stretched. Will walked swiftly, while I kept up as best I could. We skirted settlements, kept to tracks across fields and among trees. He took routes that seemed to involve climbing hundreds of dry-stone walls. The rough stone scratched my hands, and my arms and shoulders ached. The ground was uneven and my boots rubbed my feet raw. Brambles clawed at me, and every muscle in my body cried out. In the end I was keeping going more by guess than anything else. I walked into gorse bushes several times. A pothole in the road caught me unawares; it caught my foot and twisted my ankle. I fell with a cry, tearing hands and knees on the rough ground.

Will halted ahead of me, looking back, waiting for me to get to my feet. When I didn't, he turned back and crouched beside me. Tears of pain and exhaustion were starting in my eyes. Lacking a pocket handkerchief, I swiped them away with my sleeve.

'It's only a few minutes to the next stop,' Will told me.

'I can't take another step,' I told him weakly. He took hold of my arms and hauled me to my feet.

'Oh, my ankle! Ouch!' I cried as I tried to put it to the ground.

'Best to walk on it straight away,' said Will unfeelingly. 'Resting it makes it worse. You can lean on me.'

63

He offered his arm, but I pushed it away. I hobbled along beside him, sniffing, feeling sorry for myself. It wasn't long before we reached a farm. Dusk had fallen in earnest now, but Will clearly knew his way through the gloom. He led me along a rough path to a barn, where, after a quick glance around, he pulled me inside. It was a lofty building, stacked high with the autumn stocks of hay and straw. A sweet, dusty smell pervaded it, reminding me of the barns at home. I paused a moment to sniff, but Will pushed me on to a ladder.

'Climb up,' he ordered me.

'Why?'

'Just do as you're asked for once.'

I didn't suspect him of any amorous intent, so I climbed up. Once we reached the hayloft, I found I'd been quite right about Will. Far from attempting to embrace me, he dropped the sack, extracted a length of rope from it, grasped my wrists and bound them behind my back. I was too surprised to prevent him.

'What do you think you are doing?' I demanded indignantly.

'Making sure you're still here when I get back,' Will replied.

I started to fight him. 'Back from where? Don't tie me!' I begged him, struggling and wriggling, but the rope was already tight.

'I have someone to see and your company would be highly inconvenient,' Will said, pulling me across the loft so that my back was to a post. 'In other words: none of your business.' He swiftly looped the rope around the post and made it fast.

'You're a . . . *scoundrel*!' I cried, thinking of the worst word I could. 'A blackguard! How *dare* you do this to me?'

'It's more a matter of not daring to leave you untied, dear heart,' said Will with a grin. I aimed a kick at him which caught him on the ankle, but he just laughed. 'I'm sorry, really I am. But I have no choice. I won't be long.'

He turned and descended the ladder swiftly. 'Don't you dare leave me here!' I yelled. 'Don't you *dare*! I'll scream the place down! I'm warning you!' When I got no response I began to yell: 'Help! Help me! I'm tied up in the barn . . . HELP!'

Will's face appeared at the top of the ladder again, his expression reproachful. For a moment I thought he'd relented, but, as usual, it was a mistake to think well of him. He pulled my bridal veil out of the sack, tore off a portion and stuffed it into my mouth.

'Believe me, I regret this necessity,' he said in a maddeningly calm voice. 'But you brought it on yourself.' He bound the gag in place with a strip of petticoat. I watched him in silent fury. The gag was horribly uncomfortable, and I needed to stay calm and breathe steadily through my nose if I didn't want to choke.

'See you soon, Isabelle!' said Will and dropped a kiss on the end of my nose. 'Be good and don't wander off!'

I convulsed with anger but couldn't reach to strike him. My rage, once Will had left me, knew no bounds. I fought vainly against my bonds, tensing and straining my whole body to free myself, but Will had done his job all too well. Hate-filled words buzzed in my mind, longing to be yelled out loud. I raged, I fought and then I wept. At last, exhausted from my anger and from having walked further than ever in my life before, I fell asleep.

I awoke suddenly in darkness with the feeling something had disturbed me. I retched and struggled before I remembered where I was. My neck ached and my throat was raw from the gag. I was sure I wasn't alone. All the fears of the ghosts last night came flooding back. Chills ran over me. How could Will leave me alone like this?

As I sat, straining my ears to hear anything at all, a cold, ghostly finger stroked my cheek. My stomach clenched with fear, my body convulsed and I gave a muffled shriek that made me choke helplessly. In the middle of my terror, laughter reached my ears. *Laughter!* Will emerged from behind me, holding his sides. 'This place is as haunted as that old house!' he said. I rolled my eyes, desperate to be able to breathe properly. Will seemed to understand, for he loosened the gag at once, pulling the veil from my mouth. 'Sorry, Sleeping Beauty,' he said. 'I simply couldn't resist.'

I coughed; my throat too raw for the insults and reproaches I longed to heap on him. The moment he released the ropes at my wrists, I swung my numb left hand round and struck his face. It gave a satisfying slap and his head snapped to the right.

I braced myself and shut my eyes, expecting to feel a return blow but it didn't come. When I opened them, Will was rubbing his cheek ruefully and staring at me.

I glared back angrily and then I forgot everything else as the pain of the blood flowing into my numbed hands flooded me.

CHAPTER SEVEN

✳

'Where did you go when you left me?' I asked Will as we strode out into the night. 'You were gone ages.'

'You don't need to know.' His voice was maddeningly calm. He shifted the sack he was carrying to his other shoulder with a grunt. It seemed heavier and fuller than it had been earlier in the day.

'I hate you,' I told him with feeling.

'So you keep telling me. I really don't care.'

'Where are we going now? Or is that secret too?'

'We're on our way to meet *The Invisible*.'

'Where?' I asked him. Getting information out of Will was like drawing a tooth: difficult and painful.

He shook his head at me. 'Why?' I demanded angrily. 'Why does that need to be secret? For heaven's sake, you are ridiculous!'

'If we were to be captured or stopped by the king's men,' said Will, as though explaining something to a very stupid child, 'do you really think I want you to be able to tell them where the ship is coming in to shore?'

I stomped along beside him. I was a prisoner. I had no say and no choice in anything. It was intolerable.

There were lights twinkling ahead in the darkness. I glanced at Will to see if he was going to avoid them, but

67

to my surprise, he continued walking straight towards them. The dark shapes resolved into cottages, and I could tell from the stink drifting across to us that they were not well-to-do dwellings.

'What is this place?' I whispered.

'These are quarry workers,' he replied. 'They work hard but they're very poor. At the moment, times are so bad they can't make enough to live. Many have been laid off altogether.' At the edge of the waving shadow of light, he paused, stopped me by grasping my wrist and looked me over critically. He pulled my cap, which I'd pushed back, down lower over my face, then nodded. 'You'll do,' he said. 'As long as you don't speak. Stay close to me.' Then he stepped out of the darkness between the cottages.

The glow of light was emanating from a fire in the muddy space between the cottages. It was like a brick oven or some such thing, and, early in the morning though it was, a woman was bent over it tending it. As Will appeared, several small children in tattered rags and bare feet ran towards him shouting with excitement. He dropped the sack at his feet and crouched down to speak to them. I wondered why we'd come here.

Will was reaching into his sack and pulling out pieces of fruit: apples, an orange. A paper bag of raisins; a cone of biscuits. The children clamoured for them, sharp-eyed and hungry, hardly waiting until they had the food in their hands before they began to eat. Even so, a couple of the older children were making sure the youngest had their share in the scramble.

I noticed how pitifully thin many of them were. Their cheeks were hollow and shadowed with want. As Will handed out the food, he spoke a few words to each of the children and it seemed he knew them all.

Once the children had all had something from him, he walked from cottage to cottage, placing a loaf of bread or a wrapped square of cheese just inside each doorway. From some there was a nod of thanks or a word exchanged. From others a silence. From most, a stench of unwashed bodies, excrement, and mould.

Just before we left the village, a very young child limped up to me from out of the shadows and slipped a small, grimy hand into mine. I tried not to recoil at the sight of her ragged, filthy nails and at the smell of sickness. Her skin was grey, her hair lank. She smiled up at me. I looked into her eyes and was transfixed. They were huge and dark in her pale, thin face and had the look of one who had already seen the other side.

'Jess,' said Will with a smile. He crouched down where he stood. 'I wonder if there's anything left for you?' he said. He delved into the sack once more, almost empty but for ropes and gown now, and pulled out an orange. He held it out and the girl let go of my hand and limped towards him. I saw her foot was malformed, and that there was an open sore upon her leg. I shuddered and drew back, wiping my hand on my breeches, hoping I hadn't caught anything nasty. I was shaken by the sight of so much dirt and degradation. I wished Will hadn't brought me here. The girl looked back at me again, and all such selfish thoughts were silenced by her clear, intelligent gaze.

'Who's this?' she asked Will in a soft voice. It had the local twang, but it was musical. A slight blush crept into my face under her scrutiny.

'He's helping us with the trade,' said Will, still crouched down to look the girl in the eyes. 'So we can keep bringing you oranges.' I didn't contradict him.

'But this is a girl,' said Jess, looking closely at me. Will put his finger on his lips and winked at her. She smiled and Will smiled back at her. I caught my breath, looking at the two of them. This was so clearly the give and take of friendship and liking. In that moment, something changed in the way I saw Will. It was as though he was a different person. Then he stood up and nodded to me to follow him and the spell was broken.

As we left, Will was silent, a brooding frown on his face. 'I always think,' he said as we crossed a field, 'that next time I come by, Jess might not be there any more.'

'Why don't they take her to the doctor with that dreadful sore?' I asked.

'Because her mother is dead and her father drinks. And even when he can get work, the doctor costs a week's wages,' said Will.

I didn't reply. It seemed unfair to be sure, that they couldn't afford a doctor. 'But they are so dirty!' I said. 'Why do they not clean up and wash and put on fresh clothes at least?'

Will shook his head at me. 'Washing requires clean water nearby,' he said. 'Clean clothes means having some to spare. And someone having time and energy left over from working a twelve-hour day and caring for small children to do the washing. And money for soap. Decent housing would help too.'

'Well, I would never allow myself to become so . . . degraded,' I said with a sniff.

'Perhaps you would not. You've known something different, after all,' said Will. 'But what if you had ten children, three died, the rest ran wild and had no chance of education? How would they fare?'

'I would teach them,' I said, but though I kept arguing from force of habit, clinging to my beliefs, my voice had lost its conviction. I began to have some insight into how hopeless one might become in such a situation.

'I'd like to see you find the time for that, let alone the money for the materials. And even if you did, what of their children? Your daughter marries a man who beats her and drinks the money. She's surrounded by dirt and work and want. She isn't well. How long would this superiority last, Isabelle? In two generations, you and yours would become those people. There's no difference. Don't think that you are something better. Besides, take a look at yourself! Two days on the road and you are as dirty as them, and smell very nearly as bad.'

His words shocked me. I took a cautious sniff at my clothes and could smell sweat, manure from the midden, and slime from the marsh we'd skirted. I thought of the little urchin Jess, her dark eyes so clear sighted. The way her hand had slid trustingly into mine. And I did something I'd never done before. I imagined what it must be like to live someone else's life. It wasn't a pleasant reverie. Could Will be right? Was there really no difference between me and the people in the cottages?

'How did you get to know them?' I asked Will as he strode out across the turf.

'It's a long story.' Will's voice was curt and dismissive.

'I couldn't have asked for a more charming companion,' I remarked bitterly.

Will turned on me and gripped my wrist. I bit my lip as his hand tightened uncomfortably. 'You can talk,' he said. 'We saved your life and all you've told us about yourself is lies. We've given you food and shelter and risked our safety for you, and have had precious little in return. So before you criticize me, take a look at your own behaviour.'

He released me abruptly and strode off into the darkness. I stumbled wearily after him. We walked quietly through the next settlement; a poor place but cleaner than the last. It was late now and the houses were all in darkness. Will paused at one cottage, pushed open the gate and then hesitated, turning back to me. 'Wait here,' he said.

He walked to the front door, and taking a key from around his neck, he unlocked it. He stepped inside the house, leaving the door ajar behind him, and I saw him lay several things on the table, though I couldn't see what. He was just emerging from the door again, when small hands grasped his coat and tugged. He turned back and I saw him bend down to embrace a small child, kissing her on each cheek.

'I can't stay,' I heard him say. 'I'm so sorry! But you should be asleep, Beth. You can look at the parcels in the morning.'

He stepped outside, pulled the door to behind him and walked back to me without a word. As we left, I glanced up at the window and saw a child's face pressed against the dark glass of a window in the upper storey. 'Who is that?' I asked Will.

'You don't need to know,' he said sharply, pulling his cap down lower. He walked swiftly, avoiding further questions. I was puzzled. Who was the little girl? Why did he have a key to that house?

'You are a strange person,' I told him at last, breaking the long silence. 'So harsh and unsympathetic. And yet capable of kindness to those degraded people.'

Will glanced sharply at me. 'There's no contradiction,' he said quietly. 'I merely save my compassion for those in want. I don't waste it on those who already spend far too much time feeling sorry for themselves.'

His words silenced me. I was rebuked, and wondered if he would still be so unpitying if he knew my whole story.

Will struck out across fields again and then joined a cliff path, heading west. 'I don't think I can walk much further,' I told him.

'Just around the next headland, and then we walk down to the sea,' he replied.

'Down hill,' I sighed in relief. 'Thank goodness.' I was hopeful that my ordeal was almost over. We passed a barn, and I noticed a movement on the far side. A gentle whicker told me there were horses or ponies on the far side. I could hear them stirring.

At the end of the far field we climbed a gate and the field dropped away to nothingness in the gloom. I hesitated at the top, trying to get my bearings, but Will began to descend the steep slope. The land seemed to drop away at my feet into a deep ravine filled with a threatening darkness. To our left, I could make out rocky headlands stretching out into the black sea.

'Come, Isabelle,' said Will impatiently. 'The ship is in. We need to be away.'

'How can you know that?' I asked, puzzled.

'You heard the ponies waiting behind the barn. Listen!' he pointed down into the darkness of the ravine, but I could hear nothing except the plaintive bleating of sheep on the far side of the ravine. I shook my head.

'The landers are down there already,' said Will. 'I'm sure of it.'

Gingerly, I stepped down the beginning of the slope. Contrary to my expectation, the ground didn't drop away completely as I'd expected. A narrow path wound down in a zigzag through the ridged meadow. I could just make out the darker line of it snaking through the rough winter grass. I stepped out more quickly and followed Will downwards. At every steep twist in the path, I slowed, catching hold of clumps of grass to keep my balance. The drop below us made me feel giddy each time I looked down. We went down and down and down until my legs began to shake and I was afraid of falling.

'Please wait!' I gasped, as I bent over, trying to steady my trembling limbs. Will paused, restless in his haste. 'Are . . . we . . . nearly down yet?' I asked.

Will shrugged. 'Halfway?' he said. 'But it gets steeper from now on. I thought you wanted to walk downhill?'

I groaned. 'What was that?' I asked suddenly, pointing down the ravine towards the sea. Will turned to look where I had pointed, but it had already vanished. 'A blue flash,' I said.

The flare had been tiny; a mere pinprick of light, that rose silently into the air and vanished.

'That'll be *The Invisible*,' said Will. 'Signalling the landers.'

We stood close together on the narrow path, staring into the darkness. I was breathing heavily, but Will seemed unaffected by the climb.

'Why is it blue?' I asked.

'It's a pistol shot, but no barrel, just powder in the pan,' he explained briefly. 'You won't see the answering flink from here.'

I followed him on downwards. The path wound through bramble and hawthorn patches now, the narrow track slick with mud. Several times I grasped at plants to catch my balance and spiked my hands. I gasped and caught at Will instead.

'Anyone would think you were being tortured!' he said, taking my hand.

'I am,' I told him, grasping his hand gratefully and using it to steady myself as the path plunged ever more steeply down into the valley.

'Will, are the landers really going to carry the kegs up here?' I asked, pausing again. 'It's so steep.'

'It's not a route we usually use,' he admitted. 'Chapman's Pool is too steep a climb for regular runs. We have kegs only, no ankers, this trip. And a consignment of snuff. There are reasons why we've chosen it.'

'Which you're not going to share with me?'

'Which I'm not going to share with you,' he agreed. I reflected that the very steepness of this climb would probably put the Revenue officers off patrolling it. The ponies behind the barn must be the smuggling train, waiting quietly in the darkness to relieve the landers of their load.

At long last, we reached a bubbling stream that gurgled down the last steep drop to the beach. I sighed with relief, but the scramble down the stream was tricky. To my surprise, Will turned and lifted me down onto the shingle.

'You've done well,' he said briefly. I was stunned into silence, hearing even such mild words of praise from him.

'Who's there?' said a gruff voice right behind us. I jumped, but it seemed Will had been expecting it.

'Nick the Knife,' he said calmly. 'Crew member, rejoining the ship.'

'And him?' The shape in the darkness jerked his head towards me.

Will hesitated a second before replying: 'Mermaid Jake,' he replied. 'Crew member.'

The man gave a grunt and faded back into the shadows.

'*Mermaid Jake?*' I whispered indignantly.

'You don't have an alias,' he whispered. 'It was the best I could come up with on the spur of the moment like that. I could hardly tell him "Isabelle, surname unknown, unwilling shipmate".'

'It's pathetic,' I told him.

'Then think of one for yourself next time.'

'What about you? Are you some awe-inspiring knife-thrower or something?' I asked.

'No,' whispered Will in my ear. Even in the darkness, I could see his eyes crinkling in a smile. 'We had a contest once. I'm the worst knife-thrower on board. Can't hit a barn door. Hence the name.'

I couldn't help chuckling as I followed Will wearily onto the sand and shingle beach, my boots heavy with mud. But then memories of my last walk onto a shingle beach flooded back. I shivered. I was still alive. I was breathing and moving, tasting the salt air and feeling the exhaustion in my body and the pain in my feet from two days' walking. I was struck by the same overwhelming realization I'd had over and over again since that night. No matter how difficult things were now, I was so very *glad* to be alive. Just as long as I could keep the memories at a distance.

This thought buoyed me up despite my exhaustion. Besides, this beach was very different. This wasn't deep shingle, it was a mixture of sand and flat stones with large rocks scattered here and there. There were no towering chalk cliffs here either, only short black ones before the land turned into steep grassy hillside beyond. It was a small bay, sheltered and slightly spooky.

The wind gusted in off the sea, threatening to tear my cap from my head, and I clapped a hand over it to secure it. The sounds of kegs being unloaded from *The Invisible* carried across the short stretch of water between us.

The tub boat crunched onto the beach in a surge of waves and frothing surf. The landers ran forward to heave it onto the beach, swiftly setting to work to empty it of kegs. These were carried to the back of the beach and hoisted with ropes up the short cliff to the hillside above where they disappeared into darkness.

'Come on,' said Will, tugging at my sleeve. 'The walk is over.'

He and other men were pushing the boat back into the surf. I followed them, feeling my heart thump as I stepped into the water and felt the tug of the undertow at my calves. The boat was already slipping out of reach. Will leapt in and turned to beckon me. I froze, still wanting to be helped. To be carried perhaps. Gentle Jacob would have carried me, I was sure. But Will did not.

'Come on, Belle!' he called imperatively. But his shortening of my name sounded friendly and encouraging.

Strangely, at that moment when all the men were in the boat, and I had been left behind, I had no thought of making use of the opportunity to flee. I wanted to be in the boat. I took another uncertain step out into the cold, churning water. Will leaned out, held out a hand. I reached out to take it and missed. I launched myself forward and grabbed the side of the boat. Then in a rush of water and a painful thump into the side of the boat, I was somehow scrambling aboard.

'It's so much more satisfying to do things yourself, isn't it?' asked Will with a grin. He clapped me on the shoulder briefly and turned away, taking up an oar and throwing himself into rowing. He was right, yet again. I looked out to sea, towards *The Invisible*. I hadn't expected to be so glad to see her.

CHAPTER EIGHT

✳

This time when the ship docked at Cherbourg, no one locked me in the cabin. I didn't try to escape. I stayed quietly on board and watched the sights and sounds of the foreign harbour; the ships coming and going under the French flag, the small boats bringing in fish, the French women who came to haggle, bargain and carry the fresh goods home to their families.

I ate the French food that the men brought on board and some of it was familiar. My father had, after all, employed a French chef when we spent the season in London last year.

We set sail again on a bright late-October morning, nosing quietly out of the still harbour into the fresh choppy sea beyond.

Jacob approached me where I stood in the bows, looking out towards England. 'Skipper's orders, Isabelle,' he said with an apologetic grin. 'You're to take a turn with the chores.'

I stared at him, thinking he was joking for a minute.

'Chores?' I asked, mystified.

'We all takes turns,' Jacob explained. 'Helping in the galley, swabbing the decks, cleaning the latrines, mending the sails; there's always work a-plenty to be done. Skipper said to offer you a choice, but thought you might like to help out in the galley.'

I bit back the indignant objection that rose to my tongue: that these things were servants' work, and that I was a lady. That these chores would spoil my hands and break my nails. Will was far above me in the rigging, but I knew just how he would look at me if I spoke the words aloud. He never shirked his share of the work, for all he must be as well-born as I.

'We're all equals on board *The Invisible*,' Jacob added as though he could read my thoughts. Perhaps they were written clearly enough on my face for all I hadn't voiced them. 'You're one of us now, and need to take your turn.'

I looked at Jacob's rough, kindly face and realized I had no wish to be rude or offensive to him, even if Will wasn't listening. He'd been more than kind to me. 'Very well,' I said slowly, pushing myself upright from where I'd been lounging against the ship's rail. 'I'll help in the galley.'

If Jacob was surprised at my easy capitulation, he didn't say so. He merely nodded in the direction of the galley and I headed over, opening the wooden door and stepping down the steps into the low kitchen and mess area.

The cook, a thin, wiry man with greying hair, looked at me over his shoulder and went back to chopping a large piece of meat with a cleaver. I heard a disparaging sniff. 'I get the short straw then,' he muttered.

'The short straw?' I asked walking towards him. 'I've been asked to help you.'

'That's what I'm talking about. Just my luck to get the fine lady.'

'Why does everyone think I'll be useless?' I asked, annoyed.

'Because you are?' the cook returned. Then he roared with laughter at the expression on my face. 'Go on, then. Prove to me you're not. There's a pile of dishes to be done in the sink there. You can heat the water in this kettle. When you've finished those, the potatoes need preparing for dinner.'

I filled the kettle in silence and put it over the fire to heat. Then I stacked the dishes ready for washing and scrubbed all the tables which were full of crumbs and grease from the last meal. I tried not to ask the cook where anything was, hunting for it myself, determined to make him change his mind about me. Once the dishes were washed, wiped, stacked neatly away and the potatoes were carefully scrubbed and ready in a cauldron of water, I turned to the cook, knowing the work had taken me a very long time. He was leaning against the counter, watching me, his stained apron removed and thrown over a table.

'Is there anything else that needs doing?' I asked, bending down to stroke the galley cat who purred up at me.

Instead of replying, he held out his hand. 'I'm Harry,' he said.

Tentatively, I shook his hand. He smiled.

I worked in the galley every day after that. The skin on my hands roughened, the potatoes stained my skin, and my nails broke. But the strange thing was, I had a real sense of satisfaction in the work. It was far from arduous; a couple of hours a day at most. Perhaps I once might have found it too much but not now. When Will came in and saw me working, he gave me an approving nod, and forbore to taunt me. Jacob rewarded me with a smile. I was pleased and chose not to ask myself why I was seeking their approval.

The bright sun shining through my windows woke me very early one morning. I got up, combed my hair, washed my face, pulled on my shirt and hated breeches, and stepped out onto the deck. The skipper was at the wheel and gave me a nod. A man called Fred, whom I'd heard referred to as the pilot, was busy with various instruments.

It was a still morning, the sun still low but already bright in the east and surprisingly mild for early November. I stretched a little and breathed deeply, feeling inexplicably that life was good.

Will emerged from the hatch to my left. He slept below decks with the other men; a place they'd never allowed me to see on the grounds that 'it wouldn't be fit'. I was restricted to the open deck, the galley, and my own cabin.

There was a shout from far above us. Giving Will a wave, the look-out began to descend the rigging, as nimble as a monkey. Will nodded and swung himself into the rigging, preparing to climb up. He paused and looked at me. He hadn't greeted me; until that moment I didn't even think he'd seen me. There had been a tacit truce between us since our return from the haunting. 'Come up with me?' Will asked. 'There's a fine view.'

I looked upwards to the look-out far above us and shuddered. 'Certainly not,' I said.

Will grinned. 'I dare you,' he said softly.

I shook my head. 'I'm not going to fall for that,' I told him.

'It's not as difficult as it looks,' he assured me. I shook my head. 'What a shame,' he said, looking disappointed. 'I'd an idea you'd more courage than that.' He began to climb. I stood there feeling I'd failed in some way.

'Oh very well,' I sighed, grasping a rope and taking a step up. 'But you'd better make sure I don't fall.'

I glanced up as I spoke and caught sight of a triumphant grin on Will's face. I knew I'd been manipulated. But I began to climb anyway. Perhaps I was pleased that he wanted my company, or perhaps I was keen to test the new strength I felt in myself: the result of all the walking and work. It could have been a mixture of the two, but whatever it was, I found myself stepping nervously from rope to rope, grasping the hold above me firmly, and following Will's instructions as he led me higher and higher into the rigging.

'The trick is not to look down,' he told me, climbing beside me, showing me where to step. 'Just look up.'

I did as he said and kept climbing, but soon my arms and shoulders were aching with exertion. They began to tremble. 'I need to rest,' I said, puffing for breath. 'This is hard work.'

Will shook his head at me. 'No upper body strength,' he said. 'Did you never climb trees?'

I stopped climbing and stared at him in astonishment. '*Trees?*' I asked. 'You can't be serious? Walks within the grounds on fine days with great care not to muddy our gowns was the most we did.'

I saw he was laughing at me. Of course he knew I hadn't climbed trees.

'It explains a great deal though,' said Will.

I looked at him suspiciously. 'What do you mean?' I asked, expecting the worst.

Will laughed. 'Nothing unkind, for once,' he said. 'Truly, I was just thinking such an upbringing explained your weakness and lack of adventurous spirit.'

'That wasn't unkind?' I asked hauling myself up a step or two further. Will kept pace with me easily.

'But you must have felt hemmed in,' he said. 'No wonder you were unhappy.'

'Unhappy?' I echoed. 'I wasn't unhappy! I had a wonderful time. I learned with my governess, we had tea with Mama and Papa; I had kittens and many toys. I learned music. And once I left the schoolroom, there were balls, theatre and concerts, dinners, breakfasts, picnics—oh! Every manner of entertainment! I had a wonderful time and am certainly not an object of compassion.'

Will frowned at me, puzzled. 'But then why . . . ?'

Before he could finish his sentence several things happened in quick succession. A gust of wind broke the stillness of the morning, catching the sails and tilting the ship. The rigging swayed. My foot slipped and as I caught myself from falling by clutching at the ropes, I looked down. At the sight of the deck far below, little ant-sized people scuttling around on it, a burst of sick giddiness rushed at me, turning my muscles to wet

84

porridge. I swayed and moaned. My stomach churned. The strength leeched out of my hands. Their grip loosened. I was going to fall; nothing could stop me.

Will's arm caught my waist, holding me tightly against him. 'I told you not to look down!' he said in a matter-of-fact voice. I clung to him, eyes tightly shut against the dizzying drop, still fighting the nausea.

'Isabelle!' said Will sternly and shook me a little. 'Look at me!' I took a breath and opened my eyes. Will's face was very close to mine. I stared into his eyes. The early-morning light was catching them, showing up tiny green and hazel flecks in the blue. They were calm eyes and the sight of them steadied me.

'Breathe,' Will commanded. I did as he said and felt my strength return slowly. 'Good,' Will said. 'Keep looking at me. Isabelle, you can manage this climb. You're quite safe.'

'Please don't let me fall,' I whispered.

'I won't,' he said. 'But you don't need me. There are plenty of strong ropes here to hold on to.'

I kept my eyes on him, mesmerized by his closeness. I could see all the tiny flaws in his skin; a nick where he'd cut himself shaving; the fading bruise on his right cheek where I'd hit him. It took my mind off the dizzying drop beneath me.

'Can you climb again now?' asked Will. His voice sounded as though it were coming from a long way away, not right in my ear. 'We're nearly there.'

I nodded, and broke eye-contact, looking up as far as the next rope. Will released me, and slowly, painfully, I began to climb again. I was shaking like a leaf in a storm now, which made it much harder. I had to stop and rest between each step, breathing deeply, trying to calm my fears. The ship swayed, each motion magnified a hundredfold up in the high rigging.

'Just make sure you don't look down again, and you'll be fine,' said Will encouragingly. I nodded, but still couldn't speak.

After an eternity, we reached the look-out. It was little more than a rough wooden seat attached to the mast with ropes to hold on to. I climbed into it and clung tight. Will hung in the ropes at my side, apparently quite at his ease so far above the deck. When I glanced at him, he grinned. I sat on the swaying platform and closed my eyes, wishing I was safely down again. I was already dreading the descent.

The breeze was freshening, and I could feel the mast we were attached to swinging one way and then another as *The Invisible* dipped in the growing swell.

'I must have been mad,' I said wonderingly, opening my eyes. 'What on earth made me attempt such a climb? What were you thinking of, encouraging me?'

Will chuckled. 'You have a spirit of adventure and daring hidden somewhere inside you,' he said. 'Though you hide it even from yourself. I was trying to help it emerge.'

'You're entirely wrong,' I assured him. 'I have no sense of adventure whatsoever. All I want is a quiet life. I wouldn't mind if I never experienced anything exciting ever again.'

'You cannot possibly be that hen-hearted,' said Will. 'I refuse to believe it. Just look how much you enjoyed our trek across the heath and the escape from that cottage.'

I sent him a look of dislike. 'You know perfectly well I hated every moment of it,' I told him, reproachfully. 'You treated me abominably. Why?'

'Perhaps I had reasons of my own that were not entirely fair to you. But have you asked yourself why you behaved so badly yourself? And wondered whether that affected my treatment of you?'

Instead of snapping back an indignant denial, I pondered my memories of the walk. 'I was out of my depth, out of everything I've ever known,' I said slowly. 'I have been since I came aboard. I've found it difficult to . . .'

'Not behave like a spoiled beauty?' asked Will.

I scowled at him, but he was smiling and there was no malice in it. 'Come let's have peace and agree to make a new start,' he said, holding out his hand.

I peeled my fingers, numb with gripping so tightly, off the rope and grasped his hand. I remembered what Jacob had said about winning the men's trust.

The shaking was subsiding now and I was feeling less unwell. 'What happened to me?' I asked. 'I was fine and then suddenly . . .'

'Vertigo,' said Will. 'Some people get it, some don't. Most would during a first climb this high. I did tell you not to look down.'

I shuddered at the memory. 'You didn't think it worthwhile to mention that to me beforehand?' I asked.

'It might have put you off and that would have been a pity.'

I rolled my eyes.

'Don't let me go, Will. Oh please don't leave me,' mocked Will in an exaggerated, high-pitched girly imitation.

'I never said such a thing!'

'Oh yes you did! And clung to me in a most affecting way. I'd no idea you had such feelings for me.' Will grinned and his eyes were dancing with mischief.

'I should never have accepted that handshake,' I retorted. 'Would you like a matching bruise on the other cheek?'

'She's offering me violence! And after I saved her life too!'

'What is it about you?' I asked him seriously. 'From time to time, I come close to liking you. Only a very little, of course. Not the kind of warm overflowing feelings I can see you are imagining, so don't flatter yourself! But whenever I think you may have some redeeming characteristics after all, you manage to make me hate you again. A really fierce kind of loathing and repulsion that starts right here,' I indicated my belly, 'and spreads all over me. It's quite a talent you have. I've never disliked anyone quite that intensely before.'

'Oh, you don't hate me really,' said Will cheerfully, nudging my foot with his. 'You're just pretending to yourself.'

'How well you know me,' I marvelled, opening my eyes very wide.

'Indeed,' agreed Will. 'Now stop talking nonsense and admire the view with me. Look out, not down. There! You can see the coast of England.'

It was strange the difference it made to look outwards rather than down. I felt no dizziness at all. The craggy coastline was clear and sharp in the bright, early morning light; the sky above it a pale autumn blue.

'What happens when real winter comes?' I asked Will. 'Is it not too cold and stormy to sail?'

'We do most of our trade through the winter.'

I looked at him, wondering why. His gaze was fixed on the distant shore, his eyes crinkled at the corners against the brightness. He sensed me watching him and looked round, meeting my eyes. 'There are crops to tend and harvest in summer. Sheep to shear, lambs to birth. There is plenty of work. This is the time of year men are laid off. This is when they need to find other work to support their families. And it's in the winter weather that everyone wants a drop of good French cognac to keep out the cold.'

'But what about the winter storms?' I asked. 'Aren't they dangerous?'

'Of course. But they are dangerous for the Revenue officers as well. The Gentlemen have the best pilots, the best ships, and the best sailors in the channel. So we are far safer than they. There is less risk of being caught. And the long, dark winter nights are our friend. In summer we would be far too visible.'

I nodded, my gaze drawn by the distant coastline, green slopes and varying shades of rocky cliff dappled with patches of pale sunlight and shadow. The land that held my family. I wondered how they were. Were they more comfortable now they had money once more? Had they found somewhere new to live?

'While we're up here,' said Will, 'I think it's about time you began learning your knots.'

'My knots?'

In reply, Will threw me a short length of rope. 'Make that fast on this spar,' he told me.

With hands that still shook, I wrapped the rope around the spar and tied it. 'Like that?'

'Not like that, no,' he answered. He reached out and tugged it loose in one swift movement. 'You see? If we couldn't tie better knots than that, the whole rigging would fall apart.' He looped the rope around the spar, twisting it deftly. 'That's a proper knot.'

He pulled it loose and knotted it again more slowly. 'See?'

I had a go and the loop simply fell off. 'Show it more slowly,' I asked after another unsuccessful attempt. I couldn't understand why my hands were so clumsy and unwilling to make the apparently simple moves his made.

Will climbed to stand behind me and took my hands in his, showing me which way to guide the loop, twist it and pull it taut.

'Now let me try again,' I asked after a couple of demonstrations. This time I succeeded. 'There!' I said triumphantly.

Will moved away, with a smile. 'That's a bowline,' he told me. 'A simple sailor's hitch, useful for mooring a dingy, for example.'

I frowned. 'You mean there are others?'

Will rolled his eyes. 'Of course there are others. There's a different knot for every job. I'm still learning them all after two years.'

I felt daunted, but Will laughed at my expression. 'Master the bowline,' he said. 'Then ask Jacob to teach you more. All the men know the knots, but he's the most patient teacher. And he's left-handed, like you.'

A bell rang out below. 'Ah, breakfast!' exclaimed Will rubbing his hands. 'Ready to climb back down?'

CHAPTER NINE

✳

It was dark when *The Invisible* carved her way silently through the black waters into Poole Harbour. The wind was kind, allowing us to glide behind Brownsea Island. The moon was half hidden behind clouds, showing her partial face only occasionally. The ship was sluggish in the water, groaning with the weight of the ankers and kegs of spirits that had been loaded onto her in France.

'The island shields us from view of the Revenue, you see,' said Jacob softly, standing by my side at the rail. 'They be over that side of the harbour keeping watch. Even if the moon shines full on us, they won't see us till we leave the far side of the island. We used to unload in the harbours all the time, but the Preventives have got a bit sharper of late. So in the usual way, we keeps to the more remote coves.'

'But not tonight?'

Jacob smiled his slow smile. 'Tonight we're playing with fire.'

The wind spilled out of the sails, making them flap with a crack of canvas. I could see dark shadows scurrying about up in the rigging. I knew one of them was Will, but I couldn't make out which. I was glad to have the solid deck under my feet. I'd been back up in the rigging since that first time, but I wasn't comfortable there yet.

There was a sense of suppressed excitement all around me, as the men prepared to unload the contraband. I could tell their nerves thrilled to the danger they were about to face. I found myself picking up on their enthusiasm, tension holding my body as taut as if the customs officers were breathing down my neck.

On the far side of Brownsea, the ship swung in towards land, and hovered there. A tub-boat was lowered as quietly as possible into the water. The creak of the ropes and the splash of the still harbour waters on the hull made the blood race in my veins. I held my breath, but could hear no sound of alarm being raised.

A few ankers of brandy were lowered into the tub-boat and the craft set off with a creak and muted splash of oars. She was soon lost to sight in the darkness. A mist was swirling around us now and I saw the flash of Jacob's teeth as he grinned. 'They'll not see us now,' he murmured in a satisfied voice.

The tub-boat returned and was tethered behind us, the sails filled with wind again, and *The Invisible* moved further inland, gliding past the tree-shrouded island.

We were out of the lee of the island now. The wind freshened and the mist began to clear. The only sound was the water swishing against the underside of the lugger. 'We're goin' to do it,' said Jacob. 'We just need to make the dash across this stretch of open water to Rockley Point. If only this mist would hold.'

But the mist was vanishing by the moment, allowing us to see the twinkling lights at Poole. And if we could see them . . .

'Cutter launched!' the man in the look-out called down.

Jacob frowned heavily. 'The Preventives are out,' he growled. 'They must have spotted us. That's damned unlucky.'

Every available hand rushed to the sails. I thought we were going to turn about and make our escape back out to the open sea. But I was wrong. Instead, the men were unfurling all the canvas *The Invisible* carried. The ship altered course, sailing closer to the wind. I guessed they were trying to race the cutter. It was a dangerous game, surely?

Our ship quickened her pace, the timbers creaking and the canvas filling. She surged through the still estuary waters. I couldn't see a thing ahead of us in the darkness, but I was aware both skipper and pilot knew every inch of the huge natural harbour and that the look-outs would be alert and straining their eyes for any danger. When we reached Rockley Point, the moon emerged once more from behind the clouds, allowing us a brief, dazzling glimpse of a narrow channel ahead. My heart skipped a beat. The cutter was pursuing us; did we not run the risk of becoming trapped?

I looked around me, feeling anxious. None of the men looked worried; merely tensed for action. I fidgeted restlessly, wishing I knew something about sailing the ship. I wanted to help, not stand around uselessly.

There was a light thud behind me. I turned to see Will had landed on the deck. His eyes were sparkling, his breathing quick from his descent through the rigging. I realized he was actually *enjoying* the danger. He grinned when he saw me looking at him. 'We shall see some sport before this night is out,' he promised.

'Sport?' I asked. 'Are you mad? No, that's a stupid question. I know full-well you are.'

Will chuckled. The moon slid behind another dark cloud and I couldn't see the expression on his face. 'What is the penalty for smuggling?' I asked, a new fear suddenly gripping me. I was aboard this ship, and I was as guilty as any of the men. 'Is it a hanging offence?'

'Don't sound so frightened,' said Will, clapping a hand on my shoulder. 'We won't swing unless we shoot one of the officers. It's only imprisonment for smuggling.'

The ship slid into the narrow channel and slowed as we lost the wind. The sound of water under the hull lessened to a whisper. 'Only imprisonment?' I repeated. 'That's all right then. I'm sure I could accustom myself to prison.'

'They'll be hard pressed to find a jury to convict us,' Will assured me. 'And the chances of a case going to law are small in any case. The Preventives have to pay legal fees out of their own pocket, which isn't a plump one. They don't want to have to do that.'

'So why bother to chase us?' I asked, bewildered.

'Oh, it looks good. They can't sit on their backsides in the tavern all day. Most often they'll settle for a share of the cargo or a back-handed payment. But we don't want to share or pay.'

I felt a measure of relief seeping into me at the thought that nothing very dreadful would happen if we were caught.

'Of course, you get a few officers who are hell-bent on stamping out the trade, no matter what the cost to them personally,' added Will cheerfully before he strode aft to consult with the skipper.

The part of me that was a law-abiding citizen found it outrageous that the king's men took bribes instead of combating crime. But at the same time, I hoped that whoever was chasing us right now was as corrupt as necessary. I had no fancy for a prison cell.

The channel had widened. *The Invisible* heeled over as she turned sharply around a small land mass, huddled low in the water to our right. 'Otter Island,' I heard someone mutter nearby. 'We'll make it yet.'

The ship slipped behind the island, but not before I saw the nose of a ship emerge from the channel behind us. The Revenue men were hard on our heels.

We made straight for the coast beyond the island. As we approached a high grassy bank, dark shapes rose up out of the gloom and ran forward to catch ropes thrown from *The Invisible*. Our sails were lowered in a rush of canvas and we were drawn sideways to land. The kegs and ankers began to be lowered, even before the ship had been made fast. I could make out urgent, low-voiced exchanges between the smugglers and the landers. My fists were clenched. We were about to be caught red-handed landing contraband and the men on shore would doubtless be taken too.

But the unloading was completed with remarkable swiftness and in near-silence. No sooner was the last keg off the ship than the ropes were flung back aboard and we drifted from the shore.

Our men were scurrying about the rigging and the deck once more, altering the set of the sails, working to turn the ship back the way we had come. Men were also lowering buckets into the sea; I wondered what they

could be at. Jacob interrupted my musings without cere-
mony, pushing a bucket of sea water into my hand. 'Help
scrub the deck,' he ordered.

'Why?' I asked.

'Because one o' the barrels leaked and it stinks like a
tavern,' he said as he hurried to the side to lower another bucket. Someone threw me a scrubbing brush and I
went across the deck to the side where the kegs had been
stacked for unloading. Sure enough there was a strong
smell of liquor.

Before I began the work, I looked back at Otter Island, expecting the Revenue cutter to appear behind
us at any moment, but she didn't. I dropped to my
knees, slopped some of the water out and began scrubbing. Some of the buckets were being carried down
to the hold where there was clearly more cleaning to
be done. No sooner was my bucket empty than it was
snatched away and another was pushed at me. After
three bucketfuls, my back and shoulders were aching.
I straightened myself, curious to see what was going
on around us.

As I stood up, we glided around the far end of the
island and there was the Revenue cutter, dead ahead of
us. Her guns had been run out. They were aimed straight
at us, the moonlight gleaming starkly on the barrels.

Beside me, Will whistled low. I jumped, having not
even realized he was there. 'Who'd have thought a Phil-
istine could have come up with an ambush like this?'
he said, scrubbing brush in one hand, eyes narrowed to
make out the ship in the darkness. 'They'll be learning to
read and to shoot straight next.'

There was laughter around us, the men unafraid now that our cargo had been offloaded. Nonetheless, we all bent to the scrubbing again. 'What if they fire?' I asked Jacob anxiously.

'Strictly speaking, they ain't allowed to do that. Not without firing a warning shot first. They'll be wanting to rummage us, hoping for a share of the cargo, no doubt,' said Jacob cheerfully as he worked. 'Well, they're more than welcome now.'

'Will,' said the skipper curtly. 'They'll be boarding us.'

'I know,' replied Will, and disappeared below. I wondered why but there was no time to ask.

A shout to surrender from the Revenue cutter made the men laugh more. We hauled to and lowered our sails once more and the buckets and brushes were hastily swept from sight. The Revenue came aboard to find every member of the crew standing relaxed and smiling on deck. I saw Will emerge from below at the last minute and slip in amongst the other men. At least I thought it was Will. He was now red-haired and red-bearded and dressed in rough working clothes. A hat was pulled down low over his eyes.

Eight customs men and two soldiers with rifles came aboard. A slender-looking officer led them, the brass on his uniform winking in the moonlight as he moved. He wore a neat wig with a hat and looked serious. He greeted the skipper formally, and barked orders at his men to spread out and search the ship. I stood quietly at the rail, hoping my disguise was sufficient in the darkness of the night.

The Revenue men climbed down through the hatches and we could hear banging and crashing as they searched the hold. Meanwhile the Revenue officer stayed on deck, questioning the skipper. I listened nervously, wondering what account he could give of himself. It seemed to me that cargo or no cargo, we'd been caught in highly suspicious activity.

A notebook in hand, the officer had noted down the name of the ship and the skipper's name (not his true one, I suspected) and was asking questions. The skipper was answering them slowly and painstakingly. I regarded him in surprise, having thought him an intelligent man.

'What are you doing sailing at night?' the Revenue officer wanted to know.

The skipper pushed his cap forward and scratched the back of his head.

'Can't say as we was doin' aught partickler,' he drawled, his local dialect suddenly pronounced. 'We just took a fancy for a sail by moonlight, see?'

'No one takes a fancy to sail by moonlight!' scoffed the officer.

The skipper stared at him, blank-faced. 'That's agin the law now too, be it?' he asked.

'It is if you're landing contraband and I know that's what you were doing! Defrauding His Majesty of duty!'

'His Majesty's what?' said the skipper, a look of idiocy on his face.

'His Majesty's customs!' snapped the officer. 'There's duty to be paid on goods landed on this coast as you very well know!'

'Oh aye, I reckon we know that, eh, lads?' The skipper glanced around at his crew who nodded and murmured agreement.

'So what are you doing here?'

'Ah. We came looking for otters.'

'Otters?' snapped the Revenue officer, exasperated.

'Aye. That there be Otter Island, b'aint it?' he asked pointing at the island. 'Well some of me men wanted to be sighting an otter.'

'Don't be ridiculous, man. It's the middle of the night!'

'Ah. That'd explain it then.'

'Explain what?'

'Why we ain't seen hide nor hair o' one.' The skipper shook his head and sighed deeply. 'Right disappointed they be. Happen we'd better come back later.'

The Revenue officer turned away in disgust, to find one of his men at his elbow. 'I believe otters are nocturnal, sir, with respect,' the young man said.

'I don't give a damn about otters!' exclaimed the Revenue officer furiously. 'Why do you even know these things, Jones? You worry me. Help search the ship!'

The men searched everywhere, even turning my cabin upside down. I saw the Revenue officer pull my bridal gown out of the chest and examine it in some perplexity and suspicion. My heart sank. Why hadn't I thrown the thing overboard?

'What's this?' the officer demanded, holding it up so that the skipper could see. 'You have a woman on board?'

I shrank back into the shadows, pulling my cap low as the skipper shook his head slowly. 'I don't hold with women on ships,' he replied.

'Listen, man,' said the officer seriously, 'there's a young woman gone missing in such a gown on this coast. This is serious. Where did you get it?'

Will moved slightly so that he was standing in front of me, blocking the officers' view of me. The skipper paused. My heart beat fast. They wouldn't give me up willingly. I knew far too much.

It occurred to me that I could step forward and own to the gown. There would be nothing any of the men could do if I revealed myself. I would be taken away from this ship. I hesitated. Did I want to return to my other life?

'Found it in the sea,' the skipper responded at last. 'Fished it up off . . . Durdle Door, I reckon it was, eh, lads?'

A general murmur of assent.

'And did it have . . . was there no one in it?' asked the officer swallowing hard. 'No . . . no body?'

I inched further back into Will's shadow. I didn't want to leave. It was a revelation that now I finally had the chance to escape, I no longer wished to; I was as happy on board *The Invisible* as I'd ever been in my life.

The skipper looked around at his men. 'Anyone see a young woman in it?'

Again, heads were shaken. 'Not so much as a mermaid,' said Generous Joe, who had not, in fact, seen me until I'd changed clothes. 'It were like you see it now, only wetter.'

CHAPTER TEN

✳

They took my gown with them, of course. It was all the officers of the king's Revenue had to show for their rummage of the ship. A small enough prize.

I didn't care much about the loss of the muddied, bedraggled gown; only for the trouble the find might cause. Would my parents now be certain that I was dead? Would they sorrow? They must already have thought me dead for a month or more. And as far as my old life was concerned, I was. I just hoped the gown didn't set a search afoot or cause trouble for the crew of *The Invisible*.

There had been talk of an inquiry and witnesses, which made some of the crew scowl angrily at me while others stood protectively around me. When the officers left and as *The Invisible* sailed back out to sea, Will remained close to me, not taking part in sailing the ship. I felt him watching me, but pretended not to notice. At last I yawned and realized how very tired I was. I began to walk towards my cabin, but Will caught hold of my arm.

'You didn't say anything,' he said. 'Why not?'

I shrugged. 'I don't know,' I admitted.

His eyes were on me again, and I could feel myself colouring. Although it was dark, and he wouldn't be able to see, I turned my face away from him, looking out to sea. The fresh, salty night air fanned my hot cheeks. I was telling the truth. I didn't know why I had suddenly not wanted to be taken from the ship. I didn't know when things had changed. I just knew that I felt a part of the crew now. Unthinkable, but true nonetheless. I didn't feel ready to talk about it. So I looked down at Will's hand, still grasping my wrist.

'Do you mind?' I asked. 'I'm weary and need to sleep.'

He looked at me a moment longer, his gaze curious. Then he released me. 'Sleep well,' he said. There was no trace of mockery or irony in his voice. I nodded, flustered, and retreated to my cabin to lie awake, wondering if I had made the right choice not to take the escape route when it had been offered to me.

The following day dawned dull and wet. When I emerged from my cabin, rain was lashing the decks, making them slippery. I hurried to the galley, holding on to ropes, rails, hatches, anything that was handy to help me stay upright. The visibility was so poor that I had no way of knowing where the ship was, only that it was under sail to somewhere or other.

The galley was steamy and smelt of bacon with an underlying aroma of wet dog. The ship's cat greeted me enthusiastically and I bent to stroke it. Lots of the men who weren't on duty were crammed into this warm, damp space, many unwashed and dirty.

Will and Jacob made room for me on an already overcrowded bench. I fetched my bowl of porridge and eased myself between them, struggling to wield my spoon in such a confined space.

'We've got another job for you later today,' Will told me when I finished eating.

'If you need a ghost, you're out of luck,' I told him. 'My ghost costume having been confiscated.'

Jacob shook his head, a grave frown on his face. 'That were a bad error. The skipper's kicking himself for not throwing it overboard before we was searched.'

'Or throwing *her* overboard,' muttered Slippery Sam. 'Why didn't you throw that gown away?' He sent me a swift look of dislike. 'You should of thought of it.'

'Happen she wanted to be found,' snarled Hard-Head Bill.

'She didn't say a word though, when she could of,' Jacob spoke up in my defence. 'There'd have been a whole heap more trouble if she'd have shown herself to the Philistines.' I was glad to hear mutters of agreement and had a sense of some of the men closing ranks around me in the face of this criticism.

'Well, I don't reckon she's a risk worth taking,' muttered Hard-Head Bill.

'Most of us no longer agree with you,' replied Will steadily. Then he turned and addressed me as though there'd been no interruption. 'We don't need you for your acting talent today, Isabelle,' he said. 'How is your knowledge of lace?'

I stared at him in surprise. 'I don't know . . . Certainly I know fine work when I see it. I mean . . . I've worn a fair bit in my time.'

'Good. You see, I've been commissioned to buy a large quantity, but have no detailed knowledge of the stuff. I don't want to get tricked with an inferior quality.'

'For whom?' I asked. 'Why cannot they select it themselves?'

There was much sniggering about me. I looked around puzzled. Then it dawned on me that of course brandy and wine were not the only goods to be smuggled across the channel. French lace paid high duties at the port too, and was a costly item. No doubt it would be well worth smuggling.

Will sighed. 'Come up on deck,' he told me. I got up and followed him to the door. One of the men stuck out a leg and I tripped over it, falling heavily on the dirty floor. There was a roar of laughter and the blood rushed to my cheeks. I picked myself up, one knee and both palms grazed, furious and humiliated. I couldn't see who had done it, though I had a pretty good idea it was Sam or Bill.

'That's enough to make me wish I'd spoken out yesterday when the customs man asked for me,' I said fiercely.

'Oooh, I'm quakin' in my boots,' Bill cried. I left the cabin, my face burning and tears starting in my eyes. As I walked out, I heard Jacob's voice behind me.

'That weren't funny, Bill,' he said. 'And if it happens again, you'll have me to reckon with.'

The door to the galley banged shut behind me and I was out in the rain again.

'What's wrong?' asked Will who had left the galley before the incident. I told him, and he shrugged unsympathetically.

'They're angry and frightened that you and that dratted gown have put us all in danger,' he said. 'Besides, your class has put most of them through far worse many times over. You can't expect them not to take a little revenge when you are unprotected.'

'There's no need to take it out on me, though. I've never done anyone any harm.'

'Really?' asked Will sceptically. 'You've never humiliated a servant or worker?'

I was about to retort that I certainly hadn't, when a few uncomfortable incidents rose unbidden in my mind. The nursery maid I had slapped, knowing she couldn't slap me back without losing her job. The scullery maid who'd been dismissed for stealing pies my sister and I had taken. Countless small troubles and humiliations I'd heaped on others. I'd never thought of them in that light before. I'd never considered the hurt and unhappiness my actions must have caused. They'd only been servants, after all. I'd never really thought until now that they might have feelings like me.

When I didn't reply, Will looked at me closely, nodded once and changed the subject. 'As you can see, we've arrived in Cherbourg once more,' he said, throwing out his arm to indicate our surroundings. The motion of the ship had been lessening while I ate breakfast. I'd noticed it but given it little thought. I nodded, seeing the rain-washed quay beside the ship.

'But before we go ashore you need a haircut!'

'No!' I cried. I clamped my hands protectively over my ragged hair. 'You're not touching it!' I told him.

'Me? No, of course not. It's Harry who is the expert with a pair of scissors,' replied Will. 'You can't walk about the town looking like that.'

I felt unnaturally shorn as I disembarked. My hair now reached to just above my shoulders and was at present tied back into a short ponytail with a black ribband like Will's; I couldn't remember it ever having been so short.

'But like this,' Will had comforted me, 'we can tie it back to make you look like a boy or dress it to make you look like a girl. Ideal.'

I was surprised to be sent alone with Will into the town. I'd thought there would be others accompanying us and said as much as he strode off towards the town centre, with me trotting at his side.

'I'm the agent of our little ventures, you see, Isabelle,' he told me.

'What do you mean by agent?' I asked. My father had an agent who managed his estates—or at least he used to have, I reminded myself sadly—but that couldn't be what Will meant.

'It means I handle the money,' said Will, patting his waistcoat with a grin. 'I negotiate the contracts in England; which goods are required and so on. Then I carry the money and I do the buying here in *la belle France*. In some places I also arrange the rendezvous with the landers. We always agree two or three spots on the coast. If one is being watched we move on to the next the following night.'

'You're very communicative all of a sudden,' I remarked. 'Have you decided you trust me or something?'

'Let's just say I'm inclined to give you the benefit of the doubt.'

'Which is more than some others will,' I said bitterly.

'Give them time. You don't belong. And you gave us no good reason to trust you at first either, remember?'

I reluctantly acknowledged the truth of this. 'Did they mistrust you too?' I asked. 'How long have you been sailing with them?'

'This is my second winter,' he said as we passed a bakery. A wonderful smell drifted out and I paused a moment to sniff.

'They didn't trust me for a long time,' Will admitted. 'But many of them are good men. I hope they respect me now, even if I don't fit their idea of what a smuggler should be.'

We paused outside a shop and I looked at Will in surprise. 'This is a dressmaker's, not a draper's or lace maker's,' I said.

'I know. It was agreed among us while you were sleeping that you should be dressed as a lady for this excursion.'

My eyes widened with pleasure. 'So you are going to buy me a gown?'

'The skipper has authorized the expenditure,' said Will, apparently making sure I didn't think this was a gift from him.

I didn't care. I pushed open the door eagerly and went in. We were cautiously greeted by two Frenchwomen who looked at Will's plain clothes and my rough ones with some distaste and disappointment. It was clear that they didn't expect much profit from such as us.

I was less than thrilled by their dowdy establishment too. I would never have patronized it in my former life. Considering we were in France, only a few days' drive from Paris, the fashionable heart of Europe, the gowns on display were shockingly outmoded. I wandered around the shop, eyeing them disparagingly, while Will spoke to the dressmakers in rapid French. I was astounded at his fluency and rather mortified to realize how inadequate my schoolgirl French actually was. They spoke so fast, I could catch very little of what was said.

At last one of them came forward and began to speak to me more slowly, showing me fabrics and smiling. I responded in halting French, gradually gaining in confidence as I could see she was no longer hostile. Whatever Will had said to her about my boy's raiment had clearly done the trick.

I tried on several gowns and at last settled on a green one that needed only minor alterations. It was not something I would have chosen normally. But when I picked out a much more fashionable day brocade gown in pink silk with lace trimming which needed more altering, Will shook his head at me. I took the hint, ungraciously, settling instead for the green velvet promenade gown with the cream edges and gold buttons. He seemed very determined I should select a gown with a hoop too, which surprised me. Hoops were impractical for anything but fashionable leisure time. However I didn't object to having a fine gown, and obeyed him meekly enough.

Will bundled me out of the shop and led me off to a milliner next to find a hat that would match the gown. I tried on quite a few, parading in front of the looking glass while Will sighed and groaned behind me. As soon as I settled on a pretty cream bonnet, he shoved the money at the shopkeeper and dragged me out of the shop.

'What's the rush?' I asked. 'This is the first fun I've had in weeks.'

Will looked decidedly harassed as he replied: 'It might be fun for you. I've got to stand there explaining what you're doing in boys' clothing and coping with all the comments and strange looks while you preen in front of the mirror.'

I rolled my eyes and looked down at my boots. 'Shoes next?' I asked.

'Definitely not! I've had enough. Besides you've spent a fortune already.'

'But I can't wear these! I'd look completely wrong. Anyone would stare to see men's boots with the gown I've just purchased!'

Will groaned aloud. 'For heaven's sake, Isabelle, shoes don't show under all those petticoats!'

'They certainly do,' I argued. 'Every time you take a step. It was bad enough playing the ghost in the dark. I could never get away with it in the daytime.'

I got my way, of course. Within another half an hour, I was seated in a coffee house with both a hat box and a shoe box on the seat beside me. When I wanted to peek inside the boxes while we waited for the food to be served, Will pushed my hand away. 'Leave them!' he hissed at me. 'You're a boy again now, if you please. Could you behave like one?'

'How am I supposed to know how boys behave?' I asked indignantly. 'I know they're rude and unmannered, but that's about it.'

'Well, they don't constantly peep at their shopping and squeal over it,' replied Will.

'I wasn't!'

'Oh yes, you were!'

Our bickering was interrupted by a waiter bringing us our food. He was an older man and bestowed a fatherly smile on me as he put my plate before me and said something I didn't quite catch about a young lad. Will had ordered us *ragoût* with a glass of wine and light French pastries to follow. I ate eagerly, hungry after my morning's activity.

'So what happens next?' I asked cheerfully. 'I'm beginning to enjoy this smuggling lark.'

Will rolled his eyes. 'We're going back to the dressmaker's,' he replied. 'Once we have your gown we'll go to the warehouse and select some lace.'

'I don't wish to appear in any way ungrateful,' I said cautiously. 'I'm delighted to have appropriate clothing once more. But why go to so much trouble and expense for one visit to the warehouse? If my disguise is good enough to fool the waiter, wouldn't it do for purchasing lace as well?'

'Not once you start sighing over the point work and showing all manner of feminine knowledge, it wouldn't,' said Will dryly. 'You might look the part, but you're not much of an actor.'

'It's a skill I haven't had any use for up to now,' I replied, unruffled by Will's criticism.

'As a matter of fact, it's not so much the visit to the warehouse that you need the disguise for,' Will told me. 'It's more disposing of the goods on the other side of the channel.'

A small chill crept into my stomach at his words and I laid down my fork. 'Tell me at once what it is I'm going to have to do,' I asked.

Will waved my question away. 'Plenty of time for that later,' he said lightly. 'Enjoy your meal. French cuisine is so superior to English fare. You should make the most of it.'

I pushed my plate away with a frown. 'I find I've quite lost my appetite,' I said.

Will pushed it back to me. 'No tantrums now, Isabelle,' he said. 'They don't become you.'

'Do you have sisters?' I asked him.

Will looked startled. 'No. Why?' he asked.

'I'm very relieved to hear it. You would be an intolerable older brother. I'd strongly advise against having daughters too. You'd be an even worse father.'

To my surprise, a deep flush suffused Will's face and his eyes clouded before he looked away. I'd only been bantering and was surprised to see the effect my words had produced. 'I'm sorry,' I began. 'I only . . . '

'Shall we go?' asked Will, standing up abruptly. I had no choice but to gather my boxes together and follow him as he left the inn. We walked in uncomfortable silence to the dressmaker's. There the green velvet gown was fitted once more and a couple of last adjustments made. I put on my new shoes and matching hat and emerged from the fitting room, a young lady again at last.

I walked out, holding myself very straight and grand, hoping for a word of approval from Will. Sure enough he was waiting and greeted me with a smile. It was a broad smile that didn't reach his eyes and I suspected at once he was playing a part. '*Magnifique, ma coeur!*' he cried when he saw me. I thought this was overdoing it more than a little. The gown was nothing out of the ordinary and I certainly wasn't his dear heart. When he came towards me with outstretched hands I stopped short, unsure what to expect. Will caught both my hands in his, kissed them and then kissed me briefly on the cheek.

He certainly wasn't kissing me for the pleasure of it. Why would he? So I refrained from slapping him and forced myself to smile up at him complacently instead. From the corner of my eye I noticed that both the dressmakers were watching us with almost tearful expressions on their faces. As Will slid an arm around me and embraced me, one of them actually dabbed her eyes with a pocket handkerchief.

Will tore himself away from me with apparent reluctance and completed the purchase of the gown and a very bright red woollen cloak. I looked at it in some trepidation, but said nothing until we were out of the shop.

'I do hope that isn't for me,' I said once we were on the pavement once more, my hand drawn through his arm as the two ladies watched us from the shop window. I indicated the neat brown paper parcel now tied with string in his free hand. 'I can't imagine any colour that would go less well with this gown.'

'It is for you,' he said. 'But I didn't buy it with fashion in mind. For this too we have a use.'

'I see. And may I ask what the . . . the *kissing* thing was about?' I asked, injecting as much revulsion as possible into my words. I removed my hand from his arm at the same time. We were now out of sight of the shop.

Will laughed; a more natural laugh. His sudden restraint was fading again. 'I told the good ladies that we were engaged. It was a very affecting story.' He saw outrage on my face.

'I had to tell them something!' he said and had the grace to look a little sheepish. 'To explain the scandalous way you were dressed, you know. I spun them a fabulous tale about your wicked guardian who wasn't really your guardian and how we escaped from the house at the dead of night, with you up before me on the horse. That's why you needed to be dressed in boy's clothes. We are about to be married, you know.'

'I wouldn't marry you for the world,' I told him. 'Your story is a disgraceful lie from beginning to end!'

Will shrugged. 'Tell me your real story and maybe I won't need to make up lies.'

CHAPTER ELEVEN

✳

The purchase of lace was more exciting than I expected. I justified my presence by asking to have each roll unrolled fully and discovering that on some, only the first section of lace was top quality. Thereafter, the work was shoddy and would have lost us both customers and money. The merchant was grumpy about being caught attempting to cheat us, but Will drove a very good bargain as a result and left the warehouse much lighter in mood.

'Well done, Isabelle,' he praised me as we walked back to the ship, two errand boys following us, carrying all the goods we had purchased. 'Good work.'

'Thank you. I imagine the merchants try all sorts of tricks with the goods.'

'Many are honest; some will try to cheat you. There are many ploys: a common one is sampling a barrel of brandy. Traders will sometimes offer a taste straight from the barrel. It tastes excellent and you are convinced to buy. But what you've tasted comes from a small compartment at the top of the barrel. The rest is rough enough to strip your insides right out only you don't discover until it's too late. That's a ploy used for contraband on both sides of the channel.'

I wrinkled my nose in thought. 'It seems a short-sighted way of doing business,' I observed. 'You wouldn't go back to a dealer who had cheated you once.'

'Absolutely right. We work on building up trusted contacts. And on being trustworthy ourselves. It's better for trade in the long term. But there are always a few rogues about trying to make themselves a quick fistful of guineas. And that isn't limited to the contraband trade.'

'What is my next part in this?' I asked. 'In what way will I be part of this trustworthy illegal trade?'

I should of course have known that whatever my 'next part' was, it would be embarrassing and awkward. Why else would it be delegated to me? I stood in my cabin in my shift, looking at the neatly-folded quantities of costly lace and didn't know where to start.

There was a knock at the door. 'Go away!' I shouted assuming it was Will.

'Are you nearly ready?' asked Gentle Jacob's voice mildly. 'We're almost in the port.'

'Sorry, Jacob,' I replied more politely. 'Nowhere near ready.' The ship swayed and tilted under my feet as we swung round to negotiate the harbour entrance.

It was going to be an easy matter for me to walk off the ship and into the town carrying a large quantity of contraband lace, Will had assured me. I wasn't convinced.

I unfolded a large length of lace and wrapped it experimentally around one leg. As soon as I let it go, it sagged down around my ankle. I needed some way of fastening it. I picked up my garters from beside my bunk and tried again, tying it in place. That worked better.

I wrapped lace around my waist. It wasn't going to be a flattering look. There was another rap at the door; less polite this time.

'Isabelle, we're running out of time,' said Will's voice imperatively. 'We need you ashore the moment we've tied up. We can't risk the ship being rummaged while the lace is still aboard.'

I went to the door and peered out cautiously. Jacob, Will, and Harry were all waiting outside and looked around eagerly to see how their idea had worked. I shook my head at them. 'It's too difficult,' I told them. 'It's going to be so bulky and I can't tie it on to myself without an extra hand.'

'I knew you wouldn't be able to manage alone,' said Will. 'We'll have to help you.'

I blushed. 'That would scarcely be decent,' I objected.

'There's no time to trouble ourselves over that,' said Will impatiently. 'We're almost in. And you've clearly forgotten that I've undressed you once already.' He barged past me in through the door, ignoring the blush that this brought to my cheek.

'I don't know how you can be so ungentlemanly as to remind me of that,' I said. Will laughed. The other men hesitated just outside the door, more considerate than Will, or perhaps just more embarrassed.

'I'll need one other to help,' said Will. 'Jacob, come on in and close the door.'

'If only we had some other women on board,' I said, horrified at being semi-naked before two men.

'I thank God we have not,' said Will, undoing the lace on my leg. 'They would be horribly in the way. This is far too loose, Isabelle. It will fall off before you are halfway to the shop.'

'I know. I couldn't get it to stay.'

But Will could. Before long, he and Jacob had trussed me up like a chicken. They pushed and turned me this way and that, lacking the care and politeness of dressmakers or maids. I had lace wrapped in layers around my middle, around my bust and draped over my hips like petticoats. My arms and legs were bulging like bolsters, leaving me scarcely any movement in them. I stood like a statue, as unwieldy and far less elegant.

'Now for your hoop and gown,' said Will, picking them up. 'Good thing I asked the dressmakers to make them adjustable.'

I looked at him suspiciously as he tied the tapes and buckles of the hoop around my waist. 'You had better tell me the worst,' I said. 'What lies did you tell them to explain *that*?'

Will merely shook his head and continued to fasten the hoop. But Jacob started to chuckle; a rich bubble of laughter deep in his chest.

'You might as well tell her, lad,' he said. 'It's a story as will get out sooner or later.'

I looked sharply at Will who looked very sheepish indeed. 'I told them you were expecting a *petit paquet*,' he confessed.

'You told them . . . ' My voice failed with the enormity of what he had said. I lifted cold hands to my suddenly burning cheeks. 'No, Will, how *could* you? I will never be able to show my face there again. What must they have *thought* of me?'

Will threw my gown over my head. As he pulled it straight, I found I couldn't meet his eyes. Had the women assumed it was his child I was expecting? How unbearably shameful. 'And you've told everyone on board *The Invisible* what you told them. And they've all been laughing behind my back for days?'

'Only a little,' Will assured me unconvincingly. He straightened up and tilted my chin up so that I was forced to meet his eyes. 'Forgive me?' he asked. When Will dropped his taunting, there was something disarming about him.

I nodded briefly, surprised by the sudden impulse to cry this small sign of kindness caused. It caught me as I was already feeling upset; that must be why. I turned my face away to hide my emotion.

'There,' said Will, giving my gown and petticoats a last tweak. 'I said I'd never be lady's maid for you again, and here I am arranging your finery. But I think you'll do now.'

I looked down at myself. 'I look horribly stout,' I remarked, noting that I barely had a waist and my arms were bulging. But the main quantity of lace was over my hips and legs. I could understand now why Will had insisted on a dress with a hoop. It concealed it all admirably.

'Now, listen close,' said Jacob, leaning back against the cabin wall, arms folded across his chest. 'The Revenue officer ain't allowed to rummage a lady. So you should be safe. But that might not stop him being suspicious of us in general and of you in partic'lar. So you look out for him.'

'Will it be the same man as at Poole?' I asked anxiously. 'He would smell a rat at once, surely, to see me dressed as a girl.'

'No, it won't be. We've thought of that. This is a different stretch of coast and under a different section of the guard. There should be no danger of being connected with . . . whoever it is you really are.'

I nodded. 'Very well. I'm ready. I think.'

Butterflies fluttered uncomfortably in my stomach. But I wasn't going to reveal my anxiety. We'd run a cargo of brandy onto Studland beach late last night in high winds, and the whole crew had shown such bravery, battling the breakers and darkness. I wasn't willing to show less courage than they had done.

CHAPTER TWELVE

✳

We emerged from the cabin onto the deck and Jacob accompanied me to the gangplank. 'You know where you're going and what you're to say there, don't you?'

'Will has explained,' I said.

'Remember, we'll be close by you, even if you can't see us. Walk confidently and hold your head high.'

'I will,' I said and smiled, despite my nerves.

The moment the mooring ropes were tied and the gangplank was laid, I walked across it to the quayside.

Customs men were already heading towards the ship, and one in a blue coat cast me a curious glance as he walked by. I looked straight ahead, feigning not to notice.

It wasn't easy to walk, all bundled up as I was. I felt heavy and cramped. I tried to walk with my natural stride, but couldn't quite manage it. It was fortunate that it was winter now, and cold today, or I would have been uncomfortably warm. Last night's storm had dropped, but a sharp wind still swept the quay, making my hoop sway and bounce around me.

I felt everyone's eyes were on me. They must see through this ludicrous disguise and guess what I was up to. But when I gathered the courage to glance around me, no one was looking my way at all. Men were loading and unloading cargoes from various ships, women were walking with their children, and couples were pacing along arm in arm. None of them spared me a glance.

Feeling slightly more confident, I walked on towards the town. As I entered the first of the cobbled streets, a young man fell into step beside me. A quick look at him made my heart jump into my mouth. He was wearing the blue coat and cap of the riding officers. He was the man who had passed me near the ship, and been about to board. He must have followed me.

'Good morning, Miss,' he said, doffing his hat to me politely.

I swallowed hard, my mouth suddenly dry. 'Good . . . good morning, officer,' I stuttered. Badly done, I told myself fiercely. Showing him I was afraid made me look guilty. I had to be more confident.

'Nippy this morning, isn't it?' the officer said, keeping pace with me easily, though I'd lengthened my stride. He was a young man, mid twenties perhaps, with a moustache that would benefit from a few more years' maturity.

'It's very cold,' I agreed. 'Easy to tell that winter's coming.'

'And where might you be going this morning?' he asked in a chatty, relaxed manner. 'Seeking amusement in the taverns perhaps, or going shopping?'

'Oh, just a little shopping, sir,' I replied. Could it be that he was simply polite and friendly, passing the time of day? My fears and my instincts told me differently. There was a sharpness in his eyes as he glanced at my clothes. I breathed steadily and worked at not panicking. He's not allowed to search me, I reminded myself, recollecting Gentle Jacob's words on the subject. By law, women are exempt from rummaging. It wasn't hard to see why. Otherwise every officer who wished to get his hands on a pretty maid could do so. Somehow though, this knowledge wasn't a great deal of comfort.

'May I enquire as to your name?' asked the young man politely. 'I am Lieutenant Oswald, by the way.'

'Pleased to meet you,' I lied, thinking swiftly. 'I'm Miss Bryden.'

I coloured as I told him such a barefaced lie. Miss Bryden had been my last governess, and was the first name that popped into my mind. Still, at least I hadn't blurted out my real name.

'Well, Miss Bryden. As we're agreed it's an unseasonable day, and the weather uncommonly chill, will you allow me to invite you for a warming drink in this charming local hostelry?' He indicated the inn we were passing as he spoke. I caught my breath. How was I supposed to get out of this one?

'Oh sir, that's very kind of you, but it wouldn't be proper.'

'Nonsense! You won't be alone with me. There will be plenty of other guests in the tap room at this time of day. We residents of Weymouth like to extend a friendly welcome to visitors, you know.'

My feeling of panic increased. Had he mistaken what class of woman I was? Or was this really the custom in a coastal town? I kept walking. Lieutenant Oswald put a

hand on my arm to halt me. I snatched it away, terrified that he would notice the layers of lace on my arm. I
judged it wisest to stop walking so that he didn't feel the
need to touch me again.

'Miss Bryden,' the lieutenant smirked slightly and I
wondered whether he even believed it was my name.
'I would be truly honoured if you would accept my invitation. My only intention is to extend a courtesy to
you.'

'Really, I . . . ' my voice faltered. 'I don't think . . . '

'Ah, you cannot refuse me!' he cried jovially. 'You are
feeling the cold, I can see. This way.'

He drew my hand through his arm and led me to the
inn. I followed him helplessly, noting the name on the
sign: the Nag's Head. There was nothing remotely charming about either its name or its peeling paintwork. I wasn't
even sure it sounded terribly respectable. I wondered
frantically what the officer's motivation could possibly
be for this invitation. Did he hope I would betray myself
somehow by something I said? If I offended him, would
he have me arrested? He could do that, perhaps, whether
he was allowed to rummage me in the street or not. And
in prison, my secret could not long be concealed.

The lieutenant led me to a secluded table at one side of
the tap room and handed me into a seat. 'What can I get
you? A drop of warming ale? Or perhaps a glass of good
French wine to ward off the autumn chill? They have
unusually good wines here, you'll find.' He smiled wolf-
ishly, and I wondered if he'd referred to French wine as
an allusion to the smuggling trade. This inn was almost
certainly a customer of ours. I'd learned that most of the

wine and cognac served along the south coast had paid no duty at the port.

Now that I was looking directly at the lieutenant, I could see he was a handsome man. He had wavy brown hair, combed neatly, and warm brown eyes. He was tall, with a fine figure and carried himself well.

'I'd like a lemonade, if you please,' I answered him nervously.

'Lemonade? Are you sure?' the lieutenant asked. Perhaps he hoped a glass of wine would loosen my tongue and make me careless. He wasn't going to be that lucky.

The lieutenant ordered drinks and then sat down opposite me. Those warm brown eyes drew mine and held them. But I felt they were deceptive. Not mild and kind like Jacob's. There was a keenness lurking under the surface. And every now and then they left my face and flicked over my bulky figure.

Our drinks arrived, and I saw that I'd been brought a glass of wine after all.

'The landlady has no lemons, I'm afraid,' said the officer smoothly. He took a deep draught from his tankard of ale, wiped the foam from his moustache and smiled at me. Nervous knots tied themselves in my belly.

'I've been posted here for six months now, Miss Bryden,' he said. 'I've never seen you here before.'

'Oh, I don't live here,' I said. 'I've just come ashore to do a little shopping. I'm in need of a few things.'

'I see. And where are you on your way to and from?'

I hesitated, unsure of what might have been said to him aboard *The Invisible* if he'd had time to go aboard before following me. I didn't want to arouse his suspicions further by contradicting anything they'd said. 'I took berth in the New Forest,' I told him. 'At Buckler's Hard. I'm heading for Devon where I have family.'

'A strange mode of transport for an unaccompanied young lady. Such a beautiful young lady, if I may take the liberty of saying so.' He kissed his fingertips to me.

I was too used to extravagant compliments to be flustered by this one. But his air of disbelief, his detailed questions, were making me squirm. I looked at my hands on the table twisting at the napkin I'd been given, and attempted to still them. 'It must seem so to you indeed,' I agreed with a nervous laugh. 'But I have an uncle aboard. He undertook to care for me.' I laughed again. 'Indeed, he has often said he is like a second father to me.' Jacob had said something vaguely similar. Lies were easier to tell if they contained a germ of truth, I was fast discovering.

'His name?' The officer sounded a little thrown and this gave me confidence.

'Uncle Jacob,' I said more smoothly.

'And yet your good uncle allows you to walk abroad quite unaccompanied?'

'Oh, he will be keeping an eye on me,' I assured the lieutenant, hoping fervently I was right.

'And the trade that these good men ply aboard *The Invisible*? There is no sign at all of any gainful occupation, which I find most strange. No catch of fish, no goods to trade or carry.'

'So many questions, officer. Am I on trial?'

Lieutenant Oswald laughed falsely, and laid his hand over mine where it lay on the table. I withdrew it swiftly, but not before his fingertips strayed to the lace at my wrist.

'Of course you are not on trial, my dear Miss Bryden,' he said smoothly. 'I'm just passing the time of day. And I'm a little curious, I confess.'

'Then you had better ask the men yourself, sir,' I said and smiled sweetly at him. 'For I have never asked. Ladies' heads are not made for business, as you know.'

Lieutenant Oswald rose to his feet and swiftly exchanged his seat opposite me for one beside me. Before I could do or say anything to prevent him, he had slid in close to me on the bench. 'It is a great pleasure to meet you, my dear,' he said, laying a hand on my leg. 'The local people are so unfriendly to me. It is almost as though they have *something to hide*.'

I shrank back into the corner, moving my leg from beneath his hand. I was frightened now. This was certain suspicion or a deeply improper advance on my virtue. I couldn't make up my mind which.

Lieutenant Oswald sidled closer. I was trapped in the corner with no escape, panic rising in my chest. His hand was stealing around my waist, exploring the bulk of fabric at my waist. 'You would almost think the townspeople were *smugglers*,' the lieutenant whispered in my ear, his beery breath on my cheek.

I pushed him firmly away. 'Lieutenant Oswald, please!' I said loudly. 'I'm a respectable girl. You are not treating me with the courtesy you promised me!'

He moved back an inch or two, no longer touching me but his eyes boring into mine. 'I apologize, Miss,' he said. 'Your beauty caused me to get carried away.'

'Then perhaps it's time for me to leave,' I said, attempting to rise. But he grasped my wrist and pulled me back down into my seat.

'No, my dear. You have not yet finished your wine. Please! Drink up.'

I lifted the glass to my lips with a hand that trembled. Lieutenant Oswald watched me. But I had a little hope in my breast at last. As I'd half stood, I'd caught sight of Jacob lounging against the bar speaking to the landlady. A man I hoped was Will was beside him. He was never easy to recognize ashore; today he was black-haired and black-bearded, dressed like a merchant.

They'd kept their promise and not abandoned me. I was desperately relieved to see them. But were they going to help me, or did I need to get out of this one myself?

I managed to swallow a little of the wine. 'Thank you so much for inviting me, Lieutenant Oswald,' I said. 'It was so very kind of you, but I really must go now.'

'Stay just a little longer, please,' he replied, resting his hand on my arm again and stroking it. 'I still have something to ask you. You are a visitor to this charming port. Would *you* credit that people would try smuggling right under my very nose? I ask you: what kind of a name is *Invisible* for a lugger? A name that pokes fun at honest men like myself, that's what!'

I pushed his hand from my arm, but was forced to hold it away from me, as he was determined to explore my person.

'I can't believe it for a moment,' I said, my eyes innocent, looking straight at him. 'You are such a fine-looking officer,

I'm sure you set many ladies' hearts fluttering. Surely every man must respect your office?'

I was holding both his hands firmly now, speaking earnestly to him. But I was growing desperate. Behind him, I saw the landlady advancing on us with a tray of drinks.

Lieutenant Oswald freed his hands from mine and lunged at me. I tried to fend him off but he was too persistent. Gathering all my courage, I elbowed him in the face. He reeled back. At the same moment the landlady reached him and appeared to stumble, tipping the entire tray of drinks over him. He gasped.

'Oh sir!' cried the landlady loudly. 'Oh, I couldn't be more sorry! What a clumsy, good-for-nothing I am! Here, let me help you.'

She whipped out a large cloth that had been hanging from her waist and shoved it in the officer's face, pretending to wipe him. 'Leave me alone, you fool of a woman!' The words emerged muffled from under the cloth, as the lieutenant attempted to fight her off. But he was no match for the woman, who pulled him off the bench onto the floor, vigorously rubbing him dry. She gave me a significant jerk with her head, indicating the door behind her.

'Go!' she mouthed at me.

I didn't hesitate for a second. I wriggled out of my place and pushed past. There was a crowd of onlookers, already, roaring with laughter at the sight of the king's officer being manhandled.

Oswald managed to free himself briefly, pushing her roughly aside, and leapt after me. I ran for the door, which Jacob was holding open. Behind me, I heard a huge crash. I glanced back and saw a man had put out a foot and tripped the officer, shouting out 'Whoops, sorry, sir!' The landlady took advantage of him being full-length on the floor to sit heavily down on him and rub the cloth in his face again.

'Don't you rush off before I've cleaned you up, like, good sir!' she cried, drowning out his muffled shouts that he was performing his duty.

Jacob pushed me through the door the moment I reached it. Will was waiting in the street. He grabbed my hand and pulled me out into the bright midday sun. It dazzled me, but Will ran, leading me swiftly into the town. We raced down a narrow cobbled alleyway before emerging into a wider street again. Will was still holding my hand tightly so I neither tripped nor fell behind. When he finally whisked me into a small shop, I was panting in a most unladylike manner.

The woman serving behind the counter looked up in surprise, but seeing Will, she stepped forward. I was swiftly whisked into a private room where I was left to unwrap my layers of contraband lace with trembling fingers, still gasping for breath. I passed the folded lengths of lace through to Will, who negotiated a deal with the shopkeeper. I dressed once more, delighted to be free of the extra layers. As we left, Will was tucking money into his waistcoat, and the shopkeeper was disappearing into a cellar with the last of the lace. I felt absurdly light, both in my body and my mind, as we left the shop. It was over.

'That was a near run thing!' said Will quietly as we walked down the street.

'Oh, I thought I was going to be caught!' I said in heartfelt relief. 'I was in agonies!'

'Whatever possessed you to go into the inn with him?' demanded Will. 'We were frantic at the risk you were running.'

'How could I refuse when he pressed me so?' I asked defensively. 'I was certain he suspected and would arrest me on the spot if I said no.'

'He's a rare creature, that one,' said Will. 'An honest excise man with a good head on his shoulders. It's a dangerous combination.'

'For us, it is,' I agreed. 'Oh dear, I am so relieved that's over. I thought I should die of fright!'

'Didn't you enjoy it even a little bit?' asked Will curiously. 'There is a thrill in outwitting the law, I find.'

'Not at all,' I said firmly. 'I'm at heart a law-abiding citizen, I believe. I take no pleasure in danger. Besides, he had his hands all over me!' I shuddered at the memory.

'Did you not enjoy the landlady's prompt action though?' asked Will beginning to laugh.

I remembered the stout landlady sitting on the poor officer, under pretence of helping him, and smiled reluctantly. 'Yes, that was amusing,' I agreed. 'I can't tell you how grateful I was to her. And I never thought I should be so pleased to see *you* either, as I was when I spotted you in the inn!'

'Ah, you'll love us all yet, wait and see,' replied Will lightly. 'Dear me, look! It's the good lieutenant heading our way. Quickly, take my arm and let's greet him with all the courtesy in the world. We can tease him a little.'

Will drew my hand through his arm and pressed my fingers mischievously as the lieutenant approached. As we drew level, he lifted his cap politely and I stopped with a sympathetic smile.

'Dear sir! I do hope you're quite recovered from that most unfortunate accident?' I asked him solicitously, noting the bruise forming under one eye. 'You look a trifle . . . shall we say ruffled?'

The lieutenant smoothed his dishevelled hair and moustache distractedly and cast a disappointed eye over my now-slender figure. 'I'm not convinced it was an accident at all!' he blustered. 'You were very quick to abandon me, Miss Bryden.'

'I'm so sorry! But you see, I was late to meet my cousin, Ted,' I smiled up at Will, who smiled back and nodded politely at the officer. 'It was impolite of me, and I'm glad to see no harm was done.' I cast a quick look over the lieutenant's soaked clothing and sniffed the ale aroma drifting from him and smiled slightly. 'Well, not *too* much harm in any case. I must take my leave now, but thank you so much for your hospitality. Again.'

I extended my free hand to him, and the lieutenant bowed over it and kissed it. 'I'm sure we'll meet again, Miss Bryden,' he said with meaning.

'I'm sure I hope so!' I told him sweetly.

Oswald glared at Will. 'As for you,' he said, scowling. 'You needn't think I don't know you're the gang who bring in contraband from Chewton Bunny to Scratchy Bottom. Your days are numbered.'

'What's that?' said Will, suddenly distressingly deaf, one hand behind his ear. 'You're feeling funny and have a scratchy bottom? Ah, that'll be the ringworm, like as not. Get yourself a purge from the physician. That'll do the trick.'

Oswald grew alarmingly red in the face. 'Goodbye, good sir!' I cried hurriedly, dragging Will away from the enraged riding officer.

'How *could* you?' I asked him reproachfully.

Will grinned. 'Oh, that's an old joke. I couldn't resist it. Very nicely done from you too,' he added approvingly. 'Just the right blend of innocence and bare-faced cheek. Isabelle, we shall make a fine smuggler of you yet!'

CHAPTER THIRTEEN

✳

Sleep was elusive that night. The excitement of the morning had caused a fire in my veins that wouldn't die down. I wriggled restlessly on my bunk for several hours before finally giving up. I got dressed, wrapped a blanket around me and went out on deck.

It was a mild night for November. The stars were obscured by clouds and the breeze was light. The crew of *The Invisible* were sleeping or had shore leave. We'd left Weymouth behind us, many of the crew too, and were moored off Swanage Bay. We'd done a spot of fishing with our rarely-used nets to give ourselves a valid reason for being here and Harry had fried fish for us all.

The weather was utterly different to only twenty-four hours ago. The storm had blown itself out, leaving stillness behind. The rain-washed sea was leaden, moving heavily around us in a languid swell. The mournful cry of an owl sounded from the shore. I went to the rail and stood looking out to sea, while my thoughts buzzed through my mind. The fresh air and stillness didn't calm me at all. On the contrary, I felt wide awake and full of life in a most unfamiliar way. I found I couldn't keep still and slowly paced the deck.

After a while, footsteps joined mine, and I didn't need to look to know it was Will. I'd been thinking about him, so his appearance beside me in the middle of the night seemed quite natural. We walked in silence for a few minutes. 'Couldn't you sleep either?' I asked at last, breaking the silence.

'I was sleeping very well,' said Will with a yawn. 'Until someone started pacing above my head.'

'I can't have woken you!' I said, surprised. My stockinged feet had made next to no noise on the deck, I was sure.

Will grinned sleepily. 'I don't know what woke me, but once I was awake, I did hear something, and I guessed it might be you. It's all that unaccustomed excitement, I expect.'

'I think it must be. I'm restless and don't know what to do with myself. I feel so very . . . alive. No, that sounds stupid. Of course I'm alive.'

'Yes, but it's not every day one is so acutely aware of it. An action tends to have that effect. Often after a brush with the law you'll find the crew all awake late into the night, no matter how tired we are. It's what makes this life so attractive to many. That and the money, of course.'

'Not that I've had any of that,' I pointed out.

'I'm looking after your share for you for the time being,' said Will. 'In case I didn't say so earlier: you did well today, Isabelle.'

'Praise from you!' I exclaimed archly. 'I declare, I'm overwhelmed.'

'Am I such an unreasonable taskmaster?'

'Not usually unreasonable. Impatient and exacting, yes.'

'I like things done well if they are to be done at all.'

I tried to suppress a smile and failed.

'Very well, I apologize,' said Will with a smile.

'This is a night of surprises,' I told him. 'You are pleased with something I did *and* willing to apologize.' I dropped my bantering tone and added after a pause, 'Perhaps at times you had reason to be harsh with me. I look back and feel ashamed of myself for how I behaved at first.'

'There's every need to,' said Will. I caught my breath at his unkindness when I had already admitted a fault, but then saw the flash of his teeth in the dark and realized he was smiling again.

'Was I so very bad?' I asked in a small voice. I stopped pacing and leant over the rail, staring down into the water. Will leant beside me, his shoulder resting against mine. I wondered if he was aware of it, or whether it meant anything to him. His closeness burned my arm and set my nerves jingling.

'Spoiled, indulged, selfish, lazy . . . no words are bad enough for your conduct when you first came aboard,' he said. 'But you are learning and changing fast. Not everyone could do that. And you're growing stronger in body and mind with every day that passes. Tell me, are you enjoying yourself?'

'At times, I am. I don't think I could ever revel in the danger as many of you do.'

Will pulled a length of rope from his pocket and passed it to me. 'Let's see your bowline,' he said. I knotted it easily. A breeze blew straight at us off the sea, lifting my hair. It smelled fresh and salty.

Will pulled the bowline undone. 'Now a clove hitch,' he said. 'Do you miss your home at all?'

I frowned as I tied the clove hitch with practised fingers. 'I'd left my home before I came aboard,' I said.

'You're very young to have left home. What's your real age, Isabelle?'

I undid the hitch and retied it, my eyes on the rope, playing for time. 'Fifteen,' I admitted at last in a very low voice.

Will caught his breath. 'So young?'

The bleakness of my situation, which I so often pushed from me in the busy days on board *The Invisible*, rushed over me afresh. I glanced wordlessly up at Will and something must have shown in my face for he didn't press me for more. Instead he reached over and took the rope from me. 'Has Jacob shown you a running hitch yet?' he asked. 'It goes like this.' He demonstrated clearly, before pulling the knot free and putting it back into my hands.

I tried, but my fingers were suddenly clumsy. Will took hold of my hands. The sudden closeness took me by surprise and made it hard for me to concentrate. 'I'm too tired,' I protested weakly.

'No, you're not, come! I'm helping you.' Will guided my hands through the tying of the hitch, once, twice and then let me tie it alone. 'There, you see,' he said, releasing me. He went to sit down on some upturned crates and patted the wood beside him. 'Come and sit by me?' he asked. 'It's more sheltered than at the rail.'

I sat down beside him, wrapping my blanket more closely around me. 'Are you warm enough?' asked Will.

'I am,' I replied. 'I can scarcely believe it's almost December. Christmas is only a few weeks away, and yet it's mild enough to be out at night.'

'It's unusually warm,' agreed Will. 'It will change; it's bound to. Smuggling can be cold work in the depths of winter.'

'But it doesn't stop you?' I asked.

'The worse the weather, the better for us. Less chance we'll be stopped about our business.'

He paused a minute looking out over the water. I wriggled back a little so my back rested against solid wood and I could relax a little. 'Isabelle,' Will began. 'Speaking of Christmas, do you have . . . anyone you wish to be with at that season? Many of the crew will disperse for a week or so. I'm sure we could persuade them to let you go now.'

I bit my lip and closed my eyes, feeling a tumult of strange emotions. 'I have no one,' I said at last when I had mastered myself.

'And yet the story of the poor orphan was quite clearly untrue.'

'Yes, it was a bad lie,' I admitted.

'Do you trust me enough to tell me the truth? Or some part of the truth?'

'How far around the crew will it travel?' I asked with a touch of bitterness for the stories he'd repeated from Cherbourg.

'No further than the two of us, I swear.'

I thought for a few moments. My past was a burden on my mind that ached. Perhaps it would lighten it to share it. I wanted to believe I could trust Will. I needed a friend.

'My father was very wealthy,' I began. 'I grew up in luxury, I suppose. A country seat in Berkshire and a house in the best part of town. I had governesses, maids, and every piece of finery I wished for. You consider me spoiled and indulged. I am.'

'But still very young, as I now know,' said Will. 'Your father. Who is he? Titled?'

I shook my head. 'Not titled. But wealthy and of an old and proud family. His name isn't important. Not any more.'

'Why?' Will's voice was gentle.

'Earlier this year, he lost his entire fortune and estates in an investment,' I explained.

'The South Sea Bubble?' asked Will. I nodded. 'I'm no longer living in that world, and I rarely see the London papers,' he said. 'But I heard that when it burst, many families lost a great deal of money.'

'It was far worse than that,' I said. 'Many families lost everything they had. We were one of them. My father speculated. He was convinced he could make a great fortune for us. He invested everything we had, his properties and even my dowry and that of my sister. We were utterly ruined.'

My voice failed and I sat quite still, fighting tears that the memories of that terrible day brought rushing back. Will said nothing and sat quite still beside me.

'They came and took everything away. Our furnishings, our horses and carriages. Our jewels, pictures, plate and ornaments. Everything of value and even everything of no value to anyone but us. They even took my gowns, my shoes, my shawls, my hats. Everything. It was utterly, utterly humiliating.

'We had to move into shabby lodgings,' I continued, my voice reduced by shame to a whisper. 'Paid for by an uncle who was furious at being burdened with the costs of my father's recklessness. My parents saved a few items. My bride gown was one.'

'So it *was* a bride gown? I suspected as much. And yet you wear no ring.'

I paused, my voice choking in my throat and then forced myself to continue, not looking at Will: 'I was engaged to be married. Father was determined that I at least should be spared the shame of poverty.'

'I'm guessing something more went wrong?' asked Will.

'Of course. My betrothed, it turned out, had been interested mainly in my dowry. Once that was gone, he found himself obliged to end the contract to marry.'

I fell silent, unable to tell any more. Will took my hand and pressed it. I leaned back and closed my eyes. Will's hand was warm and comforting around mine after the trauma of reliving the past.

Footsteps sounded on the ladder to the aft hatch. We both let go of each other at the same time. I opened my eyes to see that dawn was staining the dark sky pink in the east. The whole night had gone by. The skipper emerged onto the deck, and gave us both a nod. If he was surprised to see us, he hid it.

'I should get some sleep,' I said softly. I was feeling bone-weary suddenly.

'By all means,' agreed Will. 'Thank you for trusting me. One more question. What was his name?'

'My betrothed?'

Will nodded.

'James Marlow was his name. He had a title too: Viscount Bedford.'

Will froze. I saw a strange look on his face for a second. 'You know him?' I asked curiously.

Will's expression smoothed to a polite mask. 'I used to, years ago. I thought he was already married.'

'He was. He was widowed very quickly. His first wife died in childbirth.'

'I see,' said Will woodenly. He turned abruptly away, walking towards the skipper who greeted him cheerfully. Will replied briefly and then swung himself down onto the ladder to the lower deck. For a moment he paused and glanced back at me before he vanished from sight.

I sought my bunk but the past had returned to trouble me and wouldn't let me rest. Scenes I had still hidden from Will lurked just out of sight behind that dreaded door. In my mind, I slammed it firmly shut, turned my face to the wall and pulled the covers over my head.

CHAPTER FOURTEEN

✳

The month of December passed swiftly. The temperatures plunged, the wind blew, and life aboard the ship grew harsher. The sojourns in Cherbourg with its cosy inns and coffee houses grew to be a welcome rest from battling tides and weather. Will was not always with us, however. On two trips he stayed behind in England negotiating finance for our runs, finding buyers to supply, and arranging collection with the land smugglers.

'May I not accompany you?' I'd asked at first.

'Certainly not. You'd be damnably in the way,' he told me, not bothering to spare my feelings. I must have looked hurt then, because he relented a little. 'You'll be safer and more comfortable on *The Invisible*,' he told me more kindly. 'And I can travel faster alone. I'll be back soon.'

It seemed empty and forlorn on board without him at first. As well as Jacob, who had been kind to me from the beginning, I gradually got to know Harry, the skipper, and one or two of the other men rather better. They all still teased me: about being a mermaid, about being the only woman on board, and for the way I spoke, so different from them. I learned to smile and laugh with them rather than taking offence, and gradually the jokes became less barbed.

I was constantly taken aback to find the depth of thought, understanding, and feelings in the rough, un-educated men. Some of them couldn't even read or write, but they had strong views nonetheless.

'You say the law should be obeyed, and happen you're right,' said Harry as we prepared the dinner together one evening. 'But who made those laws?'

'Parliament, of course!' I replied, wondering how stupid he actually was.

'And who sits in parliament?' asked Harry.

'The House of Lords and the House of Commons,' I said, wondering if he was joking.

'And are those Commons really common men, or are they gentry and suchlike?'

'I've never thought about it. I suppose they're . . . gentlemen.'

'Ah. That's right. No ordinary men like me or those I know. No working men. So those lords and fine gentry who own the land and have more money than what they need, they decide how to run the country. You can be sure they do it as benefits them, not as it benefits me and mine. Look at the land enclosures. Who was the land taken from? The common people. Who's got it now? The rich.'

I blushed to think I'd thought him stupid just a moment ago. He had thought about the subject far more deeply than I ever had. 'But the common land was shared out, wasn't it?' I asked.

'So it were: big bit for the squire, a good-sized bit for the parson and the crumbs for the rest of us. Yep. It were shared out.'

I bit my lip uncomfortably. He was probably telling the truth. I'd never heard it explained in that way before. 'The men who sit in parliament are educated and understand how to run the country,' I said more timidly. 'Perhaps working men who can't write wouldn't know enough.'

'There's plenty of working men as can write,' said Harry. 'And they understand the needs of the poor. What do your fancy lords in the fine wigs know about that? Eh? Nothing. They raise taxes to go to war. The rest of us don't want no wars. What do we ever have to gain except dying by the sword and the cannon? What do they understand how a body suffers when they can't feed their family?'

I was silent. Then even more timidly, I asked: 'Are you a revolutionary, Harry?'

Harry laughed and gave his cauldron a vigorous stir. 'Nay, lass, I'm not. I just got ideas in my noddle. It don't mean I'm going to fight for 'em.'

I nodded, my mind full of the thoughts his words had created.

A week later, I was sitting in the prow beside Fred the pilot, as we approached the coast of England once more. He was pointing out the signs of rocks and currents, revealing where dangers lurked and where we could safely sail. He pointed out the different sea birds to me and named them all. I'd seen in the past months how he could sense a change in the weather before anyone else. He was a gentle man and a steady one and I always enjoyed sitting by him.

'You read the water like a book,' I told him, a note of admiration in my voice as he called out to warn of rocks where I could see nothing at all. 'I can barely make out the signs you are navigating by, even when you show them to me.'

'Well, reading is a closed book to me,' he replied slowly, squinting against the low winter sun. 'I never went to school and neither of my parents could read. But I went to sea with my father almost as soon as I was breeched and he taught me to navigate. I learned every corner of this part of the coast.'

'I'm in awe of your skill and your knowledge of the sea,' I told him. 'Surely a pilot such as you could serve your country better in the Royal Navy?'

The pilot fell silent, his lips pressed tightly together.

'That ain't something you say to the Gentlemen,' the skipper said from behind me.

'Why not?' I asked, eyes wide. I knew they thought differently on almost every topic to me, but surely we were all agreed that the Royal Navy kept England safe? 'The Navy is our pride,' I said. 'My uncle serves in it.'

The skipper snorted derisively. 'As an officer no doubt?'

'Of course.'

'Well it may be fine for officers, but for most of the men they may as well find themselves in hell itself. Rotten food, sour beer, relentless work, senseless punishments and death lurking. If they're lucky, their family gets paid a few miserable shillings. Why do you think they are obliged to press men to fill their ships?'

I opened my mouth to repeat my uncle's words; to say that the men they were forced to press were the scum of the earth and needed to be flogged into shape, and then I shut it again. Some instinct warned me this might not be a tactful thing to say on board *The Invisible*.

'They want us in the Navy all right and tight,' growled the pilot. 'But we don't want none of them.'

'Show her,' the skipper said grimly.

The pilot hesitated, and then turned away from me, stripped off his jerkin and pulled up his coarse linen shirt. His back was a mass of ridges: weals and cuts that had healed into a knotted red and purple mess of scar tissue. I gasped in horror.

'I've a closer acquaintance with the Navy and with the cat-o'-nine-tails than I would like,' he said. 'I don't aim to renew it.'

I sat in silence, thanking God I'd said nothing about scum or deserving flogging. My world view was on its head and I just didn't know what to think about anything any longer.

We picked Will up at Winspit on a still moonless night. *The Invisible* glided into the rocky cove, the men lowered the boats and filled them with kegs of cognac, packets of snuff and sacks of cocoa beans. I waited eagerly at the rail for the first boat to return, straining for my first glimpse of Will. There! Sitting in the prow of the boat with his back to me, a cap pulled down low over his eyes. He was slighter and slimmer than the other burly smugglers and easy to pick out no matter what disguise he'd put on.

I moved towards him to greet him when he came aboard, feeling a rush of pleasure at the sight of his face, hoping for a smile.

Will was laughing as he climbed aboard, at something the skipper had said to him, but when he saw me his smile faded. I paused, unsure of my welcome. Will nodded briefly at me. 'Isabelle,' he said by way of greeting.

Then he turned from me, finished his conversation with the skipper and disappeared below without another word or look for me.

I stood at the rail, trembling with disappointment, still hoping to see him emerge once more and seek me out. But he didn't reappear. I climbed into the rigging to help set the sail as we left the bay again, and then went to my own cabin to sit listlessly on my bunk. 'I *trusted* him,' I said to myself. 'And he rewards me with silence. Why?'

Will left us again just a few days later without having exchanged more than a few words with me. I'd kept my distance from him, confused and hurt.

We were due to run a last cargo into Purbeck four days before Christmas when a fearsome storm blew up. It was the heaviest weather I'd seen and transformed the friendly channel into a heaving, raging blue-green beast. The swell tossed the lugger this way and that as though her bulk were nothing more than a piece of insubstantial driftwood. *The Invisible*'s timbers creaked and groaned as though they would spring apart at any moment. I had not been sea-sick until now, and I'd prided myself on the circumstance. But that night, I had to take several trips to the rail, clinging desperately to the wooden support, shivering, as the waves broke over the ship, sending great torrents of spray crashing down on me, and sheets of water swilling over the deck. I was not alone there, I was comforted to see. Those of the crew who had not been at sea all their lives joined me from time to time, relieving their aching stomachs into the swell.

As we approached land, the sails reefed as small as they would go, and every man on deck to bail and to be on hand to deal with trouble, the skipper shook his head grimly.

'We can't attempt this,' he yelled to the pilot. 'I won't risk the ship!'

The pilot shouted his agreement, and the ship swung back out towards the open sea, keeping away from the treacherous coastline lest we should be driven upon the rocks.

'What shall we do?' I asked Jacob when he came into the galley, streaming with sea water and chilled through. I poured him a generous tot of rum, and he drank it with a sigh of pleasure. 'Is Will not awaiting us at Lulworth Cove?'

'He is, but he'll know what's toward when he doesn't get our signal.'

'So will we try again tomorrow?'

'Aye, we will that, if the storm abates. But not Lulworth. It ain't safe for the landers to be the same place two nights running.'

'So where then?'

'I don't know where the next point is they've arranged,' said Jacob. 'Skipper'll know that.'

'But we're not in any danger, are we?' I asked timidly, voicing my real fear.

Jacob grunted. 'This weather's never safe,' he told me. 'You can't call it that. But we've weathered worse. We've got the finest ship and the best men in the channel, I reckon.'

I nodded, not entirely reassured. The floor lifted, tilting so violently that even my clutch on the table didn't stop me staggering sideways. Jacob caught at my wrist to steady me with one hand, while holding his rum safe with the other. He grinned a little. 'Looking a bit green, girl,' he commented.

'Feeling pretty green,' I admitted, willing my rebellious stomach to quieten. My head swam unpleasantly as the ship rolled and lurched once more.

Jacob downed his drink and rose to go, but I caught his sleeve. 'What about Will?' I asked. 'Is he safe on shore in this storm, waiting for us?'

'Oh, Will always stays safe,' said Jacob, patting my hand. 'He's got more lives than a cat, that lad. Don't you worry. No storm or excise man will get him. Now you stay in here where it's safe and out of everyone's way.'

He disappeared out into the howling storm, banging the door behind him. I shivered in the blast of cold air that had swirled in.

The storm raged on and we couldn't make the landing the next day either. I thought of Will waiting in the rain and the wind and the dark with a train of pack ponies for the second night running, watching this storm enrage the sea, transforming it into a white-crested roaring monster. I could imagine how the waves must be hurling themselves against the cliffs where he waited as if it wished to tear them down. But perhaps at least the Preventives would keep to their cosy firesides in such weather and he need not fear them tonight.

The storm blew itself out some time late in the second night. The sea, swift to grow unruly, was also quick to calm itself again. The swell diminished and the white horses faded from the waves, leaving *The Invisible* wallowing in a heavy swell. We could once more unreef the sail and head for the next night's rendezvous.

'Where is it we'll make shore tonight?' I asked the pilot, going to stand beside him as he pored over his charts.

Fred sighed and shook his head slightly. 'Dancing Ledge,' he said. 'It's never my first choice of landfall. It's isolated, right enough, and well-hidden. Only the quarry ships use it and that by daylight. But it's an evil stretch of coast, with rogue currents and a liberal sprinkling of rocks that would tear the hull open.'

I'd never heard him express himself with less than absolute confidence before. 'Surely there must be another choice, then?' I asked, appalled.

'It's the spot we agreed for the third night,' he said. 'And though it's tricky, the Philistines won't guess that we'll attempt it in big seas. So likely we'll come off well. And it's our last run this side of Christmas, so we could do with that. We're all looking forward to seeing our families.'

His words reminded me that I still didn't know what I was to do with the week ahead. I thought of my family celebrating quietly without me, and my heart ached with longing. The fact that they thought me dead seemed suddenly infamous. Could I not seek them out, spend some time with them?

But as always when this thought rose in my mind, I remembered that if I returned to my family, I would no longer be able to escape my duty. I hardened my heart and closed my mind to my past life.

It was in considerable trepidation that I watched the shore draw nearer that evening. The wind had freshened once more with the coming of darkness, and the decks heaved beneath my feet.

While we were still out at sea, Jacob took me up to the look-out to help him spot Will's signal. It wasn't often I climbed up here, nor was it my favourite spot on the ship, but I could manage the climb without paralysing attacks of vertigo now. I stood at the swaying look-out, feeling exposed and vulnerable each time the mast swung out across the sea, clinging on tightly as I scanned the horizon for the flash of blue we expected.

'There!' I cried at last, pointing to the spot where I'd seen it. Jacob followed the direction of my arm, and just caught the last of the blue fading away in the deep darkness.

'It's sharp-sighted you are,' he said with satisfaction. 'As for me, I must be getting old. Time was I never missed the flink.'

The bearing was taken from the flink and we approached land. As we drew closer, I could hear the roar and drag of the open sea breaking against rock. My anxiety grew as we approached the landing place. Two spout lanterns had been lit to guide us, and the skipper was battling wind and waves to stay on course.

The skipper spun the wheel, the men dropped the sails and the ship swept around in the swell. In the gloom, a bare ledge of rock loomed up, side-on to the ship. This landing place was wide open to the unruly sea. A huge fender of twisted ropes was strung across the rock to prevent ships being ground against it by the waves that pounded the shore.

Beyond the narrow berth, I could make out the swell surging over other ledges that reached far out into the sea beside us. Even a landlubber like me could see why this was a dangerous spot.

Mooring ropes were flung down to secure *The Invisible* and caught by men who emerged from the shadows. They looped them around great rocks that lay on the ledge for the purpose. The ship groaned against the fender. She still rose and fell in the great waves that washed up to the ledge, and on the far side of the ship they broke over the rail, sending water crashing down upon the deck.

One moment the ledge was below us, the next we dropped so that we were looking up at it. We were at our moorings now, but still the unloading would be treacherous. And as for leaving the shore again; how possible would that be without being dashed upon these dreadful cliffs?

I was right about the unloading. It was dangerous work. The kegs were slung overboard on ropes and the men needed to time the lowering of them very precisely so that the landers could grasp and secure them. I saw one anker crushed between the side of the ship and the fender. I watched from the rail as it burst, spilling its precious contents into the sea to shouts of frustration from the men.

At last the cargo was all ashore. I had scanned the landers, hoping to spot Will among them, but the night was dark, and I had no idea which disguise he was wearing tonight. I thought I could make him out standing on the ledge, wrapped in a dark frieze coat. He was slighter than many of the landers and carried himself very straight, but that was my only clue.

'We need men,' someone was shouting across to us. The skipper stood at the rail as the ship rose and fell, one hand cupped to his ear, straining to hear his words.

'Trouble . . . revenue . . . ' we made out. Most of the words were tossed aside by the wind. 'Plenty . . . ponies . . . four men, more . . . spare them . . . '

'He needs extra men,' the skipper relayed to those who hadn't caught the words. 'Didn't hear why, but they're short of landers to lead the ponies. Any volunteers?'

CHAPTER FIFTEEN

✳

There was muttering and shaking of heads. It was Christmas Eve on the morrow and *The Invisible* due to sail on to Poole harbour after the drop so the crew members could all reach their families in time for Christmas Day. Few wanted to risk a long exhausting journey inland leading pack ponies and dodging the Revenue.

Harry, however, volunteered at once. His home was at Swanage, only a short walk away.

My heart skipped a beat as I saw him prepared to be helped ashore. The memory of the shattered cask took on appalling significance as they looped ropes about his torso and he prepared to make the jump. Harry climbed to the outside of the rail and clung there precariously, two of his comrades holding him fast. They waited as the ship plunged sickeningly and then lifted once more. Just as it began to sink again, Harry shouted: 'Now!' He leapt, the men pushed and Harry flew towards the ledge. He was caught by two landers, staggering against them with the shock of the jolt onto the rock. He was safe.

They freed him swiftly from the rope and it was pulled aboard for the next man. The skipper looked around the assembled crew. 'No one has to go, but you know as well as I do that this venture is money in all of our pockets. The loss of the cargo would dig deep into our savings.'

Jacob stepped forward. I felt sick with fear and had to fight an urge to beg him not to risk himself. It wasn't the Revenue officers that troubled me. It was that leap into the abyss that was the transfer to shore.

'I'll go,' Jacob said. 'It's only a step home from here after the job's done.'

The men were preparing to loop the rope about him when I grasped his hand. 'Take care,' I begged him.

Jacob's eyes twinkled at me and a smile crinkled his big beard. 'I will,' he promised.

His crew-mates were clapping him on the shoulder and the back, showing their appreciation that he was willing to do this for the rest of them.

The boat rose, the boat fell, and Jacob was perched on that slippery rail, waiting for the right moment. He leapt and I thought he was going to make it. But with a lurch of my stomach, I realized he'd jumped short. He was going to fall into that dreadful gap between ship and rock. I screamed in horror, clutching the rail. Jacob fell down, down, and then just as I thought he was gone, he grasped the very edge of the treacherous ledge of rock and clung on, though the water spouted up through the gap, drenching him.

The men holding the rope strained to hold him, to help him hang on to the ledge. Then the landers ran forward and grasped him, hauling him back from the precipice and to safety. I was trembling with shock. The strength of my feelings caught me by surprise. I'd grown to care for this gentle, lumbering smuggler. How had that come about?

No one else wished to volunteer. I couldn't find it in me to blame them. Who in their right mind would risk that dreadful leap, and a night creeping through damp undergrowth, when they could be heading for a snug berth in Poole and a Christmas at home with their families?

Will, at least I thought it was Will, was standing onshore holding up his index finger and then performing a pleading gesture, hands together.

'One more,' the skipper told us. The men shook their heads. I was wondering what he would do if they all refused. Then his eye fell on me. 'Isabelle!' he said. 'You can go.'

'Me?' I gasped. Panic tore through me. 'No!'

'You're strong enough to lead a pony,' the skipper said. 'The tubs don't need carrying. And you have no home to go to for Christmas. You can spare one of the men from missing out on seeing their families.'

My protests went unheeded. I was pulled to the rail and the soaking rope was passed around me.

'Please,' I begged. I didn't mind helping to lead the ponies. If that had been all, I'd have been happy to go. It was that jump.

But before I could say more I was being helped over the rail, held fast by strong hands. I trembled as I stood there on the brink, sure I was going to die. I no longer even had a voice to plead. I would be crushed like the barrel. I knew it.

A rope was passed through my harness and thrown ashore. I could see Will had caught it and was holding it fast. His eyes were fixed intently on me, a frown on his face. Jacob stood at his side looking anxiously up at me.

The ship dipped. As it rose again to its peak and began to drop, the men holding me shouted: 'Jump!'

I bent my trembling legs and half leapt and was half thrown out into the abyss.

I must have closed my eyes as I plummeted. I certainly stopped breathing. For a moment everything fell silent. It was almost as if the sea ceased to churn and the wind dropped to nothing. With a jolt that knocked the breath from my body, I landed heavily. I felt pain from the impact shoot up my ankle, but I also felt strong arms around me, supporting me before I fell. For a moment, I didn't dare look, so certain had I been that I would fall into the gap and be squashed. When I opened my eyes, both Will and Jacob were holding me, and I gasped out loud with relief. I'd made it.

Jacob put his arm around me and supported me away from the edge. I leaned heavily on his arm, still trembling. 'I thought I was going to die,' I said with a slight sob in my voice.

'Nay, we caught you right and tight. It's almost easier to catch a slight lass like you than a grown man. But what were you doing volunteering for such danger?'

'I didn't!' I said indignantly. 'The skipper ordered it.'

'That wasn't right,' said Jacob, shaking his head.

'I'm here now. The worst bit is surely over?' I asked hopefully. I walked a few steps along the slimy pitted ledge and winced a little at the pain in my ankle.

'Injured yourself?' asked Will, joining us. 'You'll be in the way rather than a help, as usual.'

I sent him a hurt look, but he was preoccupied with watching the ship. Behind me, *The Invisible* was casting off.

I turned to watch too. She swung slowly away from the berth, dipping and bucking in the big sea, and headed away from the ledge. I was relieved to see her clear this treacherous coast.

Once she was safely heading out to sea, the men all turned, began to sling the last of the kegs over their shoulders and carry them to the back of the deep ledge. Some had already been hauled up by rope to the shelf above.

There was a path up, or something that resembled a rocky stairway, to the right. Will sent me up there while he helped rope the rest of the barrels.

The second ledge was deeper than the lower one, and much smoother. It went right back into the cliffs, where I could see dark, gaping holes in the sheer faces. It looked like a working quarry, with blocks of stone stacked up in piles. I looked up the cliff and realized the next climb up was going to be much steeper and longer than the last; especially difficult with a painful ankle.

The barrels were hauled up the second cliff too, but we climbed up a narrow, uneven track on the left of the ledge. I found myself glad of the time I'd spent in the rigging, learning never to look down.

At the top of the climb, a path ran along the cliff tops in either direction. I stopped to catch my breath, peering into the darkness.

'This is where the customs men patrol,' Will told me as we reached it. 'This is one of the few places we can land a cargo on this stretch of coast.'

'How do you know they aren't watching now?' I asked.

'Because there is a look-out on the spyway above us,' said Will with a grin. 'Wait till we get up there; you can see for miles in either direction. We're quite safe for now. Can you walk all right?'

'Of course,' I said at once, determined not to slow the train down. The pain was already lessening as I moved about.

The ponies were waiting beyond a cliff path. Many were already carrying kegs, and the rest were being loaded up now. I was given a pony by a large figure in a dark coat. 'Bless me, it's just a lad,' he said to himself in a hoarse whisper, as he handed me the leading rein.

Before we set out, I was assigned a second pony to lead. Several had three to manage. I saw many of the men had their faces blacked so as not to stand out in the darkness. All wore dark clothes. I realized I must stand out with my pale face, and resolved to keep it hidden if we were pursued.

All the organization was done in near silence, voices low and cautious, the loading and manoeuvring smooth and practised. Only a few minutes later, the train turned and set off across the short springy turf. We climbed straight up the steep hill ahead of us. The grass was nibbled short by sheep and covered in droppings. Its very smoothness made it difficult to climb, and I was glad of the ridges in the turf that I imagined had formed through land slippage and of the occasional big tufts of rougher grass too.

The two ponies followed me willingly enough, climbing the sheer hill with short, jerky steps, their shaggy heads bobbing up and down with the strain of bearing the casks on their backs. They were soon puffing harder than I, and straining to keep climbing as the slope grew ever steeper. I noticed their harness neither creaked nor jingled. I stared at it in the dark, and from what I could see, it had no metal in it at all. Had it been made especially for smuggling?

Suddenly, with a last, exhausted scramble, we had reached the top, and the fields sloped only gently upwards from here. Drystone walls that ran in long straight lines along the contours of the hills, divided the slopes into fields. I was relieved to be putting less strain on my aching ankle.

There was a brief pause while a gate was opened ahead of us. Behind me, I heard Will whisper: 'Isabelle!'

I turned, and understood at once what he wanted me to see. The view was magnificent. The hills sloped steeply away behind us to the cliffs and by the light of the moon I could see for miles in both directions. The moonlight gleamed on the vast expanse of the sea too, as it stretched out into the distance. I could still make out *The Invisible*, sailing away towards Poole.

Neither of us needed to say anything. We just stared, and then the train was moving on again, the only sounds the soft thud of hooves in the turf and the occasional snort of a tired pony.

We crossed two fields, paused at a barn to unload a couple of kegs and leave a pony behind, and then crossed two fields more before we reached a village, lying dark and quiet in the moonlight. No smoke rose from any of the chimneys and no light shone from any of the windows. We led the ponies straight through the sleeping village to its stone church. Here more kegs were unloaded and left in the porch, and we moved on, leaving one or two kegs at the inn and other houses.

I was afraid the clattering of hooves on the stony road might wake the sleeping villagers, but when I whispered my fears to Will he laughed softly in the darkness. 'Only women and children are sleeping tonight,' he whispered back. 'And they know not to look. Their men are all here with us.'

Our long line drew clear of the village into silent fields. It was a breathless, silent trek through the darkness, all of us aware of every sound around us. Even my ponies sensed the tension; their ears were pricked forward eagerly as we made our way into the denser darkness of a small wood, their hooves silent on the thick bed of leaves and moss.

It was as we emerged from the wood that we heard hoof beats ahead. The line broke up around me and melted back into the trees. With difficulty, I turned my ponies and followed them. Every man had concealed himself and his beasts as best he could behind trees and bushes or in small hollows. I withdrew quietly, but wasn't experienced at this work, and was relieved when Will came to one pony's head and helped me lead it quietly out of sight.

The hoof beats outside the wood had come closer and resolved into the clop of several pairs of hooves on the nearby road.

'Preventives?' I whispered in Will's ear.

'Maybe,' he breathed back into mine, his breath warm on my cheek. 'Who else would be out in the dead of night?'

We stood quietly side-by-side, listening intently. The horses stopped, and Will left me, creeping forward through the trees until he was lost to sight.

When he reappeared he was moving with urgency. 'They've picked up our trail,' he whispered to a huddle of men who gathered around him. I pressed close to overhear. 'We need to draw them off. Who will risk riding with me? It must be men who ride light.'

'I will,' said a slim lad I didn't know. Will nodded.

'Thank you, Tom,' he said and then looked around for another rider.

'I will,' I heard my own voice whisper. It was a surprise even to me. Why was I volunteering? Because my ankle would be far less painful on horseback, I told myself firmly. I stifled the small voice that told me I wanted to be with Will.

Will looked taken aback and not best pleased. 'Can you ride bareback and astride?' he asked.

'Of course,' I lied at once.

Will shrugged and then nodded his permission. 'You'll ride light at least,' he said reluctantly. 'But this will be dangerous work.'

I nodded, hoping I looked braver than I felt.

'We three then,' said Will after another hesitation. 'Shed the ponies' loads.'

The larger of my two ponies was swiftly relieved of his burden, and someone lifted me onto his warm back. I was glad of the darkness that hid my embarrassment at such an indecent thing as a lady astride a pony.

Men were burying the extra kegs in the leaves at the foot of an oak tree. No doubt they would be back to collect them once it was safe. 'We ride to the edge of the forest,' Will whispered hurriedly, coming to stand beside my mount. 'Until they catch sight of us. Enough to make sure they follow, but not close enough to see we carry no contraband. Then we make off as fast as we can. Stick close to me and Tom. We ride round in a big sweep. As long as we reach the bridge below ahead of them, we'll be safe enough.'

I nodded, tense with the fear of what lay ahead. I was not a neck-or-nothing rider like my sister. But my ankle was far more comfortable now I was mounted. I would take this night as it came; my luck had held until now.

I urged my pony after Will, who was vaulting onto his own mount. He led us straight towards the king's men. They were silent, clearly waiting for some sign from us to trigger their pursuit. My pony jogged along, seeming surprised by this new turn of events. At the edge of the forest, we rode in a silent line, one after the other, weaving in and out of the trees at the edge of the wood.

The moon was obscured by cloud and there was no sign yet that we'd been seen. I was just wondering what Will was going to do about that when his horse snorted loudly.

In moments, there was a shout from the Revenue men. Will urged his pony forward into a brisk trot and wove back into the trees. The jingle of the harness and the clop of the hooves on the road sounded in pursuit. Someone shouted at us to stop. Will's pony broke into a canter; Tom and I followed.

Cantering in the dark through woods is nasty work. I knew I should work with my pony, help him look out for dangers and keep firm contact with his mouth at all times. But with branches whipping in my face and tree trunks leaping out of the darkness at me, the best I could manage was to bury my hands in his mane, lean low over his neck and cling on for dear life. It was lucky that my pony wished to stay close to the other two, for I closed my eyes a lot of the time and it was little enough guidance he got from me.

We were soon out of the trees; Purbeck is mostly an open, windswept landscape. The three of us galloped flat out across the hillsides, pausing only to open gates which we swung shut again behind us. Once we jumped a broken-down section of stone wall and I was almost unseated.

When the pursuit drew too far behind, Will slowed. When they drew too close, he pushed the ponies faster. At last, both the other ponies leapt a larger wall onto open hillside. They made it look so easy. I sent mine after them. He stopped dead at the wall and I shot forward onto his neck. Then he jumped, and I lost my grip and took a tumble. I rolled onto turf but banged my shoulder on the stones of the wall in the darkness. The fall had knocked the wind out of me, and I lay gasping and shaken, not sure what was up or down.

Will leant over the wall, still mounted on his pony. 'Are you hurt?' he asked urgently. I could breathe again at last and struggled to my feet, dazed.

'Not much,' I said breathlessly.

'We can't linger,' he said, reaching down a hand. I grasped it and he pulled me up. Tom led my pony up to me and I slid onto his back from the wall. As I did so, I could hear the customs men thundering across the field behind us, and felt panic rising. They had drawn far too close. If we were caught through my incompetence, I'd never forgive myself.

'Now for a gallop across the downs,' said Will. 'Keep up!' and he was off in a flurry of hooves, clods of turf kicked up behind him. I turned my pony after his and he lengthened his stride. Tom brought up the rear, no doubt to check I stayed up this time.

My rides had never gone beyond sedate hacks around my father's estate or even more decorous outings in Hyde Park. In Bath, I'd not ridden at all. The speed of this headlong flight was terrifying but also exhilarating. We flew over the turf, black in the darkness, and I found I was able to keep my eyes open and even relish the rush of air in my face and the ground vanishing beneath my pony's hooves.

A shot exploded behind us making me jump. With my heart in my mouth, I urged my horse faster still, keeping low on his neck as Will was doing ahead of me and praying the men were poor shots, or not aiming to kill. They must surely see this isn't the train of pack ponies now, I thought, frightened and shaking. Why are they still pursuing us?

Will dropped back, urging me to go faster. A line of trees loomed ahead. Another shot rang out and Will gasped, clapping his hand to his arm. He slowed, swerved to the right, and pushed through a hedge. He disappeared down out of sight. I clung on tight as my pony scrambled through the hedge and down the bank after him. We were in a kind of sunken lane. Will led us in a swift jog down it for a spell. I could hear the pursuit behind us and grew afraid again, but Will turned and attempted a smile.

'Are you hurt?' I asked him anxiously. 'They hit you, didn't they?'

'It's only a nick,' Will said, but his voice sounded faint. 'As long as they got the message down to Farmer Benson, we're safe enough now. This next bit will be fun.'

At the bottom of a hill, a narrow bridge provided the only crossing over a deep river. As we rode out towards it, I heard restless lowing, and saw a herd of cows massed at the side of the road. It struck me as very strange that anyone should be herding cows in the middle of the night.

A whistle sounded, and a dog appeared, tail wagging and tongue lolling. Will rode past the cows, out onto the middle of the bridge, giving the farmer a wink as he rode past. We followed him and the cows followed us.

On the far side of the bridge, Will reined in and turned. I looked over my shoulder to see the whole bridge blocked by cows. The excise men had pulled up behind the herd, their horses steaming, and one officer was shouting at the farmer, gesticulating wildly. The old farmer, bent and gnarled, had a hand cupped behind one ear and was shouting, 'Beg your pardon?'

Will laughed and we rode on at an easy pace up the far side of the valley. At the top, he paused, dropped down from his pony. Leaning weakly against it, he said: 'Isabelle, I need you to bind up my arm. It's still bleeding and I don't want to leave a trail.'

I slid down from my horse, jarring my bad ankle, and limped over to him. His whole sleeve was slick with blood. 'Will, you have to get to a doctor,' I said, dismayed.

'Nonsense,' he replied breathlessly. 'Only a flesh wound. No bullet lodged. Just bind it tightly and we'll go on.'

'I have no experience with wounds,' I protested, afraid of making it worse. I looked up at Tom but he shook his head hurriedly and looked away.

'I do go sick at the sight of blood,' he muttered shamefaced.

'Please, Isabelle,' Will begged faintly. He slid down onto the ground and put his head on his knees.

I dropped to the turf beside him. I was frightened now. 'Tell me what I must do,' I said unsteadily.

'Help me get my coat off,' he asked. I did so with difficulty, easing his bleeding arm from the torn and bloodied sleeve. Will gasped with pain and swayed. For a moment I thought he was going to faint.

'I'm sorry,' I whispered. I tore the wet shirt sleeve from his arm and laid bare the wound. It was on the outside of his arm, a deep gash torn through flesh and muscle, bleeding profusely. It was bad, but even I could see that this was not a dangerous spot.

Unsure what to tie it with, I picked up the ruined coat, but the fabric was too coarse for bandaging. 'Look away,' I told both the men. When they did as I asked, I pulled off my own coat and then my shirt. Shivering in the frosty night air, I pulled my coat swiftly back on and buttoned it, then tore up the shirt. The sleeves I folded into a pad, my fingers trembling with haste and cold. The rest of the shirt I tore into strips. I pressed the pad to the wound trying to ignore Will's gasp of pain.

'Tom, you'll have to help me now,' I ordered him, realizing I couldn't both hold it in place and tie the bandage, unpractised nurse as I was. 'There's no more blood to be seen.'

Tom dismounted and held the pad in place, averting his eyes from the bloodied garments that lay strewn on the ground. I felt impatient with him; there was little enough to see in the darkness.

I bandaged the pad firmly into place over the wound. Will winced again as I tied the ends tight and leaned his head on my shoulder with a groan. Awkwardly, I put an arm around him as he rested there.

'Are you all right?' I asked anxiously.

'I will be . . . in a moment,' said Will faintly. 'Lost . . . a damnable lot of . . . blood.' He sat quite still, his breathing heavy while I cast about in my mind for what we should do.

'Is there somewhere nearby where we can take you?' I asked him.

With an effort, Will pushed himself upright away from me. 'I'm recovered now,' he said. 'I shall do. Yes, there is a barn nearby we need to reach.'

He mounted his pony again with difficulty but appeared reasonably steady in the saddle. We moved on: out across more fields and along the bed of a shallow stream. 'Keep in the water,' Will called over his shoulder.

We left the stream near a farm. All was silent around and behind us. Will paused and we halted, listening intently.

'Reckon we made it,' said Tom echoing my own hope.

'Yes,' Will agreed faintly. 'Let's hope the customs men all followed us, leaving everyone else time to get away.'

As we walked on, weariness overcame me. I sagged on the pony's back and almost nodded off.

'Wake up, Isabelle,' chided Will, riding up beside me and nudging my knee with his. I jumped awake, groggy and confused, and straightened myself. 'It's time to return the ponies,' Will told me.

We pulled up at a big old barn. Will and Tom slid off their mounts. As I followed them down to the ground and landed on my bad ankle, I cried out in pain.

'It still hurts?' Will asked. I nodded, biting my lip. 'You can rest as soon as we've rubbed down the ponies,' said Will, tossing me a wisp of hay. I set to work awkwardly, trying to copy what the other two were doing. When we were done, Will groaned and straightened up, cradling his arm. 'I have to rest, before I go on. Goodbye, Tom, and thank you,' said Will faintly, nodding to Tom, who slipped silently out of the barn into the grey, early morning light and disappeared.

'We need to be sure we're hidden from sight,' said Will, glancing around the barn. I followed him behind a large stack of hay in the far corner of the barn. He sank to his knees, while I hurriedly burrowed into the loose hay behind to make a nest.

Will unbuttoned his cloak with his good hand and threw it onto the straw and sank down with a sigh of relief. I sat down beside him and shivered. It was freezing in the barn. 'Lie beside me and cover us both with the cloak,' said Will faintly, his eyes already closed, a crease of pain furrowing his brow. I did as he said, trying not to hurt him. Under the cloak with Will close beside me, our arms touching, warmth began to spread through me and sleep followed close on its heels.

CHAPTER SIXTEEN

✦

A door. Darkness around me. Light seeping round the edges. A brass door handle glowing faintly. My hand reaches out unwillingly to turn it. As I push the door open, I see two people beyond it. I stare uncomprehending for a moment, and then cry out.

'Isabelle, hush!' whispered a voice in my ear. It was urgent. I struggled to sit up, to throw off the hand that was pressed suffocatingly over my mouth. 'Isabelle! It's me, Will! Wake up but don't make a sound!'

Consciousness returned. I stopped struggling and lay still. 'Will?' I whispered when he released me.

'You were having a nightmare,' he whispered. 'But there are men outside. Customs officers, or perhaps soldiers. Can you bury us in the hay?'

Voices reached my sleep-fogged mind from outside the barn. Dust motes dancing in the air above me. The light was low, as though it was late in the day. I rubbed my eyes. 'As quickly as you can!' Will urged me. He was pulling a sheaf down over us with his good arm. He looked dreadful; dark shadows etched under his bloodshot, bleary eyes.

'Lie down, I'll do it,' I told him, seeing him wince. As he lay down, I pulled the cloak back over him and strewed another sheaf of hay over the top. We were already concealed in a sort of nest, it wasn't difficult to pull a covering down over us. When Will was completely concealed, I pulled an armful over myself and burrowed under it, down under the cloak, pulling in my feet after me. I heard Will gasp softly and guessed either I or he had nudged his bad arm.

'Are you all right?' I whispered.

'I'll do. Hush now!'

I lay still beside him in the darkness, feeling the rise and fall of his breath beside me. I pricked my ears, trying to hear the voices, but something else began to distract me. The dust from the hay had got into my nose and I needed to sneeze. I tried to breathe and fight it, but the impulse grew and grew. My eyes were watering now, my nose tickling fiercely.

'Should we check inside, sir?' I heard a voice ask from outside the door.

'No, there's no . . .'

The sneeze exploded out of me, all the more potent for being resisted. Will flinched beside me and swore softly. Then we both heard the words we dreaded: 'Search the barn!'

Slowly, with a creaking sound, the barn door was pushed open. Will's hand gripped my wrist so tightly it was painful. We both lay absolutely still. My heart was hammering.

Footsteps crossed the barn. One of the ponies paused from munching hay to whicker softly.

'There's no one here,' said a voice, terrifyingly close at hand.

'Check more carefully. They could be hiding some-where,' said another voice, further away. 'They can't have got far. I'll swear I winged him.'

'I still don't understand why we aren't tracking the contraband rather than these men, sir?'

'You don't need to know. It's orders. The contraband is a distraction. We're searching for one man by the alias Nick the Knife. The other is a young woman dressed as a lad. Don't know what he calls himself.'

I caught my breath in fright. Will's already painful grip tightened.

'*Her*self, you must mean, sir,' said the first voice.

'He's dressed as a man, Jameson,' snapped the second.

'Yessir. Him then.'

'Search the hay. Someone sneezed, I could swear it.'

Footsteps. The sound of hay sheaves being pushed aside. I was frozen with fear and trembling. Will was silent and motionless beside me. I could scarcely sense his breathing, and tried to still my own, praying an-other sneeze didn't catch me unawares. The hay rustled right next to my head. I held my breath until dark spots danced in front of my eyes. The rustling moved further off and I sucked dusty air down into my desperate lungs.

'Is there a reward out for these characters?' asked the first soldier suddenly. His voice was still terrifyingly close, making me jump. 'Is that why you're not telling me? You want to keep it for yourself?'

'There's a reward. But there's no point discussing that if we haven't blasted well found them, is it? Curse it, I could have sworn we had them earlier.' The sound of something being kicked reached my ears. The officer was angry. I could feel perspiration trickling down my back. I was suffocating in the heat and the dust.

At that moment one of the ponies sneezed loudly on the other side of the barn. A great snorting sound with a whooshing of air and saliva. There was a silence and then a voice asked: 'Are you sure it wasn't one of these ponies as you heard sneeze, sir?'

'Damn you, you're probably right. We're wasting our time here. Come on.'

Footsteps retreated across the barn away from us. The door groaned and banged shut. I listened to the squeak of leather and the jingle of bits as they mounted their horses outside. This was followed by the thud of hooves, gradually growing more distant.

I threw off the cloak and gasped in relief to breathe cooler air. Will did the same.

'Now *that* was a close shave,' he said weakly.

I looked at him. 'How did they know so much about us?' I asked him. 'Why are they searching for us so specifically?'

Will frowned, but didn't meet my eyes. 'I don't know,' he said after a pause. 'But I intend to find out.'

It seemed to me we must have a traitor aboard the ship. I could understand why they might be searching for me. Why there might be a reward out for finding me. Not that I was a criminal as the soldiers had said, of course. But why did they want Will?

'And I didn't sneeze anything like that pony,' I added indignantly.

Will laughed shortly. 'Be grateful they couldn't hear the difference!'

Will then seemed to dismiss the matter from his mind. 'By God, I'm hungry,' he remarked. He yawned and ran his good hand through his hair. It had come untied from its black silk ribband and had bits of hay sticking out of it. I grinned at his tousled appearance, picked up his ribband and held it out to him.

'You need to tidy yourself,' I told him. 'Honestly, look at us! If anyone were to walk in now, they'd get *quite* the wrong impression.'

Will's eyes twinkled. 'If anyone thinks I'd be in the mood for tumbling in the hay with a bullet wound and customs men chasing me, they must be mad. Your turn to be maid and valet,' he said, nodding at the ribband and passing me a comb from his pocket. 'I can't do this with only one good arm.'

It felt strange to comb Will's hair free of hay for him and tie it back. It was smooth and silky in my hands. I rested one hand on his shoulder for a moment when I was finished. 'What are we going to do now?' I asked.

'The light is fading,' he said. 'As soon as it's properly dark, we'll move on. We'll need to take one of the ponies. Neither of us can walk as far as we need to go.'

'I'm famished,' I told him. 'We've eaten nothing since this time yesterday.'

'There's nothing we can do about that now,' said Will with a shrug. 'I really need to sleep another hour. Will you keep watch?'

He lay back and was asleep in moments, his usually glowing face pale and drawn. The light faded gradually in the high window on the west side of the barn. I watched Will anxiously as I waited for the hour to pass. I watched the steady rise and fall of his chest as he breathed, the dark lashes against his cheek. I could never study him this closely when he was awake.

How strange, I thought, that he should have fair hair and yet dark lashes and brows. Strange too the way he usually disguised himself when he came ashore in England. Why? The other men never did so. He seemed more afraid of being recognized than they.

It was odd to think I'd once hated him so much. I didn't dislike him now; or at least only when he was provoking me. He was a handsome young man, I decided. High cheekbones, a clear forehead, delicate lips. I looked away and blushed, and then laughed at myself softly for blushing when there was no one here to see.

I looked back, and tried to imagine Will in gentleman's clothing, instead of his rough smuggling garb. Mentally I put him into a smart waistcoat, a fine coat and a powdered, long-bottom wig, the grey curls tumbling down over his shoulders. Yes, he would look very fine indeed. I frowned slightly in an effort of memory. It was strange, but when I pictured him like that, it was almost as though he was familiar to me; familiar from my previous life as a young lady of fashion. I shook my head. That couldn't be. I would have remembered if I'd met him before.

I was just wondering whether I could bear to wake Will when he was so tired, when he stirred, yawned and sat up. He stretched and then winced. 'Time to go,' he said.

'Where are we going?'

'It's Christmas Eve.'

'I know that,' I said, although to tell the truth, the days had become a little hazy in my mind.

Will directed me to put the bridle back on the strongest pony. 'Now, would you open the barn door for me while I lead this fellow out?' he asked.

I limped to the door and opened it. Will swung himself up into the saddle and rode out past me while I fastened the door again behind him. When I turned, he was holding a hand down to me; his good arm. He kept the other cradled close to his chest. 'We're both going to ride the same pony?' I asked uncertainly.

'He's strong enough,' said Will. 'Come on.'

'What is this obsession you smugglers have with walking for miles, chasing around the country on horseback and climbing up and down rigging?' I asked, looking up at him. 'You are the least restful crowd of people I ever met.'

Will looked back down, a smile in his eyes. 'And look how much good it's done you,' he retorted. 'When you came to us, you were a pale, puny weakling who squeaked and threw tantrums at the mere thought of physical exertion.'

I scowled. 'I was a refined and delicate young lady. And what am I now? A rough, coarse criminal.'

'Not at all. You are active, healthy and stronger than you have any idea of,' replied Will. 'And you quite possibly saved my life last night.'

I didn't know where to look suddenly. 'Come, Isabelle. Are you riding or walking?' Will asked, holding his hand down to me again.

I gave him my hand, put my foot on his and he pulled me up behind him, drawing my arms around his waist. 'Are you comfortable?'

In fact I was sore almost everywhere from the previous night, but I told him that I was fine, and we set off at a brisk walk. Will avoided the roads, and took us across heathland and downs, sometimes following quiet tracks, at others cutting across country. I clung on tight, my face pressed into his warm back.

It seemed a long, weary time in the cold evening air until we reached a village that Will didn't skirt. We rode straight into it, the pony's hooves clopping on the stones of the road. Small, grey, stone cottages were gathered around a central green that was home to both a well and a duck pond. Its tranquil charm had something idyllic about it. An old church tower rose up behind the furthest cottages.

We pulled up outside a small cottage. It looked neat and tidy, but very small, with a diminutive garden in front. No sooner had we halted, than the door was flung open and candlelight spilled out onto the front porch. A huge, burly figure appeared.

'Is that you, lad?' asked a gruff voice. 'We've been worried sick! Is that the lass you've got with you?'

'It is,' replied Will.

The figure strode forward and I found myself lifted down from the saddle and enveloped in a huge hug. 'Welcome, Isabelle!' said Jacob.

I was overjoyed to see him safe and sound. He led me inside and introduced me to his wife, a tall, smiling older woman dressed in plain rustic garments. Her hair was grey and simply dressed, her face lined and her hands rough. She welcomed me kindly, however, and showed me to a seat by a bright fireside in a small kitchen.

I was happy to see the fire and glad of the seat. I sat down and stretched my fingers to the blaze while she bustled around, apparently preparing a meal. Jacob had disappeared somewhere with Will; to see to the pony, I imagined. The savoury smells of cooking made my stomach rumble.

By the time Will and Jacob returned, I'd been taken into the cramped front bedroom, which was the only other room on the ground floor, given a bowl of water for washing and been lent a rustic gown by my hostess, whose name, she told me, was Ann. It wasn't a garment I would have chosen to be seen in, and much too big for me, but infinitely more fitting for a Christmas meal than breeches that had been ridden in, rolled in mud, buried in hay and slept in.

I was sitting by the fire once more, a glass of hot punch in my hand, when Will joined me. He'd also washed and changed into a borrowed shirt.

He sat down opposite me, guarding his bad arm from any knocks, accepted a glass of punch from Ann, stretched out his long legs and grinned at me. 'So,' he said. 'What do you think of spending Christmas with Jacob and Ann? They wouldn't take no for an answer.'

'I'm overwhelmed,' I said frankly, smiling across at Jacob. 'It's so kind! I expected to be almost alone aboard *The Invisible* in a port somewhere.'

'And me,' nodded Will. 'And here we are by a glowing fire, waiting for one of Ann's fine dinners.' He sipped his own punch and sighed contentedly. 'It's a bright light in a dark world, this little cottage.'

I nodded, not thinking his words strange, for they fitted my thoughts too. I had been feeling keenly that I had nowhere and no one to go to. Ann batted Will playfully on his good shoulder as she passed him and shook her head at him. But she was smiling and pleased, I could tell.

'You're looking very . . . housewifely, Isabelle,' said Will, looking at my apparel. I shifted a little in my seat, uncomfortable in the clothes I'd been lent, but knowing it would be rude to say so.

'I could wish I had my gown from *The Invisible* with me,' I told him. But Will shook his head.

'Not at all,' he replied wisely. He lowered his voice and spoke for my ears only as Ann and Jacob set the table behind us. 'You would be out of place here in that. Ann would be uncomfortable and would treat you like a grand lady rather than a guest and friend. And it could come to the ears of the customs officer or constable that some wealthy lady was staying in the village.'

'I hadn't thought of that,' I admitted ruefully. 'But my own gown isn't *that* fine, you know!'

'By comparison, it is. Besides, you wouldn't be able to fit the hoop through these doorways or sit down on the chairs,' added Will mischievously. 'By the way, while we're staying here, I'm Nick and you'd better be Janet.'

I pulled a face, but could see the sense of it.

CHAPTER SEVENTEEN

✳

Christmas passed merrily in the humble cottage. I tried hard not to think of previous Christmases and not to wonder more than a few times a day how my own family were doing.

Will spent a couple of days with a slight fever, but then improved quickly as his arm healed. He seemed cheerful. The constraint that he'd shown after I told him my story had lessened after the night-time chase. He treated me in a friendly, teasing way, almost as though I were a younger sister.

Our hosts were generous and thoughtful and offered us plain but tasty fare. For our Christmas meal, we had goose, roasted potatoes, vegetables and gravy. Ann had made the best plum pudding I'd ever tasted. It was filled with smuggled dried fruits and laced liberally with contraband brandy she told me proudly. French wine and cognac were in abundance, naturally. I attended church with Jacob and Ann on Christmas Day. Jacob whispered to me during the service that both the parson and his sexton were good customers of the trade, and regularly hid shipments of brandy in the church tower and the vaults. I giggled and then thought perhaps I ought to be ashamed of myself for behaving so improperly in church.

To my disappointment, Will wasn't well enough to come with us to church. In fact he refused to leave the cottage at all during daylight hours, even once he was better. There was one night, however, when he disappeared altogether. He was gone at supper and slipped back into the kitchen when the rest of us were halfway through breakfast. When I asked Jacob and Ann where he'd gone, they merely said he was 'on business'. I refrained from prying.

In the cottage, I slept under the rafters in the tiny, freezing-cold attic room that was the upstairs of the cottage. The couple slept in the downstairs bedroom and Will had a bed made up on the floor in the kitchen each night. He said he had the best of the bargain, as it was the warmest room in the cottage.

At the end of a week, I found him packing his few belongings into a bag. 'Are we leaving?' I asked. I was beginning to feel a little restless.

'Jacob and I are,' he replied shortly. I stared at him, an uneasy feeling in my stomach. I sat down on the chair by the fire and tried to speak calmly.

'And what about me?' My hands were shaking.

Will looked up at me, hearing the hurt in my voice.

'It's bitterly cold,' he said. 'It'll be worse at sea. Dangerous too, if we get winter storms. Won't you be more comfortable here with Ann? She'd love to have you.'

'No!' I half-cried out.

Will sat back on his heels and looked directly at me, brows raised. 'And there was me thinking it was your aim to escape us.'

I calmed my voice. 'Not for a long time now. You know that. I'm happy on board. You're all my . . . ' I paused and glanced out of the small kitchen window, ' . . . friends,' I finished awkwardly.

Will's eyebrows rose still higher. 'Criminals, labourers, illiterates, farmers. Gentlemen of the night. You can bring yourself to call us friends now?'

I nodded silently, a lump in my throat. I thought of the skipper's lined and cheerful face, and Harry with his aromatic stews in the galley, and Fred the pilot and the way he could read the water. I would miss them all if I were to be parted from them. It was strange, but it was the truth.

Will's face was unreadable. He didn't take his eyes off me. I tried to meet that clear, penetrating gaze, but my eyes fell before his. 'Stay with Ann for three weeks,' said Will at last. 'We have a couple of particularly dangerous runs to do. And Ann gets lonely in these darkest months. There is a job you can help us with here besides.'

My heart lightened at once at the prospect of joining them again. 'What is it?' I asked at once. 'Not lace smuggling again, I hope.'

'Not that, though the skipper does plan to trade more lace if you rejoin us. But we need a living signal; someone who will walk the cliff for us at a certain time of day if the coast is clear. Do you remember that red cloak I bought?'

'I do.'

'Ann has it. We'll need you on the cliff at Kimmeridge Bay. We'll get you a message with the date and time, but it'll be later in January. If there are excise men around, you stay out of sight, and we know to do the same. Can you do that for us?'

'Easy,' I said confidently.

To my surprise Will leaned forward and kissed me lightly on the cheek. Then, as though regretting this gesture, he left the room hurriedly and could next be heard talking heartily to Jacob in the back garden. I sat quite still, wondering what he had meant by it.

I went with Will and Jacob as far as Kimmeridge that day. We walked down towards Chapman's Pool where Will and I had once rejoined the ship, but instead of descending the steep drop to the cove, we only went down a short way before crossing the stream and walking on up to the next headland.

It had snowed in the night; just a light powdering that adorned the frozen ground and made the day bright. It was bitterly cold and the ground was frozen hard. I wore my breeches, boots and coat as they were more suitable for the long walk and for the cold than a gown, and would make walking back alone safer for me. Jacob had lent me a thick fur hat that was much too big for me. It kept slipping over my eyes as we walked.

'I must look a complete fright,' I remarked.

'Who cares? The main thing is to be warm enough,' replied Will.

'I *do* look a complete fright,' I said dolefully. 'You don't deny it.'

Will just laughed. 'Well, put it this way: Isabelle-the-lady wouldn't have dressed like this. But then she couldn't have managed this walk either. She would have missed this beautiful morning.'

It really was beautiful: bright, frozen, and sparkling. We followed the cliffs along the coast for miles. Above Kimmeridge Ledges, another crew member joined us. He and Jacob walked ahead, striding out along the rough path. Will and I followed more slowly. The sun had broken through the clouds and the sea sparkled brightly to our left, hardly any waves disturbing the gleaming turquoise surface. It grew milder and I could pull Jacob's hat off my head at last. We talked as we walked, and I felt that Will was more relaxed than he had been all Christmas.

'Are you looking forward to being at sea again?' I asked him.

Will's eyes sparkled. 'I am,' he admitted. 'Christmas was very pleasant to be sure, but now I'm ready for some excitement.'

I felt a tug of sadness that he was so glad to be going away from me. Then I took myself sternly to task. Will wasn't at all the kind of man a lady like me should miss. He was wild, unsettled, and had far too many revolutionary views.

The next headland opened out a view down into Kimmeridge Bay. It was an unattractive bay compared to many on this magnificent stretch of coast. The cliffs were low and formed of crumbling black stone rather than bright white chalk. The beach was a mixture of dark sand and pebble. Slabs of dark ledge showed treacherously out in the bay with each sigh and ebb of the waves. The wind caught at my hair and whipped it back from my face. Gulls called their haunting cries as they glided over the sea below us. In the distance, a ship headed up the channel under full sail.

Beside me, Will paused. 'This is Hen Cliff we're standing on now,' he said. He reached for my hand and held it as we stood looking out at the water side by side. I didn't dare look at him.

'I'm sorry for what happened to you,' he said quietly. 'I'm sorry that your family's loss of fortune had such consequences for you. The end of your betrothal . . . I can't imagine the despair, the heartbreak that drove you to walk into the sea that night.'

I bit my lip and looked straight ahead. Oh, how wrongly he had interpreted my half-told tale. I felt ashamed to be receiving his sympathy. I didn't deserve it. Not in the way he thought.

I opened my mouth to put him right. 'Will . . . ' I began. 'It wasn't . . . I didn't . . . '

'You don't need to say anything,' Will interrupted me. He squeezed my hand and then released it. 'Look, this cliff is where we need you to come and walk,' he said, changing the subject abruptly. He turned to show me the path along the cliff, and I saw Jacob approaching.

'Explained the task?' asked Jacob.

'I'm about to,' Will said.

'This is Will's idea,' Jacob explained. 'Instead of using lanterns that could be spotted by Navy sloops or Revenue cutters, we use a human signal that's known only to us. You walk at an agreed time on the cliff in that red cloak. We know as it means the coast is clear to land the goods.'

'And how will I know if the coast is clear?' I asked Will with a touch of shyness.

'You have a clear view from this cliff,' said Will, indicating the bay and the farmland stretching behind it with a sweep of his hand. 'This whole area is like a natural amphitheatre with the bay as its stage.'

It was true. I looked inland and noted the way the land sloped gradually upwards from the bay in each direction, ending in high hills all the way around. It was open ground; pastureland with barely a tree.

'The landers will meet you here. If you're due to walk at four, be here by mid-afternoon to spy out the surroundings. Stay hidden, keep your eyes open. They'll do the same. If there's Philistines about, keep your cloak and yourself well out of sight. If not, you walk.'

'And if it isn't clear, how will you land the goods?'

'Same thing the next day,' said Jacob. 'And if that's no good either, we have a new *rendez-vous* arranged for the third night. The landers will get a message to you if need be.'

'Very well,' I agreed. 'I'll play my part.'

'Good girl,' said Jacob with a nod of approval. 'I know Ann's got some work for you before then too. I reckon you'll enjoy it. We need to be leaving you now. Can you find your way back?'

'I can,' I said confidently. It had been very straightforward getting here: we'd followed the same cliff path most of the way. Jacob gave me a great bear hug, a whiskery kiss on the cheek, tousled my hair and told me to look after myself. He turned away and I was left facing Will, unsure how to make my goodbyes to him. Should I offer to shake his hand or give him a casual nod? Will surprised me again by following Jacob's example and pulling me into a hug. I hugged him back, my heart unruly in my chest. I pressed my cold face against his warm, woollen coat as he held me close, and then it was over, no more words exchanged. I was standing alone on the high cliff, watching him stride away from me.

I felt hot tears prick my eyes and a confusion of emotions within me as I watched the men grow smaller in the distance and disappear. Will turned at the last minute and raised his hand in farewell, but before I could respond, he'd vanished from sight.

CHAPTER EIGHTEEN

✵

The long, lonely walk home in the fading afternoon did not serve to resolve my tangled feelings into any kind of order. I'd led Will to believe I'd been driven to take my own life due to a broken heart. When the truth was . . . much more sordid. In the first weeks and months aboard *The Invisible*, I'd been too angry and confused to think things through and later, too content and too busy with my new life to face up to the mess that I'd left behind me. The thought tortured me. I resolved that next time I saw Will, I would confess everything to him. I would be truthful. No matter how hard it was.

Perhaps he would think it was me that had behaved badly. Maybe he would despise me. I'd changed so much that it was hard to connect the girl who was the belle of the ballroom with the person I'd now become. My former life was remote and unreal.

Ann greeted me with supper when I returned. Freshly baked bread, a piece of cheese and some ham pie were set out on the table. I stepped from the frosty dusk in through the kitchen door, and sighed with relief to be back in the warmth and glow of the firelight. Ann took my coat and asked after the day. It eased my heartache to feel her kindness.

I slept badly that night. I tossed and turned on my narrow bed, shivering under the blankets and going restlessly over and over in my mind how I could explain everything to Will. I tried to imagine how I would tell him the dreadful, humiliating truth. Sometimes I thought Will would turn from me in disgust. At others, that he would understand. I would lose myself briefly in a happy dream of the future. But this always ended with one unanswerable fact: by my own actions, I had made sure there could be no happy ending for me.

When I finally fell asleep, the dark door loomed before me, light seeping around the edges. I knew my usual craven impulse to flee; to run from what waited behind it. But this time, I didn't. I walked up to it boldly, put my hand upon the door handle and turned it. But then as light flooded over me, I lost my courage, closed my eyes tight shut and screamed. I screamed so loudly that I woke myself and brought Ann running into my room in her nightgown and cap. 'Whatever is the trouble, child?' she asked, looking sleepy and confused.

'Just a nightmare,' I told her. If I couldn't tell Ann the truth, how was I going to tell Will?

I expected the following weeks to be empty and dull and wondered how I would get through them. But Ann had some surprises for me. The third day I was alone with her, I came down to the kitchen to the aroma of bubbling sugar. A large cauldron of some sweet substance was hot on the fire, filling the kitchen with its caramel scent. Pouring this golden substance into two urns, Ann took one herself and gave another to me to carry. Wondering what this was, and what kind of work could take us out of the house on such a cold, dark winter's morning, I wrapped myself up, and followed her.

I learned that morning that the brandy we brought across from France was clear, but that the English liked it a golden honey colour. So the women on shore set up little workshops in barns, caves, and vaults and doctored the bulk of the cognac with caramel. I also learned that the near-proof brew we brought was so strong it could blind you. I helped dilute it, pouring it carefully into larger barrels to be taken inland to Bath and Salisbury by cart. The women explained why the Cousin Jacky was brought over so strong: even concentrated as it was, there was so much carrying involved in bringing it secretly up from the coast. It made sense, but I'd had no idea how many women were involved in the trade.

The domestic life I experienced at Ann's was also an eye-opener for me. It wasn't desperate poverty. But it was poverty nonetheless. She made and scraped, saved and took great care to waste nothing. Even when my family had been in reduced circumstances, we'd not known the need for such economies. In fact, when I thought of the lavish meals that had been set on our table throughout my life, I squirmed. We'd always had far more than we needed and so much had always been sent away again uneaten. Presumably the servants had consumed much of it, but I didn't know for sure. I'd never given the waste a thought until now.

'If it weren't for the trade,' Ann said simply, 'we'd starve come winter. Be thrown on the parish too, like as not, for poor relief. Oh the shame! And those as starve all winter, ain't strong enough for work when it does come in spring.

'But with Jacob bringing home money from the trade, and the hens, the pig, and our bit of a garden for growing some onions and so on, we can get by.'

'But doesn't he bring home a great deal of money?' I asked, thinking of all those runs we'd made; great cargoes of brandy, snuff, lace, and other goods besides.

'Not as much as he should,' said Ann bitterly. 'It's the financier that gets the lion's share. Ain't that the way of the world? Them that's rich gets richer and them that's poor does all the hard work.' She shook her head and then added, 'And it's even harder now they're saving . . . but mum for that.' She refused to say more.

CHAPTER NINETEEN
✳

The day of the run into Kimmeridge dawned cold and clear. Ann shook her head at the bright sky and muttered under her breath that heavy cloud would have been a deal more to her taste.

'It's new moon, though,' I said comfortingly. 'There'll be little enough light to betray them.'

'There'll be enough,' she said darkly. 'We worry, Isabelle. Those of us left behind. We sit here helpless, and there's little we can do to keep our men safe. Just keep our mouths shut and pray.'

I nodded, but tonight I *was* doing something to help, and the blood pulsed quicker in my veins at the thought. I wondered at myself. It seemed strange for me to be delighting in the prospect of danger. But then, as I'd already acknowledged to myself, I'd changed.

I parted from Ann with much affection, embracing her and thanking her for having me to stay. I wished I could have given her some parting gift for all the care she'd lavished on me, but Will had left me no money, and I hadn't thought to ask for any.

'You can say your goodbyes all you like,' said Ann cheerfully, 'but you may be back later for all that. The run doesn't always take place on the first night, nor yet the second.'

'I know,' I agreed. 'But I've a good feeling about to-night.'

I set off full of eagerness. The bright day lifted my mood still further, and the walk was exhilarating. I had a packet of food and some water in a basket, together with my bright red cloak and a tinderbox. This last item Ann had come running after me with, telling me to tuck it into my basket 'in case of need'. I hadn't been able to imagine what I'd need a tinderbox for, but I'd accepted it without question, tucked it into the bottom of the basket and promptly forgotten about it. My thoughts were all on rejoining *The Invisible* that night.

I reached Hen Cliff much earlier than was necessary, found a relatively sheltered spot from which I could see both the beach and the surrounding countryside and set-tled down to watch and wait. The brightness faded as I ate my meal and the sun dropped towards the west. Soon it would be time for me to walk back and forth along the cliff top, to signal *The Invisible*. All seemed quiet and safe. I'd seen no one but a shepherd pass by in the hour or so I'd been here, and no one could approach the beach without me seeing. I just needed to wait for the landers to contact me to let me know they were in place to receive the contraband.

I unpacked my red cloak and laid it on the ground beside me. Wrapping my arms about my body, I rocked myself back and forth, hoping I could start to walk soon. It was cold and exposed up here.

I stroked the cloak, and as I looked back up again, I caught a slight movement out of the corner of my eye. I stared down at the beach, puzzled. Something had moved. What was it? A crab? A dog? I was certain I'd seen something.

The beach was a long stretch of rock and shingle, empty and deserted in the pale winter light. A fresh wind was blowing and there were white-crested waves rolling onto the beach. But I was almost certain it wasn't the waves that had moved. I ran my eyes slowly along the beach, noting the large patches of seaweed and driftwood lying strewn across the shingle. The seaweed all lay in a long strip, marking the high-tide line. Except that now I looked more closely, it didn't. Some was heaped further back in piles. That was where I'd caught sight of the movement.

Footsteps behind me and the sound of someone clearing their throat made me jump out of my skin, and slip dangerously close to the edge of the cliff. The man behind me grabbed me by the arm and pulled me back to safety.

'Cousin Jacky's arriving,' he said with his eyes on the red cloak lying on the grass beside me.

'I'm here to meet him,' I responded as I'd been told. He nodded, apparently satisfied. I took stock of him. He wasn't anyone I remembered seeing before, but then landing almost always took place under cover of darkness. He was a broad stocky man, not tall, but undoubtedly strong. He had a beard and wore a cap pulled down low over his eyes. I knew better by now than to ask his name or give mine.

'Been here long?' he asked.

'An hour or so. You?'

'Just got here.' He nodded his head to a line of men walking down from the far side of the bay. 'Those are our men. You seen anyone?'

I shook my head. 'Only a shepherd. But just now, I thought I saw . . . '

I looked back down to the beach, remembering that puzzling certainty I'd had that there was something out of the ordinary down there. Nothing stirred except a gull, walking along the beach.

'What?' asked the lander.

'What could be making the seaweed move?' I asked him.

He peered short-sightedly down into the bay and then shrugged. 'The gull?' he asked.

I sighed, an uncomfortable feeling still knotting itself in my belly. 'Perhaps,' I agreed. I got up and shook out my cloak. 'Is it time?' I asked. The day was already dimming. Soon they would no longer be able to see me from *The Invisible*.

The man nodded and made off to ready his men. I slung the cloak about my shoulders and began to stroll casually along the top of Hen Cliff. The wind caught at my cloak, making it billow out behind me like a flag. I smiled in satisfaction. I must be easy to spot through a telescope. I walked the full length of the cliff, turned and walked back. As I drew nearer the beach again, I looked down closely at it, still wondering what it was that had moved. I had no real apprehension that it was human, and therefore a danger to the venture. There were quite clearly no people on the beach. I stared at it for a long time, but saw nothing. And then, at last, when I was about to give up, a pile of seaweed twitched.

I frowned, staring down at the place where I'd seen movement. Could a seal be hiding on the beach among the seaweed? The hairs rose on the back of my neck. Not seals, but . . . could there be customs men hiding down there under the seaweed?

They would have had to have arrived hours ago and dug themselves down into the beach. All those hours lying in the cold damp shingle? Surely not. Was there a customs man in existence that was that dedicated?

I stood frozen with indecision on the cliff. What should I do? Raise the alarm? It was a drastic measure on so slight a suspicion. Everyone would be so angry with me if I were to postpone the run for nothing.

And yet. If there really were king's men lying there, Will and Jacob and the others could all be caught. They could be hurt or imprisoned. And the valuable cargo lost.

At the thought of Will being shot or injured, I began to run. I ran in the direction the lander had taken, hoping to find him and to persuade him to search the beach. My feet flew over the sparse turf of the stony ground and my heart hammered in my chest.

If I was right and there was an ambush down there on the shore, then it would have been I who had drawn *The Invisible* straight into it. I had signalled to the ship that the coast was clear. But perhaps it was not.

I slipped and scrambled down the steep path that led from Hen Cliff to the bay itself. Once or twice I nearly missed my footing and tumbled, but I recovered and kept hurrying. At the bottom of the path, I ran along the back of the beach until I almost tripped over the landers who were lying in the long vegetation.

I cried out with shock, and one of them grabbed hold of me and clapped a hand over my mouth. I fought him. The light was fading fast now, the setting sun firing the sky in the west with reds and oranges.

I stopped struggling and the hand eased cautiously from my mouth. 'What's wrong?' asked the man.

'I gave the signal,' I replied frantically. 'But I don't believe that the beach is safe! I saw movement.'

'There's no one there. We've checked,' he said impatiently. 'You're putting us all in danger running around and screeching like that!'

'I believe they've hidden themselves in the seaweed,' I cried. 'Will you not at least let me go and look? Otherwise you could all be caught and the cargo lost!'

'Hidden in the seaweed? Are you mad?' chuckled a man in a smock and straw hat.

'Excise men are far too stupid for such a ruse!' scoffed another, a tall thin man in baggy clothes.

'There are too many of us,' growled my captor. 'We're a match for them whatever they do.'

'But they'll be armed. They could have soldiers with them,' said another. 'Men could be lost.'

The man I'd spoken to earlier who seemed to be the leader looked around his men doubtfully. 'Someone should go and look, to be sure,' he said at last. 'We need to warn *The Invisible* off if it's true.' A man looked out to sea, shielding his eyes with one hand and reported: 'She's in sight.'

In the end they let me go. I wrapped my cloak close about me and pulled my hood over my head to hide my features. Then I crunched out onto the shingle beach, my basket on my arm. My heart was hammering. If there really were excise men down there, what would they do when they realized I had rumbled them? Would they capture me or leave me be?

Trying to behave as a beachcomber might, I paused to turn over driftwood and seaweed and pretended to be hunting for items of value. I looked up once and saw *The Invisible* sailing straight towards the bay, her sails bellied out before her. I could clearly recognize her at this distance. Hurriedly, I bent and turned over another piece of driftwood. All the time I was drawing closer to those suspicious piles of rubbish above the tide line.

Before I even reached them, I trod on some shingle that gave way and grunted under my feet. Horrified, I stepped back. The stones had slipped where I'd trodden and I thought I could see a patch of blue uniform poking through. Was it merely a piece of old fabric? Or a dead body?

I stepped carefully around whatever it was, and crouched at the first patch of seaweed, carefully turning it over in my hands, piece by piece. I felt sick with fear.

I pulled away a strip that exposed a pair of dark eyes staring back at me in the gloom. I caught my breath and flinched back in shock, but not before the pile had erupted, a strong hand had shot out and grabbed my wrist.

I stifled a shriek of terror and tugged vainly. 'Hush! You've no need to be frightened,' said a hoarse voice rusty with disuse. He cleared his throat and spoke again. 'What are you doing here?' he asked.

'Lookin' for stuff,' I said, imitating the voices of the village girls I'd heard over the past weeks. 'I ain't doin' nothin' wrong.'

'Well, it's far too late for you to be out. It's getting dark! There could be trouble here very soon. Go home and say nothing to anyone! Do you understand?'

'Yessir . . . ' I said, backing away, the moment he loosened his grip on me.

'Not that way!' he hissed as he saw me retracing my steps. 'Go further up the beach!'

I obeyed him, feeling sick with fear. It occurred to me there could be soldiers about that he didn't want me to run into. If they'd got here before me, they could be concealed somewhere.

I struggled across the shingle as swiftly as I could, my feet slipping in my hurry to leave the beach. I found a path that led up behind it and began to run. I needed to tell the others there was danger. They might not have seen what I found. I reached a small hummock and climbed it, panting with exertion now.

Below me and to my left, I saw with a jolt of shock that the landers were now sitting huddled into a group. Crouched down, surrounding them, muskets trained, was a ring of three dragoons. Another soldier was waiting in the long grasses, his muskets trained on the beach. Where had they lain hidden?

Instantly, I dropped down into the grass myself, hoping none of them had noticed that I'd spotted them. This had been an ambush. We had a traitor among us. There was no other possible way that the soldiers could have known so precisely when and where the run would be.

Cautiously I raised my eyes to look once more. None of the soldiers were looking in my direction. I breathed a sigh of relief, but it was short-lived. I realized none of the landers could now signal the ship. I turned and looked out to sea. She was close now. I could see every sail, every mast, and I could even make out tiny figures moving about on the decks in the dusk.

My friends were sailing straight into a deadly trap. And there was no sign of it from out in the bay. There was no one but me to warn them, but what could I do? My cloak was useless now that it was dark. I had no lantern.

I pressed my face into the damp, cold ground, panic gripping me. Then I gave myself a shake. I couldn't give in, I had to do something. Think! I told myself furiously. What would Will do?

In a moment, I'd grasped my basket and was fumbling in it. At the bottom was the tinderbox that Ann had given me. Now I knew what that 'need' might be. I had a vivid memory of the gorse bushes that had been fired the night I'd been taken aboard *The Invisible*. A warning, bright enough to be seen from sea.

Abandoning my basket, I ran for the cliffs, clutching the tinderbox to me. I threw myself up the steep path, racing frantically upwards, leaping from rock to rock, to get the best possible footing on the steep slope. I had to get to the top before anyone saw me. Darkness was falling fast now, so I could hope no one would spot me, or think anything of it if they did. My breathing was coming in desperate gasps before I was halfway to the top of the cliff.

I paused and risked a glance behind me. No one was following. But out to sea, *The Invisible* had lowered her boats and was loading kegs and men into them. I had to warn them away before they reached the beach.

I turned and began to run upwards once more. By the time I reached the top, I was gasping raggedly and the sweat was pouring off me. Where was some suitable gorse? I needed a bush that grew right on the cliff edge and would be clearly visible from the ship.

I almost stumbled into a sharp bush in the dark. I dropped to my knees beside it, ignoring the prickles that stabbed into my knees and scraped my hands. With desperate, clumsy fingers, I fumbled with the tinderbox trying to get it to work. The first spark fell upon my cloak and almost set it alight. Beating it out with my hands, I tried again.

The first boat had left the ship now and was heading in towards the beach, loaded with incriminating evidence. Anyone caught with kegs of French cognac could be thrown into gaol. Worst of all, they might fight to defend themselves and lives could be lost.

Several more sparks flew, but failed to light the bush. At last, one landed on a branch and glowed. I bent over it, cursing the painful scratches I was getting, and blew softly on it. It glowed brighter and then caught in a tiny flame. The flame grew. It spread along the branch and began to crackle.

I'd done it. But was I in time?

I backed away and looked out to sea. The first boat was halfway to the beach. The second had left the ship. On the dark beach, I could see no movement at all; no sign that an untold number of men lay concealed in the shingle.

I looked anxiously back at the gorse. The fire was taking far too long to catch. I clenched my hands in an agony of fear and frustration. There was nothing more I could do now. It was out of my hands.

As I waited in painful uncertainty, a gust of wind blew in from the sea. It fanned the flames on the gorse bush. The fire leapt and engulfed the whole bush in a moment. It burned like a bright beacon, almost blinding me. I could see nothing but yellows and oranges dancing before my eyes wherever I looked.

I half-laughed, half-wept with relief. I had succeeded. Though I could see nothing, I was certain I had warned the crew away from that dangerous beach.

Moving cautiously away from the fire, staying away from where I thought the cliff edge might be, I stared out into the darkness, waiting for my eyes to adjust. Behind me the blaze faded to a glow. When I could see again, both boats were heading back out to *The Invisible*. On board the ship, men were in the rigging, raising the sails, making ready to flee.

But I was left behind. My heart lurched with the realization. I'd been so busy warning them, I'd forgotten about myself. There was no way I could have got to the ship. I'd done what I could. I stood and watched them leave, feeling bereft.

The sound of heavy footsteps and loud breathing approaching reminded me I mustn't be caught here. I fled away along the cliff path, away from the soldiers, and didn't stop running until I was lost in the darkness.

It took a long time to reach Ann's cottage. I stumbled and fell more than once and became hopelessly lost. When I finally got there, the windows were dark and Ann already abed. I knocked softly and when she didn't hear me, I crept around the back. I climbed the low wall behind the cottage and let myself in through the back door that was never fastened.

I was just pouring myself a cup of water, when I heard soft steps behind me and the dim light of a shaded candle came into view. 'Who's there?' demanded Ann's voice sounding frightened.

'It's me, Isabelle,' I said. 'Don't be afraid!'

'Isabelle!' exclaimed Ann. 'What went wrong?'

'They took the landers!' I said, my voice catching. 'There were soldiers hidden on the beach. And I'd signalled the all clear, so the crew from *The Invisible* were very nearly caught too!' And then because I'd been through so much excitement and fear, I burst into tears.

Ann put her arms around me and held me tight. 'Dear Lord! But they didn't catch them?' she asked urgently, giving me a little shake. 'Tell me they're safe!'

'They're s . . . safe,' I sobbed. 'I . . . I fired a gorse bush with the tinder . . . tinderbox you gave me. They got away . . . just!'

Ann let go of me with a sigh of relief and patted my shoulder. 'I think a small beer is called for. You can tell me all about it,' she said. 'Then we need to get word out to help the landers as was taken.'

CHAPTER TWENTY

✳

As she poured the beer for breakfast two days later, Ann told me that a messenger had called in the night.

'You're to be at Lulworth Cove tonight at eleven of the clock,' she told me. 'It's a long trek from here, a fair step beyond Kimmeridge, but they've fixed you a ride in a carrier's cart as far as Tyneham where you'll be met.'

'They're attempting to land the cargo again?' I asked. I'd been thinking of them constantly, hovering in the channel with their dangerous cargo, evading the Navy and Revenue ships that patrolled it. It hadn't been considered safe to follow our original back-up plans. Yet again, someone had appeared to have inside information about the run.

'Yes, but they won't risk the cloak signal again so soon in case anyone spotted you last time. You never know. A customs man as can dig his men into the beach might have the brains to work out you were signalling. The landers will use a spout lantern tonight.'

I nodded as I sipped my beer and buttered some bread. 'I bet it was that Oswald fellow. He seemed sly enough for anything. What about the men that were caught?' I asked. 'Any news of them?'

'They've all been released without charge,' Ann told me.

'Really?' I must have looked astonished, because she laughed.

'Without the cargo, there was nothing to charge them with. There's no law against being on the beach at night. There are laws about signalling ships, but they were all under guard when the bush was fired. The excise men have to pay prosecution expenses themselves, so they never prosecute unless there's clear proof.'

'Are you saying that I rescued all those men too? As well as everyone on *The Invisible*?' I could feel myself swelling with pride.

'You did.' Ann began to pack me some food for my journey and wrap it in a clean cloth. I nibbled a piece of bread and grew thoughtful.

'Ann,' I asked, in what I hoped was a casual tone, 'how close is Lulworth to Newlands?'

'Newlands Manor?' she asked curiously. 'No more than a step. It's above Durdle and that's the next bay along. Why?'

'Oh. No reason,' I said, unwilling to explain why I didn't want to go back to that place. 'Do you think it would be better if I went dressed as a lad today? It's a long way for a girl to go alone, isn't it?'

Ann shook her head, looking mystified. 'Well, I suppose so,' she said. 'It's as you like. But pack the gown in case you should need to be a girl again.'

Changed into breeches, my hair concealed in a cap, I bid her farewell once more and climbed into the cart. The carrier was ferrying a load of furniture for someone who was moving house. I sat on the seat at the front of the cart with him as he drove the horses.

The driver was a taciturn man, so I watched the countryside go by and examined the other travellers we passed on the road. Mainly though, I thought ahead to tonight. I hoped there would be no danger like last time and that I would reach the ship safely. I told myself I longed to see everyone again, but it was Will's face that rose most often in my mind.

When the creaking, lumbering cart rolled into the village of Tyneham, the light was beginning to fail. A yokel was sitting idly on a low wall, chewing a straw and watching us approach. He was dressed in a grubby smock with a straw hat pulled low over his eyes, so I barely glanced at him. But when he stood up and addressed us, I realized with a shock of pleasure that it was Will himself. He winked at me as the cart pulled up beside him with a 'Whoa!' from the driver.

I jumped down from the seat and Will passed a few coins to the carrier. I thanked him, he touched his cap to me and proceeded on his way. Will and I looked at each other, and I felt shy all of a sudden. 'Come on,' Will said. 'There's a fair way to walk yet, but then a good supper ordered at the inn at West Lulworth when we get there.'

I followed him gladly; happy to be striding at his side once more. 'I understand we owe you thanks,' said Will once we were clear of the village. 'You spotted the soldiers and fired the gorse bush. That was quick thinking.'

It felt strange to be praised by Will instead of criticized. 'I should have checked the beach earlier though,' I added honestly. 'I had such a feeling there was something odd down there. If I hadn't given the signal in the first place, it wouldn't have been such a close-run thing.'

Will shook his head. 'You have to admire the riding officer,' he said. 'If it hadn't been for your sharp eyes, he'd have got the lot of us and earned himself a fine reward from His Majesty's Treasury. We are so unlucky. Most places along the coast have little or no credible watch. The officers are lazy, infirm or open to bribes. The contraband is run openly in broad daylight. But we get the one officer who can add two and two together and get four and has the dedication to lay an ambush.'

'I can't imagine how cold and uncomfortable it must have been to lie so still all those hours,' I agreed. 'I've thought about it often the last few days. Those men could have taken severe chills.'

'Indeed.' Will laughed. 'We've heard Oswald *is* laid up with a bad cold in his head. And the soldiers have all left the area again after such a failure. So we intend to strike while the iron is hot and run the goods in tonight.'

The new moon was high in the night sky by the time Will and I met the landers on the hill behind Lulworth Cove. Knowing Lieutenant Oswald was laid up, they all seemed quite unconcerned about the brightness of the night, and took no trouble to conceal themselves. One man held a lantern which he was lighting ready to signal the ship out to sea.

'Is she in range?' asked Will.

'Aye, that she is,' he replied. 'We spied her before dark, but have been biding till the time was right.'

'Have you checked the beach?' I asked, mindful of the last near-disastrous run.

'We've checked it,' confirmed another man.

The signal was sent and returned. We could make out *The Invisible* setting her sails and heading in towards us, though she was soon hidden by the cliffs.

We all made off down to the cove in a long train, the men leading the pack ponies along the sloping track that led down towards the sea. I walked at Will's side, amazed at the relaxed, buoyant mood among the men. It was almost as though we were heading for a party, not a secret and illegal venture.

As we emerged from the track into the cove, I caught my breath. I'd sailed a considerable stretch of this coast now, and seen many remarkable bays and beaches. But Lulworth was splendid.

Almost a perfect horseshoe, it curved before us; only a narrow exit to the sea visible straight ahead. We were surrounded by looming white cliffs, glowing in the pale moonlight, cut off completely from the countryside on the one side and almost as completely from the sea. There was an eerie stillness down in the cove, broken only by the crunching of men's and ponies' feet on the shingle. As we all settled to wait, the stillness was complete. The waves were tiny and lapped softly on the fringe of the beach. An owl hooted somewhere inland, its mournful cry drifting to us in the dark, still air.

A tall, dark shape loomed at the entrance to the bay. I caught my breath as *The Invisible* glided silently into the cove, the moonlight shining on her sails. Her grace and beauty were undeniable. She looked like a living creature; a swan perhaps. Hearing my intake of breath, Will looked down and smiled. 'Glad to see her?' he asked.

'You can't imagine how glad,' I replied softly. I felt almost tearful at the sight of the ship. Will took my hand and pressed it in the darkness. I felt the heat rise in my cheeks and was glad of the darkness that hid it. I hadn't spoken to Will as I'd promised myself I would and felt a stab of guilt at the thought. But he'd been so friendly and relaxed this evening, I'd not wanted to spoil the short time we'd had together.

The Invisible sailed close to the beach, and the boats had already brought us our first load of kegs when there was the sound of hooves behind us.

'Hi!' called an outraged voice. 'You can't land that here!'

My heart jumped into my mouth. We all spun round, some men paused in the very act of unloading contraband, to stare into the moonlit darkness at the back of the beach. I couldn't believe it: after barely escaping last time, we were all to be caught anyway. 'Damn,' I heard Will mutter beside me.

Two junior riding officers rode towards us, their horses foundering in the shingle. My heart was hammering, but the men around me seemed unperturbed. Seeing only two of them approaching, knowing that Lieutenant Oswald was ill and the soldiers gone, they went back to work, splashing through the shallows, carrying the heavy kegs.

'I said halt!' cried the junior officer angrily. 'I can't allow smuggling here!'

There was laughter at this. 'You going to stop us?' demanded the man who'd lit the lantern.

'Yes, I am,' he replied bravely, riding his horse right up to us, and trying to get between the men and the boats. 'Stop! Stop now, I say! This is an illegal trade!'

His companion, an older man, hung back, looking nervous.

'Give up, do,' said the lander. 'You've got no one to back you up. You can't stop us tonight. And we don't want to hurt you.'

'I'm an officer of His Majesty King George and his representative in this place!' cried the officer, barging a man who was trying to carry a keg past him. The man stumbled and fell into the sea, dropping the keg. This angered the landers, setting off a low growl. As one, they abandoned their work to haul the officer down off his horse.

'Don't interfere with us and we won't interfere with you!' the men told him.

'I won't stand by and watch!' he cried.

It was a foolish argument. He should have backed off when his initial warning was ignored. These were rough men with hungry families to feed at home. They weren't going to obey him. Instead of fearing for the smugglers' safety, I began to feel concern for the customs men.

The second officer backed off, clearly thinking about fleeing, only to be stopped by other men who had spread out and surrounded him. 'You wouldn't run off and leave your friend all alone, would you?' they asked him. He kicked out at them as they closed in on him, but he too was pulled from his frightened horse, and none too gently at that.

I sought out Will in the dim light. 'They won't hurt them, will they?' I asked him anxiously.

'They might, but they know not to go too far,' Will said. I wasn't comforted.

The two men were dragged back out of the cove, and up the road they had ridden down. All around me the men that were left carried on with the job of unloading the kegs from the ship. There were several crates of fine wine too, that were loaded into a small cart that had been brought down the slipway to the edge of the beach. I sat on the shingle, feeling sick at the thought of what might be happening to the two officers who had only been performing their duty.

I didn't have long to wait to see what was in store for them. There were shouts from the top of the low cliff to the right, and two dark shapes descended over the edge. It wasn't easy to see in this light what was happening, but after a few moments I made out the two officers, tightly bound, hanging from their ankles from the cliff top.

My heart almost stopped at the sight. 'Oh no,' I breathed. But everyone else was amused; there was laughter around me. The officers hung there, watching the last of the kegs being unloaded and tied to the pack horses. When everything was ashore and ready to go, there was a discussion about what to do with them.

'Don't have to stand by and watch us now, do he?' remarked one man cheerfully. 'He can dangle and watch instead!' There was a shout of laughter.

'Leave 'em there till morning, I say,' one man suggested.

I tugged at Will's sleeve: 'Please do not,' I whispered. 'They could die.'

'Interferin' busybodies!' said someone else. 'They deserve what they get.'

'A good beating would be more to the point,' suggested another. 'That'd teach them to keep their noses out of our business next time.'

'That might get the law after us,' said another man, to my relief. I'd been thinking the same thing.

'How about you hand them over to the skipper for a holiday in France?' suggested Will.

This caused a great deal of hilarity. The bound officers were hauled back up the cliff and carried back down to the beach, strapped onto their own horses. There was some rough horseplay as the men were first dropped into the water and then loaded onto one of the boats and rowed out to the ship. Their horses were turned loose; the landers vanished quietly into the darkness with their train of ponies.

'Come, Isabelle,' said Will. The last boat was waiting for us in the shallows. I crossed the shingle to join him.

'What will happen to them now?' I asked.

'The Preventives? Nothing too terrible,' he said, jumping into the boat.

'But what is a holiday in France?' I asked as I climbed in after him. 'What does that signify?'

'We'll drop them off with nothing but the clothes they stand up in,' said Will. He grinned at the thought. 'It's unkind. Most speak no French and will have to find a way to get back to England. But it does no real harm. I thought it the least of the evils. Don't forget they'd have flung every last man of us into gaol four nights ago if they'd had their way.'

'I suppose so,' I said reluctantly as I helped to push the boat out into deeper water. As the boat floated free of the shingle the last men jumped in and others bent to the oars, taking us swiftly out to *The Invisible*. Despite my concerns for the riding officers, I was delighted to be at sea once more.

CHAPTER TWENTY-ONE

✳

The officers were duly dropped off in France. They'd been blindfolded and tied to the mast during the crossing and though I'd felt sorry for them, I'd been forbidden to approach them or speak to them, even though I was back in breeches.

'Them boy's clothes you wears might fool people as don't look at you too close,' Jacob said. 'But if they hear and don't see you, they'll know we have a woman aboard.'

I agreed reluctantly to keep my distance. I was troubled by the treatment meted out to the men. No one hurt them once they were on board, but they were offered neither food nor drink. And to be abandoned in a strange country, a country with which we were at war as often as not, seemed a harsh fate. Especially as one of the men tearfully pleaded, as we left him alone on some deserted beach, that he'd 'never learned to speak frog'.

'It's often done,' Will assured me with a carefree laugh, as he swung up into the rigging. 'If you think about it, they shouldn't recruit customs men who speak no French. See it as an educational trip for them. They will know a few words for next time!'

The skipper approached me once the ship was moored in its usual berth in Cherbourg. 'Isabelle,' he asked, catching me while I was energetically scrubbing the tables in the galley. 'A word.'

I sat down opposite him, pushing the cloth to one side, wiping my hands on my breeches and tucking some wisps of hair back out of my eyes. 'What can I do for you?' I asked him rather breathlessly.

'It's how much you dare,' he said. 'I've a large order for French lace if I can get it into the country.'

'Oh,' I said reluctantly. 'I have to say, I didn't enjoy it much last time.'

'How about if we ensure that Lieutenant Oswald is not in the vicinity?' asked the skipper. 'It just doesn't do to send lace through the usual channels, you see. It must be kept dry and clean and must reach quite a different market.'

I wasn't unwilling to do my part. Especially as Will had promised me that there was money waiting as my share of the ventures we'd undertaken. It gave me some hope of being able to survive once the season was over. I hesitated, however, still remembering the terrors at Poole. 'If you are quite sure he won't be there,' I said at last. 'For I'm certain he would recognize me and find my presence most suspicious.'

'Thank you, Isabelle,' said the skipper, waving aside my objections as though they were irrelevancies. 'I'll send you and Will to the warehouse today.' He half got up, and then paused and smiled slightly down at me. 'You've been an asset to us,' he said awkwardly. 'I never thought I'd admit it. But you have. It's good to have you back.'

He hurried out onto the deck before I could reply, obviously feeling he'd embarrassed himself in some way.

I was glad of his words. It was good to feel useful and wanted.

'Don't let it go to your head, Isabelle!' called Harry, breaking in on my thoughts. 'He'll soon be shouting at you again!'

I laughed, got to my feet and resumed cleaning the tables.

The quantity of lace Will bought in the warehouse made me thoughtful. It was more than twice what I'd smuggled last time, and I didn't think I could possibly carry so much in one go. Will was in a more than usually teasing mood. 'You need to earn your keep, you know,' he commented. 'We can't have you eating up the whole ship's rations and doing nothing useful any longer.'

'What about my work in the galley? And that day on Kimmeridge beach?' I asked indignantly. 'I saved your skins for you!'

'Oh, I don't know,' said Will with a shrug and a laugh. 'Who's to say we wouldn't have had a good turn-up and seen them off? Instead of which we were obliged to dodge the Navy for several days and run the cargo all over again another night.'

His voice and face were quite serious, with no sign that he was joking. But I could see by the slight creases around his eyes that he was enjoying himself.

A wonderful revenge came to mind, so instead of continuing to argue with him, I tucked a hand into his arm and spoke coaxingly to him: 'Will, you know this money you're saving for me?'

'Ye-es,' Will replied, clearly suspicious of this change in tactics.

'Could I have some of it for a new gown?' I asked.

'Certainly not!' exclaimed Will. 'What? Should I allow you to waste it all on fripperies and leave you nothing for the summer?'

I frowned a little, wondering how to persuade him to change his mind. And then I remembered that I *had* another gown on board: the gown Ann had lent me would be ideal for the purpose I had in mind.

'Very well,' I agreed, suddenly docile. 'You are very good to me, Will. Thank you.'

Will cast a suspicious glance down at me and I smiled sweetly in return. He was going to hate me presently.

Back on board, I took the skipper aside. 'There is a great deal of lace there,' I told him bluntly. 'We'll need a second woman if you wish to take it ashore in one go.'

'We don't have a second woman,' said the skipper, frowning. 'And it can't be kept on board. The customs men will rummage the ship as soon as we make port.'

'You may not have two women on board,' I pointed out. 'But we do have two gowns.'

The skipper's quick mind grasped my idea at once. 'Who do you have in mind?' he asked.

'Well,' I replied, pretending to ponder the matter. 'We need a young man, with no beard, someone slight and small enough to pass for a tall woman. I would suggest . . . Will perhaps?'

The skipper chuckled. 'Send him to me,' he said.

I stepped across the gangplank onto the quay at Poole, feeling even bulkier and heavier than the last time I'd gone ashore here. My maid followed: a great strapping girl, too stout for beauty, her head wrapped in a shawl.

'Morning, ma'am,' said the junior customs officer walking towards me and executing a small bow. 'Welcome to Poole.'

I could see him looking at us both closely, a small crease between his brow at our bulk and at my maid being so hidden in her shawl. But I was confident in the knowledge it was not in his power to search us. 'Lieutenant Oswald is not here today?' I asked.

'No, ma'am,' replied the young man. 'He's at Studland today.'

I already knew this, but pretended to look disappointed. 'Oh,' I said. 'He was so kind to me last time I was here. I wished to ask him where I might find a tooth-drawer. My poor maid here has a tooth that needs pulling. She's in so much pain.'

At once sympathetic and eager to be helpful, the young officer explained to me where I could find the local tooth-drawer. Thanking him prettily, I left my compliments to Lieutenant Oswald and moved on, leaving the young officer to go aboard *The Invisible*. He would find nothing, of course. We'd already run our tubs into Swanage the night before.

Walking towards the town, I attracted one or two curious looks. My maid attracted even more. 'Keep up, Betty,' I chided her, as she stumbled along, appearing to have difficulty with her petticoats and shoes.

I got a baleful glare from under the shawl that made me grin. As we rounded the corner into the High Street, a middle-aged man apparently the worse for drink stopped and stared at my maid. 'Now there's a strapping wench!' he exclaimed. As we passed, he reached out and clapped her on her well-padded bottom.

My maid whipped round and growled: 'Try that again at your peril!'

Startled, the man backed off. He stared at the face half-concealed by the shawl. 'That's the deepest voice I ever heard on a lass,' he said suspiciously.

'Poor Betty has *such* a sore throat,' I explained hurriedly, catching hold of Betty's arm and dragging her away with some difficulty. 'You cannot start a brawl in the street,' I hissed fiercely. 'Behave yourself, Betty!'

'Call me Betty one more time and I'll start a brawl with you,' muttered Will at me from under the shawl.

'You have no idea how to walk as a woman.' I continued telling him off. 'I thought I'd taught you better than this! Take smaller steps! Don't look so bold! Everyone's staring now.'

'I will never, ever forgive you for this,' said Will as we turned into a narrow alley where the lace merchant had his small store. 'Not if I live to be a hundred.'

I chuckled. 'Yes, you will,' I assured him. 'Just think of all the things I've forgiven you for.'

When we returned to the ship, the lace safely delivered to the purchaser, Will was greeted with wolf whistles and laughter.

'Well, here's a pair of pretty maids!' cried Harry.

'The maid is the most comely for my money,' shouted another. 'Come and sit on my knee, my pretty.'

Will shook his fist at him. 'You'd soon regret it, my friend,' he said. 'I'm no dainty piece.'

'A bit flat around here, aren't you, my beauty?' suggested another, cupping imaginary breasts in his hands. Some of the men were wiping tears from their eyes they were laughing so much. I blushed a little at their crudeness, but couldn't help but be amused. Will was trying to take it well, but there was no hiding his humiliation. He soon hurried below to throw off the offending garments.

'So how did he manage?' asked the skipper once he was gone. 'You had no trouble. Did he make a convincing girl?'

'Convincing enough,' I replied. Then my sense of mischief got the better of me and I added: 'He might have been born to the role, in fact.'

'I'll be bound,' sniggered Hard-Head Bill.

The wit was still flying back and forth when Will re-emerged some ten minutes later. My heart lurched at the sight of his slim figure, his strong legs encased in breeches, his broad shoulders filling out his coat, his fair hair caught back in the nape of his neck in his black ribband. He might not be especially tall, but there was nothing girly about him. The men couldn't leave their teasing, though.

'So our two girls are going into the lace trade then, eh, Betty?' they asked.

Will stalked off to the prow to be alone.

'Don't take any notice of them,' I told him, joining him there. 'They will have their fun and forget it again.' I smiled as it occurred to me that this was very similar to the advice he himself had given me just a few months ago.

'Even you are laughing at me!' he exclaimed.

'No, not at all. I'm just amused to be repeating your own advice back to you,' I explained. 'And if I did laugh, is that so bad?'

'You have no idea,' he growled. 'Dressing me like a maid . . . ' he glowered at me. 'How could you?'

'How is that worse than dressing me in those dreadful breeches?' I exclaimed indignantly. 'I was so ashamed at the immodesty of it, I didn't know where to look or what to do. You should be ashamed at making such a fuss!' I looked at his still-indignant face and began to laugh again.

Reluctantly, Will grinned back. 'I'll never hear the last of it from the men,' he said.

CHAPTER TWENTY-TWO

✳

The profit we turned on the lace was considered so worthwhile, and the demand for the costly commodity so great, that Will was obliged to play the maid several more times. He grumbled, but did as he was asked. He had a considerable talent for acting and soon moved easily in woman's garb.

Slowly, the days began to draw out. Time passed and still I waited for a chance to speak to Will. The ship was crowded and busy and somehow there never seemed to be a time when we wouldn't be overheard. I began to wonder whether Will deliberately avoided being alone with me; certainly he never took me with him on his solitary trips ashore. Or perhaps I was being cowardly, for I surely could have told him I needed to speak privately, but I didn't do so.

Soon we all knew winter was fading. Some days the sun had a little warmth in it when it broke through the clouds.

'Just another month before we're all toiling in the fields again,' said Will, shielding his eyes as he looked towards the green coast of England.

'Is that what you do in the summer too?' I asked, surprised.

'It is. But unlike the others, I go to France,' said Will.

'What's wrong with England?' I asked.

'I prefer France,' said Will, not meeting my eyes.

I could make nothing of his enigmatic remarks or his secrecy. I wondered not for the first time what I would do when the crew dispersed. Where would I go? All winter I'd pushed aside the thought of my own situation. The time was fast approaching when I could escape it no longer.

It was ironic that our destination tonight brought me, in a sense, full circle. Our penultimate venture of the dying winter took us into the beach at Durdle Door. The very place I'd fled in such despair five months earlier. Since then, my despair had left me. Life was still complicated, but it was precious to me. For a while I'd found a purpose, or at least a merry distraction, aboard *The Invisible*.

The dilemma kept me awake during the crossing that night. I thought of all the things I'd like to do, and none of them were realistic. Then I thought about Will, and all the aspects of his behaviour that made no sense. Spending the summer working as a common labourer in France. Disguising himself whenever he went ashore in England. I remembered that he hadn't ventured out at all at Worth Matravers over Christmas. And yet on board the ship and in Cherbourg, he wore no disguise at all. What reason could he have for concealing his identity in England? The other Gentlemen never did so. They came and went quite openly; apparently fearless of prosecution. So it could scarcely be due to the smuggling itself.

A cold feeling crept over me. Was he . . . it was hard to frame the words even in my mind. But I needed to: was he wanted by the law? For something other than evading duty? Those men had been searching for him before Christmas and had mentioned a reward. There was obviously something I didn't know. I wriggled, the very notion filling me with darkness. I couldn't lie still any longer. I had to get up.

The weather was calm and bright, and I found my way to the open deck to think and watch away from the constrictive discomfort of my narrow bunk and stuffy cabin.

I had a shock when I saw that Will was at the helm. I wasn't sure I wanted to see him right now. He lifted his hand in greeting, but was too much occupied to speak to me. That suited me; I craved solitude for a spell.

The moon was high in the clear black sky, casting a brilliant silvery light over the quiet waters of the channel. Stars frosted the heavens, like shards of ice scattered by an idle hand. Wrapped in my shawl, I contemplated the natural world around me and drew strength from its divine beauty.

Almost sub-consciously, I picked up the loose end of rope and began to practise the knots I'd learned. Right hand over left; twist, tug. I went through them all: clove hitch, anchor bend, sheet bend, bowline, mooring hitch, buntline hitch. Sometimes they fell apart in my hand or tangled. Each time, I started again.

As I practised, Will faded from my mind and I went back to thinking over my own future. Unfortunately, inspiration stayed far from me. No matter how hard I thought, there was no solution to the mess I'd made of my life. My aim had always been marriage and status. I never remembered wishing for anything else. That had been compromised by my father's stunning loss. What did a person do when their life-long goal failed them? I had no idea. I'd fled the disaster, but I'd not escaped. The problems had followed me.

'Isabelle,' said Will's voice behind me. I started and turned to face him. As always in recent weeks, the sight of his handsome face made my breath come short. It was no good. I had to get the better of feelings that could only lead me into trouble. 'You're getting better at those, I see, though you've tied that one left-handed again.' I hurriedly pulled it free and began again. 'Is this the right time of night to be practising?'

'Will,' I said, with a fair assumption of calm. 'You've left your post?'

'My turn on duty is over,' he replied, indicating the skipper at the wheel behind us. 'It's time for me to snatch a few hours sleep, but I'm curious as to what has kept you so still in the prow for over an hour when you should be sleeping.'

'Ah just restless thoughts,' I said with a small sigh, looking away from him out to sea.

Will leaned on the rail beside me. 'Tell me?' he invited. 'As a friend.'

I swallowed, unsure how to speak, or how to put my doubts into words. 'Very well, as a friend,' I said after a long pause. It was hard to say the word, difficult to meet his eyes. 'I truly have no idea what is to become of me next week.'

'Your family?' asked Will. 'Would they not be overjoyed to see you? They must think you dead.'

I bit my lip. 'No doubt they do,' I agreed. 'There are reasons I cannot return to them.'

'Tell me,' Will repeated. 'You can trust me, you know.'

Could I? I knew he meant it kindly. But would he not judge me if he heard the truth? I dreaded seeing his expression change; the warm concern that filled his face now fade and be replaced with shock.

'Truly, when I think back to the person I was five months ago,' I said abruptly, 'I positively loathe myself. It drenches me with shame.'

Will laughed softly, but not in an unkind way. 'You were hard to like,' he said. 'A lesson to all of us in how a perfectly good person can be ruined by indulgence.'

I buried my face in my hands. 'But I'm not sure I am a good person,' I said. It came out as a muffled groan.

Will ruffled my hair casually. 'We know better,' he said lightly.

I merely shook my head. I dropped my hands, but kept my face averted, still looking out to sea though I no longer saw the beauty of the night.

'I need to tell you . . . ' I began, but Will spoke at the same time.

'Never fear, Isabelle,' Will said cheerfully. 'We won't leave you to starve. I won't . . . '

His voice tailed off. I didn't know what he had wanted to say, or what had intruded to prevent him completing his sentence.

'I don't deserve it,' I said.

'So what has brought on this sudden remorse?' Will asked me in a bantering tone. I could tell he was trying to cheer me. 'You certainly made life uncomfortable for yourself and everyone else when you were first on board. But we're all friends now. So why repine?'

'Perhaps because we're going back,' I said.

Will sobered suddenly. 'Ah! Durdle,' he said. 'Yes, I can see that the scene could be painful to you in more ways than one.'

We both fell silent. We stood quietly side by side thinking each our own thoughts. There was more of my story I should tell him. I tried to make myself speak the words but my tongue cleaved to the roof of my mouth.

'Did you love him so much?' asked Will softly, shocking me out of my abstraction.

'What?' I asked confused for a moment. Then I recalled that Will thought I'd walked into the sea that night for the love of the young viscount. He didn't know the truth. I blushed scarlet.

It was Will's turn to look confused. 'James Marlow . . . the man you were going to marry,' he said uncertainly. 'Who else?'

'I . . . yes. I mean, no,' I stammered. 'I thought myself in love with him certainly. But looking back, seeing it more clearly now, I hardly knew him. I believe I was more in love with his rank, his fortune, with the idea of marriage. I longed so much to be a bride. To make a good match. And that one was brilliant . . . '

'What is it, Isabelle?' Will asked when I faltered and stopped. A sudden gust of wind blew over us, filling the sails and pulling the boat forward in a great lurch.

I turned to him, resolute, determined to be brave. 'Will, there's something I need to tell you. It wasn't because of him. That's not why you found me in the sea that night. At least, he was only a part of the reason. There's something else. Something that happened afterwards that you should know about.'

Will was looking at me half eagerly, half anxiously. Another gust of wind swept across us, this time so fierce that the ship heeled and we both caught at the rail.

'Will!' the skipper shouted. 'Ring the bell; get some more hands on deck! We need to reef the sails!'

Will dropped a hand on my shoulder and squeezed it briefly. With a regretful backward glance, he ran to the bell. I watched as he rang it and then swung himself up into the rigging. I followed him, and side by side we worked to reef the mainsail, tying the fastenings off securely, using the knots I'd learned. I worked until men began to stumble sleepily onto the deck from below. The fresh wind that was now squalling over us and a sudden burst of rain soon woke them, and the ship bustled with activity. They joined us in the rigging, stronger and more experienced than I was. I was soon pushed aside as they took over.

I wasn't needed any longer. Feeling hollow, I climbed back down to the deck and went to my cabin. But until the dawn was flushing the sky pink, I still couldn't fall asleep.

Having been up all night, I slept much of the next day and awoke hungry and with a headache. It was already growing dark when I left the cabin, and we were close in to the coast. I cast the land an uninterested glance, and sought Harry in the galley and settled down to a hunk of bread with bacon to assuage my hunger.

Below, I could already hear the men shifting the kegs ready for unloading and I'd seen the look-outs in the rigging. We were waiting for the signal; preparing for the landing. 'Should be a straightforward one tonight,' remarked Harry, sliding onto the bench beside me.

'That's good,' I mumbled.

'You look terrible,' Harry told me. 'Where've you been all day?'

'Sleeping,' I said shortly. 'Harry, how did Will come to be with you? He doesn't seem the type to be aboard a smuggling vessel.'

Harry laughed shortly. 'Neither do you, come to that. He joined us at the beginning of last winter. We don't own *The Invisible*, you know. It's sad, but true. We're free-traders, but not free men. We get paid by the venturer who owns this ship. He sent us Will to be our agent and negotiator. We suspected he was here as a spy. You know, to make sure none of us were cheating the boss. We gave him a hard time.'

I wondered if this was the mystery that Will had been alluding to. 'And was he?' I asked curiously.

'None of us know. But he's a damn good agent. We never had so many runs, so many customers. He's negotiated us better pay too. Everything's run like clockwork since Will came aboard. He's risked his life for us a number of times. Whatever he is to the venturer, most of us trust him now.'

'I see,' I said, puzzled. Will was an enigmatic character, half comrade, half . . . what? The puzzle of what a gentleman-born was doing among smugglers was far from explained.

I went up on deck to help watch for the signal from the beach. It was bright and clear tonight and I wasn't the only one to spot it. The boats left us, heading into the dark and the sound of waves on shingle. I saw Will leave on a boat full of casks and when the boat returned he was gone.

'Where's Will?' I asked the skipper as he gave the order to set sail.

'We're picking him up tomorrow in Lulworth,' the skipper replied briefly.

Tomorrow. That wasn't so very long to wait. I would speak to him as soon he returned. It was important to me to tell him the truth now.

But when Will returned to the ship the following night, he stared at me as though I was a ghost. When I approached him, he shied away as though I carried some deadly disease. I'd left my tale too late.

CHAPTER TWENTY-THREE

✳

The mood was abruptly different on board. It was not only me Will kept his distance from. He was silent and taciturn throughout the voyage, keeping to his work, meeting no one's eyes and spending long spells alone, either aloft in the rigging or in his hammock below.

I also gathered, from conversations I overheard, that both the goods and the destination for the final run of the season had been altered.

'No lace,' Harry said. 'So Will's in a bad mood—won't get to don his gown one last time!' He laughed as though it were a joke, but there were others who didn't take this change of plan so lightly.

'Something's up,' muttered Sly Pete. 'I never trusted him.'

'Nor me,' agreed Bill. 'I always said he was a spy and a traitor. We nearly got caught running into Kimmeridge. We never found out the sneak. What does anyone wager it was him?'

'Come, lads,' said Jacob, his brow furrowed and his face troubled. 'How can you talk about not trusting him after all he's risked for us?'

'Well, perhaps he had his reasons up to now,' snapped Sly Pete. 'And now the time for trust is over. I don't like it, I tell you. We never go to the same drop twice running. What's he thinking of?'

Jacob shook his head. 'He has something weighing heavy on his mind,' he said. 'That doesn't make him a traitor.'

'Guilty conscience; that's what it is,' Sly Pete insisted.

I paced the deck as the ship dipped and rose in the swell, wondering what the truth of this was. Will had been ashore to the very beach I'd fled. Had he heard the truth about me? Was that what troubled him? He wouldn't speak to me.

At that moment, Will swung himself down through the rigging from the look-out and landed lightly on the deck. At the same moment Sly Pete, Harry, Bill and some of the others emerged from the galley and confronted him.

Hard-Head Bill went to walk past Will, but instead barged him with his shoulder. Will turned swiftly and landed a punch that sent Bill to the deck. He fell heavily with a groan as the breath was knocked from his body.

'Stop this at once!' shouted the skipper, taking the steps from the quarterdeck two at a time. 'What in God's name is going on? I won't have brawling aboard my ship!'

'The man's a traitor!' shouted Bill through his bloody nose. Lying on the deck, he pointed a finger at Will. 'He's turned us all in and we're sailing into a trap!'

'What nonsense is this?' demanded the skipper, turning to Will. 'Explain!'

'I've been listening to damned lying accusations since I came back on board,' said Will with a shrug. 'I've had enough!'

The skipper looked from one to the other, an exasperated expression on his face. 'What's your reason for this suspicion?' he asked the group of angry men. 'You've worked with the man for two winters. Why now?'

'Haven't you seen him slinking around?' demanded Bill. 'Not looking at anyone? We all know there's a traitor in among us somewhere. Look how many times they've known where to take us this winter! And now he's changed our run. He'll betray us and collect the reward.'

The skipper looked at Will, waiting for his denial. We all waited. Everyone on deck paused in what they were doing to hear what Will was going to say.

'I would never betray any of you,' said Will steadily. 'The change of drop was arranged by the venturer. We must trust him, mustn't we? It's his money and ship at stake after all. There's a reason why I'm distracted but has nothing to do with betraying the crew.'

The skipper didn't move. His eyes didn't leave Will for a moment. 'I think you should tell us what's wrong,' he said levelly.

'Very well,' said Will. He turned to me. I froze in shock and had the strangest feeling that the ship was foundering under my feet. Will's eyes were accusing and angry.

'Our mermaid,' said Will, indicating me with an angry gesture, 'failed to mention to us that she is the bride of our venturer. That she married him for his money and then having got it, ran off and left him on his wedding night, making him the laughing stock of the county. I've never seen a man so angry. There is a reward out for her.

And all this time, we've been sheltering her! If he were to discover what we've done, he'd be revenged on every last man of us!'

Absolute silence followed Will's words. One by one, they all turned to look at me. I flushed hot with shame and embarrassment. Then my stomach turned and I thought I was going to be sick. It was all over. I was utterly exposed.

'Isabelle?' said Jacob's wondering voice. 'Tell us that's not true.'

He sounded quite bewildered, bless his good heart. As though he couldn't believe it. I wished I could tell him there was some mistake. I turned to Jacob and spoke to him rather than face Will's accusing gaze.

'I didn't know he was your venturer,' I stammered. Had I really married a smuggler?

'Don't stand there looking so innocent,' snapped Will. Anger and hurt flashed in his blue eyes as he glared at me.

'I really didn't know. But it's true,' I whispered. 'At least, it wasn't quite as simple as that but . . . Oh, I'm so very sorry.'

'Why, Isabelle?' Jacob asked. His voice was still gentle and the sound of it brought tears to my eyes.

'I didn't mean any harm . . . ' I faltered, my voice breaking as I choked back the tears.

'You hid the truth—lied! You've put us all in danger,' said Will, still in a hard voice. I tore my eyes from Jacob's puzzled but sympathetic gaze to face Will. He stood rigid, blazing with anger. 'You came aboard under false pretences.'

234

'I didn't ask to be rescued,' I said miserably. 'I wish you hadn't, if it will cause so much trouble. I'm sorry I didn't have the courage to tell you. It . . . wasn't easy for me.'

I stumbled to a stop. Will hated me now. But I truly hadn't known what to do or where to turn. It had all gone so horribly wrong. Unexpectedly, Jacob put a protective arm around me. 'Never fear, Isabelle,' he said. 'We'll stand by you.'

I couldn't speak. Instead, I nodded, tears spilling over. I dashed them away. Behind me, outside the safe circle of Jacob's arm, I heard an argument raging. Some wanted to hand me over and collect the reward, others to keep me with them and protect me. I was hurt and moved in equal measure. I heard no opinion from Will, and knew only that he was furious with me. And somehow that was worse than all the rest. It was worse than anything that might happen to me now. In fact, if Will hated me, I no longer much cared what became of me.

'What if the reason they've been chasing us so hard all winter is cos of her?' shouted Hard-Head Bill. 'What if they've guessed she's here? They found her damn dress aboard, didn't they? It's put all of us in danger!'

The skipper's voice reached me once more through the babble of voices. Everyone fell silent to listen to what he had to say.

'I ask you again, Will. Did you tell Holbrook that we had his bride aboard *The Invisible*?'

'I told him nothing. Until yesterday, I hadn't seen him face-to-face since the autumn. Since before . . . it all came about.' Will, it seemed, could no longer even bring himself to mention my name.

'Did you tell anyone at all that we had a woman aboard?'

'I did not.'

'Did he give you any clue he might suspect it?'

Will shrugged. 'I'm not sure.'

'In that case, I don't see what all the fuss is about,' said the skipper firmly. 'Isabelle is a member of our crew. For safety's sake, she should stay in boy's clothing. But no one but us knows anything. So as far as I can see, nothing needs to change. Now back to your stations everyone.'

The men dispersed, talking among themselves. 'A word, if you please, Isabelle,' said the skipper. 'In private.'

Jacob patted me kindly on the shoulder as he released me. I followed the skipper across the deck towards his cabin. I saw with pain that Will turned his face away from me as I passed.

'Sit down,' said the skipper as I followed him into his cabin and shut the door behind me. I'd never been in here before. It was a grander cabin than my own small space. Besides his bunk, there was a table, spread with charts and maps, and some chairs. A large chest stood against one wall and a chart hung on the wall above it. There were barometers and other instruments mounted on the wall, and the spring sunshine shone in through a porthole. I sank into a chair, shocked and dispirited.

'So, my girl. It turns out after all this time, that you've put us in a difficult position,' the skipper said sitting down opposite me.

I nodded, sadly. 'I'm truly sorry,' I told him.

'As you said, it wasn't your fault Jacob brought you aboard. You certainly came most unwillingly. But you would have spared us this trouble if you'd told me the truth that first night.'

I nodded, shame-faced. 'But you would have taken me back,' I said. 'I dreaded that above all else.'

'Aye, the chances are I'd have done so,' admitted the skipper. 'It's breaking the law to conceal a wife from her husband. And when that husband owns this ship and pays all the men on board, that complicates life even further.'

'But I didn't know that,' I pointed out miserably. 'How could I know I'd married a smuggler?'

'Strictly speaking, he ain't,' said the skipper. 'He's the money. But that's a technicality. As you know, this is our last run. The ship goes into dock for cleaning and repair and the crew disperses for the summer. You've been a valuable crew member, and I feel a certain loyalty to you, despite this. Therefore I see no reason why we should make any changes tonight. You leave us tomorrow, and where you go and what you do after that is your business. But there is one thing I must ask of you.'

'Yes,' I said, relieved by his words. He wasn't going to take me back. I wasn't to be coerced into doing anything. But still. From tomorrow I was alone. That was a very bleak prospect indeed.

'You can never mention to anyone that you've been aboard this ship with us,' the skipper told me earnestly. 'This was a promise I would have needed to ask from you in any event. But it becomes doubly important now. If your presence became known here, our lives and livelihoods could be in danger. We risk revealing our trade and we

237

could be condemned for harbouring you. The one could lead to the other. So I must ask you for your oath.'

'I solemnly swear,' I said earnestly, 'that I won't reveal to anyone where I've been this winter.'

'That's good. Thank you,' said the skipper, shaking me by the hand. 'We'll put you ashore alone in Purbeck tomorrow. It'll be up to you where you go from there.'

He went to his chest and unlocked it, selecting an oilskin wrapped package which he brought to me. 'This is your share of the winter's work,' he said, handing it to me. 'You've earned it.'

'Thank you,' I said, accepting it and tucking it into my shirt. I rose to leave.

As I reached the door the skipper spoke once more. 'Isabelle,' he said. I paused, my hand on the door handle, and turned. 'It's been a pleasure,' he said with a wry smile.

'For me too,' I said, choking on the words. Then I fled to my cabin. There, I flung myself face-down onto my bunk and wept bitter tears.

CHAPTER TWENTY-FOUR

✳

It was all over. I no longer had any future with *The Invisible*. Jacob, Harry, and my other friends were lost to me. Worst of all was Will's fury. He had cared for me. I'd lied to him. Now he would never trust me again. I could understand his anger, but that didn't make it any easier to bear. I wept until my eyes hurt and my throat was raw. Then I sat up and tried to master my despair.

What should I do the next day? I had no more idea now what should become of me than I'd had the night I walked onto the beach at Durdle Door. The only difference was, this time when fate counselled me to despair, I knew better than to do so. Life could always improve. That thought alone gave me the fortitude to dry my tears and try to marshal my wits. I had learned so much this winter. I was no longer the spoiled, idle wretch I'd been in the autumn. I was stronger, healthier, more able. I'd find something to do. I didn't doubt it, though at the moment I couldn't see what or how.

The light was fading. Before long, we'd be sailing into Durdle with the last run of contraband. I would be needed above decks to look out for the signal, and I intended to be there as though nothing had happened.

I bathed my tear-stained face and my red eyes in the tepid water that lay from this morning in my can.

I packed my two gowns neatly into a small canvas bag and laid it on the end of my bunk. Then I combed my hair and hid it neatly in a boy's cap.

I was ready to face them all again. Taking a deep breath, I stepped out into the spring evening. There was a mildness in the air that surpassed any of the signs of spring we'd felt up to now. The fresh breeze blew on my heated cheeks and cooled them.

Harry looked up as I stepped into the galley. 'You look like you could do with a tot of rum,' he remarked, shaking the half-full bottle at me.

I shook my head. 'You know I don't like liquor,' I said. 'Do you have any small beer? I'm very thirsty.'

Harry glanced again at my reddened eyes, but said nothing; instead turning way to pour me a mug of the weak ale.

The door banged open and Hard-Head Bill, Sly Pete, and Slippery Sam all came in and took seats at the furthest bench. Hard-Head Bill sent me a look of dislike as he passed. Why did they have to come in now? This was one of the last times I would see Harry.

Without being asked, Harry began pouring out a measure of rum for each of them.

I picked up my beer. Behind me, I could hear the men starting to talk about Will. Their voices were low but still angry. I couldn't catch more than a couple of words.

Harry pushed three beakers towards me and nodded towards the men. 'Hand them theirs will you, Isabelle?' he asked. 'Sooner they drink up, the sooner they'll go.'

I carried the cups across the swaying floor of the galley. Sam was shuffling a pack of cards, looking bored, Pete was leaning forward listening intently to Bill who was still muttering fiercely. 'I tell you, I know who he is. I've known all along. And what's more I know *what* he is.'

'Heard it all before, Bill,' said Sam, flipping a card as I approached the table. He glanced up at me, but Bill was sitting with his back to me and didn't notice.

'A *murderer*!' he growled at Sly Pete, ignoring Sam. 'That's what.'

I went cold and then hot in shock. For a moment I was still, the rum shaking in my hands. Then I banged the beakers down on the table in front of him. He didn't jump; he simply raised his eyes to mine.

'Liar,' I said softly.

'Listen to yourself,' snarled Hard-Head Bill. 'Spoiled beauty, defending your lover-boy. Well, he's been busy looking out for you all winter, hasn't he? What sort of favours have you been giving the murderer in return, eh?'

'It's not like that!' I said angrily.

'What is it like then? Married girl too good to fall in love with a handsome young lord?' Bill taunted me. He looked at his friends. 'What do you reckon, lads? Do we believe her?'

The colour rushed to my face at the knowledge of how easily I'd betrayed my feelings. Did every man on board believe me in love with Will? What did Will himself think? I cringed.

'You shan't tell such vile lies about him,' I told Hard-Head Bill, ignoring his taunts.

'Lies, is it?' Bill grasped my wrist, pulling me down to his level. He spoke softly, his rum-soaked breath on my face. 'Why don't you ask him?' he sneered. 'Ask him what happened to the young lord went missing after a maid and her baby was murdered. Ask him what he knows about how rich toffs hush up scandals and get their sons away from trouble when they go bad. Go on: ask him what he's doing here where no one wants him and his like. We don't want you, neither, bringing trouble on us.'

'What's up, men?' asked Harry from the other side of the galley. Hard-Head Bill released me. I shuddered and fled back to Harry.

'Don't listen to Bill,' he said, pushing my mug back into my shaking hands. 'He's full of it.'

I tried to sip, but my hands trembled so the beer slopped out of the cup. I felt sick. 'It's nonsense, isn't it, Harry?' I asked. 'Will isn't a . . . a murderer!'

Harry shrugged. 'Not that I ever heard,' he said easily. 'Besides, I judge a man by what I see, not by gossip. And what I've seen in Will is a good shipmate.'

I was still shaken and unsteady when I went back out on deck. 'You looking out for that signal, lass?' Jacob asked as he saw me. 'Due in about ten minutes now.'

I nodded and swung myself up into the rigging, climbing towards the look-out. As I pulled up towards it, however, I saw Will already standing there. I froze for a moment, furious and embarrassed that I'd not checked who was up here. Then I swung away, crossing to the right and hanging in the rigging, my eyes fixed on the shore. Will didn't call to me and I took care not to look in his direction again.

We both spotted the all-clear flink at the same moment; calling out simultaneously and pointing. We studiously ignored each other. The estrangement between us caused me to wink tears away again. I gritted my teeth fiercely. No weakness; I must show no weakness now. I owed it to my pride to show a brave face.

'Isabelle!' Will's words, even spoken softly, reached me over the wind and waves. I looked up at him. Meeting his blue eyes gave me a jolt somewhere in the region of my heart. 'Why did you lie to me?' he asked.

'I didn't lie,' I told him desperately. 'I even tried to tell you . . .' I looked away. This was too painful.

Will swung down off the look-out and stood beside me on the ropes. 'Am I so hard to trust?' he asked, his voice hurt.

'At first you were,' I retorted. Will turned his face away, biting his lip.

'I mistrusted you,' he admitted. 'And resented you.'

'But you expected me to trust you?' I asked him.

'Later perhaps. We were friends, weren't we? I'm beginning to doubt everything.'

'We were friends,' I replied in a constricted voice

Unexpectedly, Will laid his cold hand over mine. I felt my heart lurch with pleasure. How dare Bill put such dreadful doubts in my head? Will was both honest and true, I was certain of it. You only had to look into his clear eyes to see it.

'I'm sorry for my anger towards you earlier,' said Will. 'But Isabelle. *Married*. It's such a . . . it's so . . .'

'Final?' I asked him. It was a relief to speak openly at last and it was a relief to speak about anything that drew my thoughts from Bill's dark, accusing words. 'I know.'

'You weren't wearing a ring,' Will said, his voice unsteady.

'I was. It must have slipped off my finger in the cold water. It was a bit loose. I'm . . . I'm so sorry, Will.'

Will nodded, not meeting my eyes. 'So am I,' he said quietly. 'But, Isabelle, why did you marry him? If it made you so desperate that you wished to take your own life afterwards? Did your parents force you?'

I shook my head, my lips tightly pressed together. 'I wanted to marry. To help them. He had agreed to make a generous settlement. They wouldn't be so poor. But then . . . Oh, I can't tell you,' I said, tears starting in my eyes. The door that haunted my dreams loomed large and dark in my mind. The door I had shut everything behind; that I never wanted to open again. My face started to burn. 'It's too . . . too dreadful,' I whispered.

'Try?' asked Will gently.

I shook my head vehemently. I was too ashamed to even look at my memories, let alone share them. I'd hidden so much for so long. I started to cry.

Will put an arm around my shoulder and spoke into my ear, his breath warm on my cheek: 'You are not the first person to sacrifice their lives for their family. It seems like such a noble act, but it can be harder to live with the consequences than you expected.'

Dimly, I thought he sounded bitter; as though he had experienced something of the kind himself. But I was too wrapped up in my own distress to question him. 'You should have explained,' Will whispered. 'It wasn't fair.'

His words suggested he felt something for me. Something that could never be. I couldn't bear it. Tears spilled hot and salty down my cold cheeks. I was leaving tomorrow and we would never see each other again. There was no choice. No alternative.

What was worse, I now knew that any hope I might have nurtured of being taken back on board *The Invisible* next autumn was gone. There was no chance at all that the men would risk my husband's wrath.

I fought to control my misery. I needed to be glad that whatever rage Will had felt against me for my deception was over. But it was a bleak comfort. The parting, unavoidable and irrevocable, still lay before me.

The ship heeled as we came about to head into the bay, throwing me against Will. His arm tightened around me, holding me close against him in the cold wind.

We were sweeping into the bay by the time I was able to look up again, the sea creaming white beneath our keel. I mastered my tears. Will let go of me to pull out a telescope and through it he surveyed the shore. I watched him, and felt indignant, remembering Bill's words. 'Do you know,' I began indignantly, 'what Bill is saying of you?'

'What?' asked Will absently.

The grey stone arch loomed out of the water to our starboard side, glinting in the moonlight and casting a black shadow onto the water. I could see the landers on the beach, standing waiting.

'He said . . . ' I stared at the landers and forgot what I'd been going to say. The sight of them standing on the beach struck a discordant note. Normally they didn't show themselves so openly until we were in and unloading. Something was wrong.

I stared at them in the gloom, straining my eyes to pick out familiar figures. They were definitely landers, not soldiers. I could make out the shape of their smocks. There were no uniforms there. 'There's something strange,' I murmured out loud. Will was still scanning the beach through the telescope. Then he left my side, clambering swiftly higher to get a clearer view past the sail.

We approached closer to the shore. The beach shelved very steeply here and we could get to within a few feet of the shingle. I glanced up at Will above me and saw he was studying the men one by one. I wasn't the only one who was uneasy, though the men below were making ready to unload as usual.

One man on shore had something sticking up behind him. It wasn't ropes. It was surely a rifle strapped to his back?

'Will, they aren't . . . ' I began urgently.

Before I could finish my sentence, Will shouted 'Ambush!'

For a moment, there was chaos on the decks. Some men froze, others began at once to take various evasive measures, not all compatible. The skipper looked up at Will and at me.

'Soldiers!' shouted Will frantically. 'Disguised as landers!'

The skipper looked at me. 'Isabelle?' he asked. I hesitated. I'd not had the close-up view that Will had had and it was too dark to be certain. But I too felt something was wrong. 'I think he's right!' I called down.

'Turn the ship about!' bellowed the skipper. He ran to take over the wheel, whilst the crew swarmed up into the rigging to raise the sails once more. The boat that had been lowered into the water was tethered and left. With infuriating slowness, *The Invisible* swung around into the wind away from the shore. But we'd come close in; right into the bay, almost to the shingle.

The men on the beach could see now what was happening. Doubtless they'd heard our shouts too. At first they had continued to play their part; standing innocently on the beach waiting for the contraband. But as soon as we began to move off, they fell into a well-disciplined line, dropping onto one knee, and pulled the rifles onto their shoulders. Despite their smuggling apparel, there could no longer be any doubt what they were.

'Halt in the king's name and surrender!' shouted one of them. I felt sure it was Lieutenant Oswald and cursed him silently. When we continued to glide away from the beach, picking up speed, a volley of shots were fired. I felt one whistle close to my left ear and ducked in shock. The sound of splintering wood echoed around me as the balls lodged in the timbers of the ship. Sly Pete dropped from the rigging to the deck below me with a cry, clapping one hand to his shoulder. I swung down the rigging, seeking the relative safety of the deck.

'All canvas!' shouted the skipper. 'Full speed!'

We were pulling away now, the open sea before us, promising us safety. But before we could clear the cove, a ship hove into sight on our starboard side. She cleared the headland to the right of the bay and sailed into plain view, her guns already run out. Will's telescope was immediately trained on her. 'Navy sloop!' he cried out, having seen the colours she was flying.

The skipper turned *The Invisible* to port, hoping to slip out past her. We were swifter than she was, and more manoeuvrable with our fore-and-aft rigging. 'We may yet have the advantage,' said Jacob anxiously, looking critically at the passage between the sloop and the open sea.

A Revenue cutter slid out from the other headland. We were trapped. 'Treachery,' muttered Jacob. 'We've been betrayed.'

'But surely it wasn't Will?' I asked uncertainly, recalling the arguments.

Jacob shrugged. 'I don't want to believe it,' he said. 'But if not he, then who?'

The skipper was staring helplessly at the two ships approaching. We were caught in the jaws of a trap: two ships in front of us barring our escape route, and the soldiers lined up on the beach ready to shoot any who tried to escape that way.

'So much trouble for a few free-traders,' he muttered. 'This isn't normal.'

'We've been too successful, damn it,' said the pilot. 'And this time there's no clever way past them. They're determined to put a stop to us.'

The skipper shook his head. 'It's not just that,' he said. 'People in powerful places have pulled strings here. The Revenue can't command all this firepower to capture one ship.' He sprang into action, turning to face the crew. 'Ditch the kegs!' he called out. 'All the contraband over the side.'

'Aren't we going to fight?' demanded Slippery Sam 'We've got guns as good as theirs.'

'No,' ordered the skipper decisively. 'If we could fight and run, then maybe. But we're trapped. Firing the guns would make this a hanging matter. We need to get everyone off safe now. To hell with the ship. It's not ours anyway.'

The splash of kegs going overboard reached my ears. 'Surely they'll find it all?' I asked.

'A Dorset jury likely won't convict us if it wasn't found on board,' said the skipper. I hoped he was right.

'So then . . . we have nothing to fear?' I asked uncertainly.

'Bar a spell in prison waiting for the hearing, no, I hope very little,' replied the captain. 'Do you hear me, men? We've been fishing. We know nothing of any contraband or free-trade. We don't speak no French, nor we haven't just been to France. We all plead not guilty.'

There was murmured assent. 'What about her?' asked Hard-Head Bill nodding towards me. They all turned to look at me. I felt a knot in my stomach.

'What should I do?' I asked. 'I don't want to cause you trouble.'

'Surrender!' came a shout from across the water. We all looked towards the Navy sloop approaching. 'Surrender and give up your cargo and you won't be hurt.'

'We have no cargo!' the skipper shouted back. 'We're fishermen.'

I glanced at the nets lying in the prow of the ship; nets that we almost never used, that barely smelled of fish. They were our protection; our excuse to be at sea.

The captain of the Navy ship was speaking again. His words struck a chill into me: 'Prepare to be boarded and searched. You are to give up the two fugitives from the law you have on board. They will be placed under arrest.'

I gasped. 'Fugitives from the law?' I echoed, horrified. Was that me? I remembered the men in the barn at Christmas. But I'd broken no laws that justified pursuit by the Royal Navy. Had Will?

'They're after her!' exclaimed Hard-Head Bill, seizing me by the shoulder and shaking me. 'That's what all this is about. Let's hand her over. She's nothing to us.'

'He said two fugitives!' growled Sly Pete. He turned to face Will and raised a finger, pointing at him. 'It's you, isn't it? Another one we should never have taken aboard. Bill was telling the truth about you!'

'Make up your mind!' said Will, looking pale, but still speaking with his usual nonchalance. 'Am I the traitor or am I the fugitive? I can't be both, you know.'

'Who cares, just give him up!' snarled Hard-Head Bill.

'Wait!' commanded the skipper. 'I'm not handing anyone over willingly. We try and negotiate.'

He strode to the rail and called across the still water. 'We have no fugitives aboard. We're fishermen.'

In reply, the Navy ship fired two of their guns. I saw their mouths spit fire before I heard the boom of the shot. The balls tore into the side of *The Invisible*, and the force knocked most of us off our feet. I crashed onto the deck, landing on Slippery Sam, who broke my fall. Someone was screaming. The ship was rocking in the water, in the aftermath of the shock.

Stunned and disorientated, we were still scrambling back to our feet when the captain of the sloop called again. 'That was a warning. We want the cargo and the fugitives. Surrender now!'

I clutched Jacob's arm. He took my hand from his sleeve and put a protective arm around my shoulders. 'Never fear, lass, they won't get you.'

But the ships were closing in fast now. The shots had injured at least one man and damaged the ship. The possibilities were vanishing fast. 'Hand her over!' shouted Hard-Head Bill.

'NO!' snarled Slippery Sam. 'We'll all be had up for harbouring her! We must get rid of her before they board us.'

CHAPTER TWENTY-FIVE

✴

Just as I thought everything was over, as I thought I was sure to die or be arrested, Will grabbed my arm. 'Come on, Isabelle,' he said. 'We'll take the tub-boat through the Door and into the next cove. Neither the sloop nor the cutter can follow us that way. You'll be safe and so will everyone on board. You can't stay.' He said nothing about his own safety or needing to escape. Was he the second person they hunted?

'I'll go with you,' said Jacob. 'I can't let no harm come to our mermaid.'

'Wait! Take our hope with you!' said the skipper, hurrying to the cabin and returning with an oilskin package that he thrust into Jacob's hands. It resembled the one already concealed within my clothing, only it was far larger. 'Buy us legal help, aid us any way you can, but above all, this is our next season.'

Jacob stowed the bulky package inside his jacket. Slippery Sam gave a cry at the sight of it. 'You'd trust him with that?' he demanded. 'Him and them? We'll never see it again!'

'I'd trust Jacob with my life,' retorted the skipper. 'With all our lives.'

'More fool you!' muttered Bill angrily.

'They'll find an excuse to take it from us if it stays aboard,' replied the skipper. 'You know they will! How would fishermen come by such a sum?'

'And if they're drowned or taken?'

'Like I said, it's surely lost if we keep it on board,' snapped the skipper. 'Go, Jacob. God keep you safe.'

He embraced him then pushed him away. Briefly he clasped Will's hand and kissed my cheek. 'God speed and safe passage to you. Go quiet as you can.'

The ladder was swiftly thrown down to the rowing boat at the stern. Where it lay in the water, it was shielded from the Navy ship by the bulk of *The Invisible*. We would have a good start before we could be spotted. I looked up to see the moon, which had been bright before, now obscured by clouds. Lady luck, though not our friend tonight, had given us one small gift at least.

Firm hands helped me onto the ladder. Jacob was already in the boat; Will ready to follow me.

'Mind the currents at the far side of the Door,' Fred warned him, clasping his hand. 'There is a fair swirl there. If you can get beyond it, you are safer than in this bay.'

And then I was climbing down the swaying ladder, Will's feet above my hands. 'Come on, Isabelle,' Jacob encouraged me when I reached the boat. 'We'll make it away safe enough.'

I crouched low and Will dropped down after me. Both men seized oars and the painter was thrown down to me from someone on board. I coiled it neatly in the prow. My heart was thudding in my chest with fear. The last run of the winter; how could we have been so unlucky? But it wasn't luck, was it? Someone had betrayed us. Clearly it wasn't Will. Just as clearly, Hard-Head Bill wasn't the only one to suspect him of foul crimes. He was wanted by the law. No wonder he disguised himself. I shivered in fear and doubt as the boat crept out from the friendly shadow of *The Invisible* into the dark bay. I could hear the waves breaking onto the shingle not far from us.

The two pairs of oars dipped into the water with barely a splash. We were surrounded by deep darkness, cocooning us from sight. Behind us we could already hear the sound of *The Invisible* being boarded, but we were away.

I was just breathing a sigh of relief when two things happened almost simultaneously: the moon emerged from behind a thick cloud, bathing the bay in glittering, silvery light; then shouts from the shore told us our escape was no longer secret.

The stern of *The Invisible* had swung away from us, leaving the Navy sloop with a clear view of our flight. There was no warning at all, unless you could count the distant shouts and activity aboard the Navy ship. I was trying to gauge the distance we still had to cover before we were past the great stone arch and away, when the Navy ship spat fire and a great boom assaulted my eardrums. The boat was thrown sideways and we were all flung into the sea.

I couldn't believe the cold. I gasped as I plunged down into it. For a moment, I was helpless against the force of the explosion and the shock of the icy sea. When my senses returned, I began to struggle frantically, fighting to get my head above the surface to breathe. My limbs thrashed uselessly in the murky, freezing soup. I had no sense of up or down and no notion how to propel myself anywhere if I had. I was drowning all over again. Terror gripped me.

Hands grasped me under my arms and pulled me backwards. My head broke the surface and I gasped the air. 'Stay calm, mermaid,' Jacob whispered in my ear. 'Stay silent! Our lives depend on it.'

Jacob had saved me again. Slowly he began to swim, towing me backwards through the water. I could hear the hush of the waves through the stone arch behind us. I knew where Jacob was heading. I moved convulsively. 'W-Will!' I stammered frantically. 'Where is he?'

'Here,' I heard Will murmur just behind me.

'Hush now!' ordered Jacob. 'Kick your legs, Isabelle, if you can do it without splashing; help me swim.'

I tried to do as he said, but quite apart from the numbing, icy cold that was stealing into my very bones, one leg wouldn't respond properly.

Jacob had taken a firm hold of me, floating me on my back, swimming strongly away from the wreckage of the boat. I was shuddering convulsively as the glacial water penetrated my clothing and gripped my head in a vice. The long winter of dark, freezing weather had lowered the temperature far below what it had been when I stepped into the waves last October. This was bitterly, icily cold.

Will was following, swimming swiftly, only his head showing, leaving a small wake behind him that merged with our larger one. Surely no one could see us?

I was consumed by cold. I wanted to scream with it. My teeth chattered so loudly, I felt someone might hear it all the way from the ships or the beach.

Will was speaking to me. I could see his lips move but no sound reached me. My hearing had shut down. He swam closer. 'Kick your legs, Isabelle,' Will ordered me urgently. His words reached me faintly this time, and gradually their sense penetrated my numb brain. I kicked my good leg and kept kicking. I have no idea whether it did any good, but it helped me fight the bitter, aching cold.

We passed under the archway of the great stone door. The waves swirled around it, drifting seaweed reached out for us in the black water and tried to snag us, but we kicked free, swimming onwards into the churning sea beyond.

A wave swamped us and Jacob's grip on me slipped. I went under. As I came up, choking and shocked, Will grasped me. Panic-stricken, I flung my arms around him and we both went under, flailing in the black expanse. Jacob pulled me up by my hair. It reminded me so strongly of his rescue in the autumn that I cried out as soon as I was above the surface.

'Listen to me,' said Jacob in a slurred but urgent voice. 'If you fight us or grab us, we'll drown. Let Will take you now. Don't fight!'

I didn't want to drown. I didn't want Will or Jacob to drown. I lay still and allowed them to tow me once more. Jacob swam beside me, casting anxious glances behind us and up at the cliff.

'If we survive this,' Will muttered through clenched teeth, 'I'm going to teach you to swim, Belle.'

At last, I heard waves again, and then Will and Jacob were dragging me out of the sea between them, water streaming from us, onto another shingle beach. I staggered as I struggled ashore, coughing and shuddering.

'Quiet!' Will muttered, shaking my arm. 'We mustn't be overheard.'

'My leg,' I gasped. I looked down and saw my breeches were torn. I thought my leg was bleeding, but couldn't see in the dark, and fought to follow them along the beach, limping and dragging my hurt leg, my limbs numb from the cold water.

As we crunched along the beach, a shout far above us alerted us to the fact that a sentry had been posted. I looked at my companions, aghast.

'If we can make it round into the next cove, there's another way off the beach,' said Jacob, his voice low. 'Bit of a climb, but we can make it if the tide is right.'

We broke into a stumbling run. I could hear the soldiers' boots on the steep stone pathway down to the beach. I couldn't believe that after we'd risked that dangerous swim, we were going to be captured anyway.

We reached the end of the beach to find only the narrowest passage around the point. There were no soldiers here yet, but neither was there much space. The waves washed right up to the bottom of the cliff. The rocks we had to climb over were slippery with wet and weed.

'Go ahead, Jacob!' called Will. 'Get yourself and that money away! It's vital for all of us. We'll follow as best we can!'

Jacob hesitated briefly. Conflicting emotions flitted across his face. I remembered I'd once thought him an oaf, incapable of complex or intelligent emotions. Shame surged over me at the memory. 'Go, Jacob,' I said. 'Save yourself! I'll be all right. Give my love to Ann!'

Jacob turned and climbed swiftly away from us. When he reached the point where the water met the cliff, he waded out into the water once more and swam strongly onwards towards the next stretch of beach.

I kept climbing slowly across the rocks, battered by spray, my hands numb, my hurt leg dragging. Will helped me when he could, but I was painfully slow. The tide kept surging higher up the narrow gap that remained, until it was gone and we were fighting our way through rising, surging water. All too soon, we heard shouts behind us.

I risked a glance back. Four soldiers with guns were clambering over the rocks far faster than we had done. We were trapped. I turned back to Will. 'You should go,' I told him. 'Follow Jacob. You can make it, but I can't.'

'No!' exclaimed Will vehemently. 'I won't leave you to be captured!'

'You don't have any choice,' I told him. 'You can't save me. I can't swim and I won't be able to run or climb if we do get round. My leg is damaged in some way.' I winced with pain as I spoke. 'They'll catch us both. Please, Will!'

'I can't leave you and save myself!' cried Will. 'We can make it. I know we can. I'll carry you if I have to!'

I paused, my breathing ragged with exertion. The voices were closing behind us. 'Will,' I asked, 'are you the other one they want?'

Will hesitated and then nodded. 'I am,' he said, compelling me to climb on, over the next rock. A wave broke over it, drenching us in spray. I shivered.

'It's not true that you murdered anyone, is it, Will?'
I asked him. I could hear the pleading in my voice. I
wanted him to tell me it wasn't so.

'I'm wanted for murder,' said Will shortly.

'That's not the same thing! Is it?'

Will didn't reply. He turned and helped me down into a
pool of water and then pulled me up onto the next rock.
'Not now, Isabelle! Focus on getting away. We can talk later.'

As I hauled myself up onto the next rock, my bad leg
gave way and I fell heavily. I cried out in pain. 'Go, Will!'
I begged. 'Leave me! I can't do it.'

'Then swim!' Will ordered, tugging at my hand. 'Or
you'll be taken back to . . . to your . . . ' His words trailed
into silence.

'I know.' I looked at the water swirling black and hungry about my legs and shuddered. I couldn't face plung-
ing into that icy embrace again. I felt sure I wouldn't
survive it a second time.

Instead, I pulled my oilskin package from my shirt and
pressed it into his hands. 'Take it,' I told him. 'Maybe you
can help me later. You'll not be able to help me if you're
in prison too. And Will; whatever you've done, I don't
want you to . . . ' I couldn't bring myself to say the word
hang, but we both knew what I meant.

The soldiers were close now, slipping on the rocks in
their haste to reach us. Will caught me in his arms and
held me close in a cold, wet embrace. 'I'll go,' he said.
'But only in the hope of rescuing you.'

He pulled away so that I could see his face. 'Isabelle,
it wasn't me who betrayed your presence on board,' he
said. 'I swear it. I knew nothing of this attack tonight.'

I reached up and touched his cheek. 'I know,' I said simply.

He stepped away from me and waded out into the water. At that moment the soldiers clattered round the corner almost upon us. There were four of them now. They stumbled to a halt and raised their guns. The senior officer ignored me; instead, looking straight at Will, he shouted: 'William Marlow, you are under arrest for the wilful murder of Eliza Jones and her infant!'

Will's eyes met mine for an agonized moment. I was frozen in shock and disbelief. He was wanted for the murder of a young woman and her *baby*? Just as Hard-Head Bill had said. William *Marlow*? I couldn't take it in. My brain felt as though it had received a massive electric shock. Will's clear blue eyes held mine.

'Hands up, Marlow!' shouted the officer when Will didn't move. Will looked away from me and slowly raised his arms. He stood there, half-in, half-out of the sea while the waves washed around him. His fair hair was plastered to his head, his clothes hung limply off him. No disguise, no acting this time; just a young man facing danger with courage. I wondered what I truly knew of him. I couldn't match this terrible accusation with the man I'd come to know.

I saw Will tense and glance towards me. I realized he wasn't planning to surrender at all. He was going to make a bid to escape. He was going to risk those guns.

Impulsively, I got to my feet and limped towards the soldiers. 'Was it me you were looking for, officer?' I asked. I walked as bravely as I could, straight towards the guns.

'For the lord's sake, boy, not in the line of fire!' shouted the officer.

'I'm not a boy,' I contradicted him. 'I'm Isabelle Holbrook.'

There was an audible gasp from the soldiers. Two lowered their guns instinctively, and Will took the opportunity to plunge into the sea. 'Out of the WAY!' yelled the officer, rushing forward to push me aside. I fell onto the rocks with a cry, while the officer called: 'Fire! Don't let him get away!'

His men did as he said, and fired a volley of shots, but I'd gained Will a few vital seconds. Three shots hit the sea near Will, but as far as I could tell, they'd missed. Certainly he swam on as strongly as ever, distancing himself from the shore. The soldiers began to reload, but their officer turned to shout at them. 'Too late! Too late! Bring her.' He pointed at me. 'Smith, get back up to Lieutenant Oswald and tell him Marlow's in the water. They need to try and cut him off when he tries to come ashore.'

I was grabbed and hauled roughly off the rock and into the sea, back towards the bay. 'Your friend won't get far!' they told me. We reached the dry beach again at last, breathless and soaked, but I wasn't allowed to rest for more than a moment. They marched me along the beach, half dragging me between them. Stabbing pains shot through my leg every time I put my weight on it. Climbing the cliff path was agony. Slowly, painfully, I half-walked and was half-pushed up it. As I drew towards the very top, two men stood waiting for me. I saw their boots level with my eyes as I dragged myself wearily up the last of the steep path.

'Well, well,' said a familiar voice. 'I do believe it's the beautiful young lady from Poole. In some most unsuitable clothes, what's more.' I looked up and saw Lieutenant Oswald standing looking down at me, a smirk on his handsome face.

I cast him a look of dislike. 'Do I know you?' I asked disdainfully.

There was a second man standing beside him and when he spoke my heart skipped a beat with shock: 'You certainly know me. Unless I've already slipped from your memory?' he said with heavy sarcasm. 'Welcome home, my dear. You've been away quite some time, haven't you?'

Filled with dread, I looked straight into the face of my husband. The mystery of our traitor was solved. It hadn't been anyone on the ship after all; it had been our venturer himself, it seemed. He gave me a smile that had neither pleasure nor kindness in it. Weary, chilled, and in unbearable pain, I felt a wave of sick dizziness flooding me. Gratefully, I gave into it and fainted away.

CHAPTER TWENTY-SIX

✳

After tangled dreams of forced marching and slow drowning, I awoke. I surfaced slowly, languorously, as though I'd been asleep for a lifetime.

I opened my eyes and even the comparatively muted light of an unfamiliar bedchamber stabbed at them. I was lying in a plain, bare room, the type you might find at an ordinary inn. I wondered where I could be.

I closed my eyes again. I was weak and content to lie quite still in the bed and search my memory. Gradually, it all came back to me. *The Invisible*, Will, the swim through the dark. The soldiers. My capture. I groaned softly as I recalled that my adventure was well and truly over.

But what had become of me? There had been talk of capital crimes and a hanging. My husband had been there. I struggled to sit up, to get a better look at the room in which I lay, but I found I had no strength in my body at all.

Just as I was wondering if I should call out, the door opened and a woman came into my room. She was middle-aged and motherly and as she came closer, I noticed a distinct whiff of spiritous liquor about her.

'Ah, you're awake, deary!' she said looking pleased. 'I'm Maggie Smith. I've been nursing you.'

'Where am I?' I asked puzzled.

'In the Cat and Fiddle, to be sure. Your parents brought you here. You've been very sick. An inflammation of the lung and an injured leg. Don't you remember?'

I frowned, searching my memory. I thought I could recall snatches; being very hot, feeling ill. People coming and going. 'Not much,' I told her.

'Well, you're on the mend now,' she said. 'Can you eat something, do you think? I can fetch you some broth.'

'I'll try,' I promised.

Maggie Smith helped me sit up. I was shocked by how weak I was. My arms, as they lay on the sheets, were as thin as sticks and I felt breathless from the least exertion. How long had I been lying here?

'You've been ill several weeks,' Mrs Smith told me when she returned. 'But there was another nurse before me. I don't know much about what happened to you.'

Several weeks! I sipped the hot broth slowly and without appetite, wondering what had become of the others. Had they been put in prison? I hoped not. And what of Jacob and Will? I prayed they had escaped, and not, like me, succumbed to illness as a result of the swim in the cold sea. Or been shot. I shuddered as I remembered the soldiers firing at Will in the water.

I quickly grew stronger. The next day I could leave my bed for a couple of hours to sit in a chair by the window. There was a tree in leaf outside and song birds were hopping about on the grass. I could see it was late spring now. So much time had slipped by. The fate of my friends began to prey on my mind. If only there was someone I could ask.

Later that day, my parents came to see me. I was shocked to see them both so aged. 'Oh Isabelle, we have been in such affliction!' wept my mother, embracing me. 'Captured by pirates all that time! My poor dear girl, however did it come about?'

I stared at her blankly as she released me. 'Captured . . . what?' I stammered.

'Stolen from the house by those wretches and held captive throughout the winter,' she said, stroking my hair back from my brow. 'Did they treat you very cruelly?'

'Nothing of the sort,' I said. 'No one captured me! I wasn't held prisoner!'

My parents exchanged glances. 'Hush, now,' said my mother. 'Don't become agitated.'

But it was too late. I was sitting up in bed, exclaiming: 'What story is this? Who says so?'

'I say so,' said my father firmly. 'You must know, Isabelle, that your husband has been suing for desertion. He claims you only married him for the settlement and always planned to run away. He accuses you of stealing valuables from his house and running off with them to meet these pirates who were in on the plan.'

'But this is all nonsense!' I exclaimed.

My mother dabbed at her tears with a lace pocket-handkerchief and continued as though I hadn't spoken: 'He has been pursuing us in law for the return of the settlement, Isabelle. And he has had soldiers after you since your gown was found aboard their ship!'

'But none of that is true!' I exclaimed. 'What, have the crew been accused?'

'They've been arrested as accessories,' said my father. 'The ones they caught. They are in prison awaiting the assizes. Two got clean away; one of them a wanted felon, too!'

I drew a deep breath of mixed panic and relief. Will and Jacob had escaped at least. 'But Papa, Mama, surely you don't believe this fairytale? Surely you know it's all lies?'

'My dear, we know, of course, that it is not true,' wept my mother. 'You had no opportunity to become acquainted with pirates while you were living with us. You were most carefully chaperoned.'

'And are you accused?' I asked bewildered.

'No, my dear,' replied my father. 'Though, you understand that the loss of the settlement would be a very great affliction. We would be ruined . . . again.'

'But we *know* that you did not wish to leave your wedded husband. That would be nonsense! You must have been coerced!'

'I *did* wish to leave him! Papa! These men are not pirates! They neither kidnapped me nor arranged any plan with me! I had never met them before that night.'

'Of course you hadn't!' cried my mother. 'One does not become acquainted with pirates at Harrison's Assembly Rooms! You only know gentlemen. Of course we know that these desperate criminals broke into the house and stole you and the goods away.'

'No, they did not!' I cried. 'You're not listening. I ran away. But I stole nothing. Then they—the crew—saved me from drowning!'

There was an appalled silence. My parents exchanged looks. 'That's not possible,' said my father firmly.

'No, indeed, for why would you need saving when you were newly wed?' added my mother. 'It's all a great mistake. Of course you were kidnapped.'

'But Mama, I wasn't!'

'Hush! And of course you long to return to your husband. We've told him so. Though he doesn't seem all that eager, to be honest, to *take* you back . . . '

'Mama!' I exclaimed, exasperated.

'Your memory has been affected by your illness, my love,' said my mother tentatively.

'It has, but not that part of it,' I argued. 'I'm . . . '

'You would be well advised to be guided by us, Isabelle,' interrupted my father. 'Your version would bring nothing but shame and loss of fortune on us all. We need to stick together.'

'And you are so very confused as a result of this long illness,' said my mother caressingly. 'An inflammation of the lung *and* a wounded leg. You lost so much blood! No wonder you barely remember the details.'

'I remember everything until the moment of my capture by the soldiers quite clearly!' I assured them.

'Isabelle,' said my father. There was both anger and pleading in his voice. 'Your parents know better than you in this instance.'

They got up to go. 'You need to rest, now,' said my father. 'You have a few more days before the hearing.'

My mother bent and kissed me tearfully. 'We need you to do this for us,' she whispered. 'You would hate the poverty we would otherwise endure even more than we would. Make up your mind to go back to your husband, Isabelle. You married him of your own free will.

And you will be utterly ruined if you do not.' She shed a few tears over me and left.

I lay pale and shaken after they had gone. My nurse checked my pulse and tutted over me, shaking her head. 'Too much excitement,' she said. 'Rest now!'

But it was impossible to recapture the peaceful lethargy from before my parents' visit. I could not see how to be loyal to both my parents and my shipmates. My husband I cared nothing about. He had forfeited any right to my concern. But no matter what he'd done, I hadn't earned the marriage settlement. I'd left him practically standing at the altar.

Should I tell my parents' version of the story? It would secure my family's financial future, but it would condemn me to returning to my husband. And it would mean sacrificing the crew of *The Invisible*. Unthinkable!

If I told the truth, or something near it, I could spare them all. My family would be sacrificed instead. And had we not brought our poverty on ourselves? No one but us should suffer for my father's speculation and loss.

With this painful choice before me, and with the uncertainty of whether Will and Jacob had even survived that terrible night, I turned restlessly all night long, sleepless and uncomfortable.

CHAPTER TWENTY-SEVEN

✷

The day of the hearing dawned soft and mild, the gentle sunshine and light breeze caressing and entirely out of keeping with the storm of uncertainty still raging within me.

I was conveyed in a carriage by my parents and my father's lawyer, a thin, anxious-looking man with down-turned lips and a grey complexion. He talked all the way to the hearing about how important it was for me to say just what I'd been told and no more. He'd been to see me twice and had coached me in my story. He'd assured me that it would do no good to tell the court that Mr Holbrook was the financier for the smuggling runs.

'He'll have himself well covered,' he assured me. 'He has already claimed the men were hiring his boat for fishing and he later became suspicious that they were running contraband. He was the one who reported them. Not to mention that half the magistrates are on dinner-invitation terms with him. No, that is a line that will lead precisely nowhere.'

He'd told me I needed to look innocent, appealing and to dress in a very feminine way, as the jury would no doubt be told the shocking story that I'd been dressed as a man when they found me.

My mother sighed over my hair, which she'd done her best to dress prettily, but with less success than she'd hoped, for it was still scandalously short.

'Well, no one need know when that happened,' I pointed out reasonably. 'I've been ill, and people sometimes have their hair cut right off when they are ill.'

When I took my place in the courtroom, my hands, encased in delicate white kid gloves, trembled in my lap, and clutched a lace pocket-handkerchief. I was wearing a modest white silk gown, giving an impression, my mother had explained, of youth and innocence. A silk shawl, edged with lace, was caught over my elbows, and a simple pearl necklace had been fastened around my neck. I should have felt like myself again. The clothes were certainly pretty. I had no objection to wearing them. But I couldn't help thinking that they probably cost more than a whole summer of wages for a man like Jacob.

My husband was called to speak first. I looked at him as he stood there, slightly stooped, his hair greying, and unwanted memories crowded into my mind. He caught my eye. There was a calculating, smug look in his. He counted me defeated already. I wondered how I'd ever thought it was going to be all right to marry him. I'd been a naive child, promised treats and riches, and I'd fallen for it.

My husband explained how I'd disappeared from my room as soon as we'd arrived at the manor. How my shoes had been found on the beach. He told the court that at first it had been thought I'd drowned. But then my gown had been found aboard *The Invisible*. A reward had been offered and several witnesses had come forward who believed they had seen me, including Oswald, the riding officer. My husband's solicitor put forward the notion that he'd been deliberately tricked by me. My husband agreed sorrowfully. He played the hurt, deserted husband.

The skipper of *The Invisible* was called next. He was detained on two charges. The first, smuggling, was to be heard the following day. But he stood here now accused of conspiracy to defraud Mr Holbrook of the marriage settlement.

He spoke simply and well. He explained that he and his crew were fishermen. Some of his crew members had found me in the sea and rescued me. That I refused to tell them who I was or where I was from, so it had been difficult to know what to do with me.

'She told us she was of age,' concluded the skipper. 'So I could see no reason not to let her stay with us for a time.'

Asked whether I'd been with them all winter, he returned a negative. I'd spent spells on land; he'd understood I was with my family.

It all sounded very reasonable, I thought. Surely no one could blame the men for their part in my disappearance? When he denied the accusation that he had kidnapped me, he did so most emphatically. But the prosecution ridiculed him and made him look like a criminal. I started to feel sick.

At last I was called. I stood up on shaking legs and walked to the front. I took an oath to tell the truth. Then I stood in the witness stand. I forced myself to look out over the court. I looked at my parents; anxious and bowed. I looked at the skipper, and I even met my husband's eyes. His eyes ran over me coldly.

When the defence asked me my name, I looked up again, and spoke out clearly that I was Isabelle Latimer, now Holbrook, and that I was ready to speak. My mother caught my eye and her eyes gave me an anguished plea. My heart twisted inside me.

I agreed that I had married Mr Holbrook willingly and accompanied him to his mansion. As I was speaking, someone else caught my eye. It was a tall, angular-looking woman in an ill-fitting pink dress and an outmoded red bonnet that clashed horribly. I was just wondering who would choose such an appalling combination, and thinking that the face looked rather familiar when the woman winked at me. Unmistakably, she winked. How very strange. I looked harder.

'Did you hear me, Mrs Holbrook?' asked the solicitor again. The judge rapped sharply with his gavel, startling me, and I returned my attention hurriedly to my solicitor.

'Sorry,' I said. 'I didn't hear.'

'I asked whether you were coerced to leave the manor that night or whether you left of your own free will,' he repeated.

I looked back at the woman. She tilted her bonnet back and grinned at me, then drew it down again. But in that second, recognition had come to me. Will was here in the courtroom. He was safe! But what a risk he was taking coming here. He was a wanted man and he had walked right into the lion's den.

The sight of Will made everything clear to me. I must tell the truth; more of it than I had intended to tell.

'I climbed out of my bedchamber window,' I said in a clear, carrying voice. I was speaking to Will. Everyone else ceased to exist for me. 'It was impossible for me to remain a moment longer with my husband.'

'Did you have any plan? Did you know where you were going to go?' the solicitor asked. He sounded jumpy, seeing I was deviating from the part he had coached me into over the past few days.

'I had no plan at all. I just walked out.'

'And you didn't steal anything?'

'I took nothing at all but the clothes I was married in,' I said. 'No one kidnapped me, I saw no one either in the house, the grounds or on the beach. There was no one involved in what I did but me.'

'What . . . what did you do next?' asked our solicitor weakly.

'I followed the path across the fields and down to the beach,' I said. 'When I reached the beach, I walked along the water's edge.'

I was aware I was lying now, and it made me uncomfortable. But if I confessed I had attempted to drown myself, I would face imprisonment.

'A very high wave caught me and swept me into the sea,' I said. I wasn't sure I sounded very convincing. There were mutters from those present.

'I was pulled out of the water,' I continued hurriedly. 'I was rescued by some fishermen.' I pointed at the skipper. 'This man was in charge of the fishing boat,' I said. 'I told them I was an orphan and they kindly let me stay on board. It wasn't their fault I didn't tell them the truth.'

The judge rapped for silence. My solicitor looked bemused, as though he no longer knew what to ask me. He made a visible effort to pull himself together: 'What possible reason could a new bride have to run away?' he asked feebly. 'She should be perfectly happy.'

My mother was crying softly. But I kept my eyes on Will as I spoke: 'I had a very good reason to leave.'

He looked at me, half eagerly. This was the truth I'd been too ashamed to tell him until now. The door I'd been keeping so tightly closed flew open. I looked straight at the images that had haunted me and found they were not so frightening now as they had been. Will was here.

'At the wedding reception,' I said, 'I left the room for a breath of fresh air. It was so crowded and I was feeling faint. I walked down a corridor and opened the door to another room. I thought I could find some quiet and hide away for a few minutes. But someone was already in there. My husband. And he was . . . ' I hesitated, suddenly remembering that others besides Will were listening. This realization almost stole my courage for a moment. I gathered it, gripped my hands tightly together and went on: ' . . . locked in an embrace with another woman. His vows to me of less than an hour before clearly meant nothing to him.'

There was shock in Will's eyes. And gasps around him. A great rustling and shuffling and the judge rapped for silence, but didn't get it.

In the commotion, someone tugged at my sleeve and told me the hearing had been adjourned. I looked across

274

at Will. He nodded to me and then got up and slipped away.

The next hour or so passed in a blur of questions and people rushing about arguing. The next thing that made any sense to me was coming face to face with my husband with only our solicitors for company. I stared at him without remorse and he scowled.

'None of what you said just now makes any difference,' he told me. 'I broke no law. No one cares what I did. You still stand accused of stealing, smuggling, and desertion.'

'So why are we here, talking?' I asked him. 'Why aren't we still in court?'

It wasn't easy to face him. Six months ago, I couldn't have done it. But I was so much braver now. I looked him over. He was dressed expensively but without taste in breeches, silk stockings, a colourful waistcoat and a coat with whaleboned skirts. He held a costly cane in one hand and a valuable snuff box in the other.

I thought how hard his men worked for him, the risks they took and the damage the smuggling inflicted on their health. The cold of the winter nights, the strain of carrying the kegs; all these things took their toll upon them. So that this man could dress expensively and yet still betray them. He disgusted me. I tried to put the thought aside and meet his eyes.

'You have to drop this,' I told him.

He looked taken aback. 'Drop it? Madam, you've made a fool of me.'

'So you would have me and the men who've risked their lives for your profit all winter hang for your pride?'

I asked him. 'There were no goods stolen from your house. That is pure fabrication to give you a reason to pursue me.'

Mr Holbrook didn't reply for a moment, he looked at me measuringly. I saw him quite differently now. Once I'd seen him as a harmless older man; quite kind even. Now I saw a man who was happy to exploit the men who worked for him; even to betray them to get his way. Who had almost certainly attempted to turn his own agent in to collect a reward. It shouldn't surprise me that he would lie to see his young bride hang. All because he couldn't keep his hands off even younger women.

My mother was wrong, I thought to myself. You *do* meet pirates at the Bath assemblies. I married one I met there in the mistaken belief he was a gentleman.

'No,' said Mr Holbrook at last. 'You *have* robbed me, you know.'

'The marriage settlement? That's true, though it was never my intention. If I engage to return that to you, will you then drop the other charges against me? And against the others?'

Mr Holbrook thought again, his wily eyes watching me closely. 'Maybe,' he said at last.

'Maybe isn't good enough,' I told him. 'I need your written promise.'

'I can drop the charges against you,' Mr Holbrook said. 'Marlow and the other smugglers are out of my hands.'

'But not beyond your influence, I think.'

He smiled smugly. 'Perhaps. But I cannot give any kind of written promise.'

'No, I can see that,' I frowned. 'But will you agree to release me?'

'From the charges I will. And from our sham of a marriage. I already have the annulment papers. I have no wish to take smuggler's leavings.'

I ignored the unjustified slur upon my virtue. His words couldn't hurt me. I wondered whether I should point out that his own considerable wealth appeared to come from smuggling, even though he didn't carry the kegs himself, but I refrained. There was no need for a petty exchange of insults. Especially when he might be doing what I wanted. Instead, I fixed upon the point that interested me most. 'The marriage can be annulled?'

'Being unconsummated.' Mr Holbrook winced. 'Yes, it can.' He flicked open his snuff box and inhaled a pinch, dusting his fingers off on a fine lace pocket-handkerchief afterwards. I recognized the handkerchief as one of a batch we'd smuggled across from France before Christmas.

'So I'd be free?' I asked him.

'You sound unnecessarily pleased, madam. Please restrain such vulgar joy in my presence. And if you dream of a bridal with young William Marlow, you can put that out of your mind for good.'

He paused, clearly enjoying the shock that I hadn't succeeded in hiding from my face. 'Oh yes, I know all about you two cooing and billing like lovebirds on board that ship,' he said harshly. 'Marlow is not my only man aboard.' My mind was darting about at once, trying to guess who else on board had been directly in Holbrook's pay. But Holbrook leaned forward, drawing my attention back to himself: 'Marlow *will* hang sooner or later,' he said softly.

I shivered at the menace in his voice and the terrible image of Will swinging at the end of a noose. I swallowed and managed to keep my voice almost steady as I replied: 'You know nothing about me or my dreams.'

My father's lawyer cleared his throat and shifted uncomfortably in his seat. I looked towards him and he rustled his papers. 'Shall we look at that annulment form?' he asked Mr Holbrook.

'Let us do so,' he responded.

The negotiations lasted some time. I was dropping with tiredness by the time my parents bustled me into a chaise and we set out for the inn they were staying in. My father was regarding me with deep reproach. I looked away.

'I hope you are pleased with yourself, Isabelle,' he said sternly. 'You have reduced your entire family to poverty on a whim. We can no longer even afford to stay in such an inn as this.' My mother began to weep, a handkerchief held to her eyes. 'You have broken your mother's heart,' my father continued. 'Your sister's prospects have been utterly ruined. All for what? We could have got you off the charge, if only you had kept to the story we prepared for you.'

I took a deep breath and pulled my cloak closer around me with hands that shook. 'I would have had to perjure myself and betray my friends,' I told him. 'They would have been punished for what I did! I would have had to remain married to a low scoundrel old enough to be my father. A man who couldn't even be faithful to me on the day of our wedding!'

'All men stray, Isabelle,' said my mother tearfully, emerging from behind her handkerchief. 'A well-bred wife does not heed such trifles.'

I looked at her in disgust. It was on the tip of my tongue to tell her who that other woman was. 'Even if all this were true,' I said instead. 'It was still possible I would have been convicted and hanged. Would you have preferred that, Papa?'

'It wouldn't have come to that. And now what shall we do? We face poverty. And you are the last person in the world to tolerate that patiently.'

'I've changed,' I told him. The chaise pulled up outside an inn and the steps were let down. I was weary through and through. But I had one more thing to say before we left the privacy of the carriage: 'You brought me up to value wealth, Papa. You and Mama were the ones who spoiled and indulged me and taught me to be heedless and extravagant. And it was you who lost our fortune through speculation. Not me. I would have made amends for you if I could. If the bargain had been bearable. You cannot blame me for this family's fallen fortune. It was your doing and yours alone.'

I stepped out of the chaise into the noise and bustle of the inn yard. Had my words been too harsh? I knew I had caused my family great anguish this winter; they loved me and had always loved me, despite my spoiled, wilful behaviour. For months they had feared I was dead or kidnapped. I loved them too, of course, with all their faults. But I had spoken nothing but the truth.

As I entered the inn, I realized I was too tired to be reasonable. Without further words, I climbed the stairs to the bedchamber that had been allotted to me and fell into an exhausted sleep.

CHAPTER TWENTY-EIGHT

✳

I was up early the next morning with many things on my mind. It was I, not my father, who received the solicitor. He brought the news that I was not required to attend court that morning after all. The case had been dropped.

'That's such a relief,' I sighed. 'And against the other men? Has the charge of theft and conspiring with me also been dropped?'

'It has.'

'And the charge of smuggling?'

'That still stands. It's a different charge and will be tried separately.'

'I see. Yes, that was unavoidable, I suppose. Thank you.'

He got up, bowed and went to the door. There he paused a moment. 'Please tell your father I shall still need him to remain in Poole for the next couple of days. There will be papers to sign, money to transfer and so on.' Then he left.

After he was gone, I paced the room restlessly. I was free. It was over. For me anyway; not for the skipper and the others. But I wasn't in a position to help them any further.

I needed to find Will. I needed the money he held for me. Besides, the questions I longed to put to him burned inside me. I needed to know the truth; the truth about who he was and what he'd done. But there was no way I could find him in a town like Poole. Especially not when he would be hidden behind a disguise and a false name. He would have to come to me.

But the morning went by and he didn't appear. Eventually, I went outside and walked up and down the street, wondering if he would come and speak to me there.

'Isabelle, what do you think you are doing out here?' demanded my father after half an hour or so. He'd come out to fetch me, looking annoyed.

'It's so stuffy in the inn,' I complained. 'I needed some fresh air.'

'Then for pity's sake go into the garden or open a window!' he exclaimed. 'Do not make a spectacle of yourself in the busy street!'

He ushered me back inside, but as soon as his back was turned, I slipped outside once more. I was rewarded almost at once, not by any sight of Will, but of Gentle Jacob who approached me with a smile. 'Jacob!' I cried joyfully.

I would have thrown my arms around him in front of everyone, but he forestalled me by tipping his cap to me. 'Best pretend you don't know me, Miss Isabelle,' he said quietly, falling into step beside me.

'You're safe then!' I said, trying to restrain my delight at seeing him. 'You made it ashore!'

'I did. Climbed up on a ledge beyond the cove and stayed hid till everyone had cleared off. Then I climbed the cliff and went home.'

'Did the cold water make you ill?' I asked.

'Not I,' said Jacob with his rumbling laugh. 'Got up the next morning and did a full day's work.'

I smiled with pleasure. 'And the money?'

Jacob lowered his voice. 'That's safe. I'm paying some law man to do what he can for our friends. That's about all I can do. I'm headin' home today. I stayed in the hope of seeing you.'

'Oh, I'm so pleased you did! And you are safe? You won't be arrested?'

Jacob's eyes twinkled. 'I wasn't there, was I?' he said.

'What about Will?' I whispered. 'I saw him. In the court.'

'He's had to go. He nearly got took.'

I clutched Jacob's arm in alarm, but he patted my hand reassuringly. 'He's safe in France by now,' he said steadily.

'Jacob,' I said hesitantly.

'Yes?'

'Did he do it?'

'The murder?' Jacob's voice was so low, I had to lean close to him to hear. I nodded.

'I truly don't know. There's been rumours of all kinds since he first come aboard. But there's not one among us knows the truth. All I can say is, it don't seem likely to me.'

'I need to know,' I said, my voice low.

'I'd be pleased to be clear about it myself,' admitted Jacob. 'But he won't say a word. And the evidence looks black against him.'

'I think there could be someone who knows him better than we do,' I told Jacob. 'Mind you, I'm far from sure. It's a very long shot.'

'Who?' Jacob looked curious.

'There was a cottage where we stopped on the way to Chapman's Pool. Will had a key. There was a child who knew him. Do you know who they might be?' The thought had been turning over in my mind for a while now. I couldn't say when it had first come to me. During my illness at some point. I felt there might be someone in that cottage who could shed light on this.

Jacob shook his head blankly. 'No idea,' he said.

'I'd like to go there. To ask them if they know anything of his past. Will you take me? It's on your way home. I'd go myself, only I'm not sure I can find it.'

'Will your parents allow that?' asked Jacob, surprised.

'I wasn't planning to ask. Any minute now, my father will come out and take me back inside. Tomorrow or the day after, we are going to a completely different part of the country. It's now or never. Can we go?'

I tucked my hand into Jacob's arm and led him down the street, away from the inn.

'Isabelle, you madcap!' he protested. 'You ain't so much as got food nor nothing! Your pa and ma'll be mad with worry.' But he didn't stop walking and I pressed on quickly.

'I know,' I told him. 'But I have this shawl for warmth, luckily. I may have to borrow a few pennies from you for food.'

Jacob stopped. 'You can do that,' he said. 'But you let them know you're safe or I'll not take you.'

In the end, we sent a boy with a message that my parents were not to fret, and I'd be safely home by the following evening. Jacob fetched his gear, all of which fitted into a small satchel that he slung over one shoulder, and we set out.

Jacob begged a ride across Poole harbour in a fishing boat, which he said would save us the best part of a day's walk across the marshes. Then we struck off across the hills, talking as we went. I described the place I'd visited with Will. Jacob thought it might be near Harman's Cross, some way inland from his own village. He also told me a few facts about the jury that would try the smugglers.

'Ten of the twelve buy their Cousin Jacky from the Gentlemen,' he told me gleefully. 'Some of 'em are our own customers. One of 'em is one of our landers. They won't find it easy to prosecute.'

The spring weather was fresh and bright and the walk took us high up onto the downs. I breathed the clear air deep into my lungs and sighed with pleasure. 'Ah, it's good to be out again!' I said.

Jacob smiled. 'Are you strong enough for this, though?' he asked. 'You've been very sick.'

'I don't have as much strength in me as before the illness,' I admitted. 'And my leg still aches. It was badly torn when we were shot out of the boat. I'll need to rest from time to time.'

I needed to rest more than I'd expected and night had fallen long before we reached Harman's Cross. Jacob headed away from the village, straight for Worth where he said Ann would get me some hot food and a bed for the night.

To tell the truth, I was grateful for it, as well as happy to see her again. She exclaimed over how thin I'd grown, and set to heating a pie for me. I ate well and slept better, and so it was mid-morning the next day before I was knocking on the door of the little cottage I'd seen Will let himself into. I'd asked Jacob to stay nearby but not to come with me, in case his large size was intimidating to the people who lived here.

'Can I help you?' asked the kindly middle-aged woman who answered the door.

I smiled at her, wondering where to begin. 'Hello. My name is Isabelle. I'm a friend of Will's,' I said.

As I feared, a shadow crossed her face at once. She tried to close the door.

'Please!' I begged, pushing at it. 'Please! I mean no harm. I just need to talk to you!'

'I know no one called Will,' cried the woman alarmed.

'Then what do you have to be afraid of?' I asked. 'I only want to help.'

She stopped trying to push the door shut. 'Please,' I said again. 'He trusted me enough to bring me here once,' I told her quietly. 'He's safely in France now, but there are some things I really need to know.'

The poor woman's brow was furrowed with doubt and suspicion, but she fell back a step and opened the door.

'You'd better come in, I suppose,' she said uncertainly.

I walked in through the door straight into a tiny kitchen. It was clean and bright, with a scrubbed table and some chairs. A fire was burning in the grate and there was a rich smell of baking.

Scattered on the table was a primer, a copybook, and a pencil. Someone had been learning; I guessed the child I'd seen last time I was here.

'What is it you want from me?' the woman asked. She had wrapped her hands in her apron and looked scared. I wondered if she could be the child's mother, but thought she looked too old.

'May I sit down?' I asked. She nodded nervously and sat herself on the edge of one seat while I took another. I was glad to take the weight off my aching leg.

'I've been with Will all winter,' I said. 'I was with him when he came here and left some things once. I saw he had a key. He spoke to a child called Beth.'

At these words, the woman glanced nervously at the stairs that led up from the back of the kitchen. I continued as though I hadn't noticed. 'I think perhaps he came at Christmas too. We were staying nearby and he disappeared for the night. I guessed he came here.'

Her eyes were fixed warily on my face. 'So why don't you ask him what you want to know yourself?'

'I was with Will on the coast a few weeks ago. They tried to arrest him for murder. He got away. We—that is two of his other friends and I—care about him very much. We wanted to know more about this accusation. It doesn't seem to fit the person we know. I thought perhaps you might know more than we do.'

'If he wanted you to know, he'd have told you. I can't go spilling his life story to strangers,' she said tearfully. I was upsetting her, I could see.

'I'm so sorry to come here like this,' I said. 'I don't mean to cause trouble. I just want to understand.'

'In love with him, are you?' she asked suddenly.

I blushed and turned my head away. 'We're just friends,' I said.

'Hmm.' The woman turned away and put a kettle onto the fire. 'Tea?' she asked unexpectedly.

'Thank you,' I faltered. I watched as she bustled about getting down cups from the dresser, a milk jug and tea from the larder and setting them onto the table. When the water boiled she poured it into the pot and sat down at the table. She looked straight at me. 'What do you want to know? I don't promise to tell you everything; and there's a lot I don't know myself.'

'First of all, who are you and how do you know Will?' I asked her, relieved that she no longer seemed afraid of me.

'I was . . . nursemaid in the household where he grew up. My name is Jane Moorland.'

'And that household was . . . ?'

She shook her head.

'Please,' I begged. 'I wondered . . . whether he was by any chance cousin or brother to . . . James Marlow?'

Her eyes widened. 'So you know that, do you?'

'I guessed. I heard his surname when they tried to arrest him. And then I remembered that he'd been startled when I told him . . . told him that I'd once been engaged to . . . ' I coughed, embarrassed. 'To James Marlow,' I admitted.

'Engaged?' Jane frowned. 'But the viscount's married.'

'That's what Will said. He was a widower when I knew him. His wife had died in childbed.'

'I live so out of the world,' said Jane, shaking her head. 'That sort of news never reaches me. But you didn't marry him?'

I shook my head. 'No. My father lost his fortune. He speculated in the South Sea venture.'

'Ah,' said Jane. 'Then he didn't want you? Well, it always was money with James.' Again she shook her head. 'Since you know so much, I might as well tell you that William is James's younger brother.'

It made sense to me. It explained the feeling I'd had once or twice that I'd seen Will somewhere before. I'd known his brother. 'I had no idea James *had* a brother,' I said, puzzled.

She shrugged. 'I've heard they never mention him now. He was very young at the time. He was still at Cambridge when all this happened four years ago. He wasn't known in what you would call *the fashionable world*.' She spoke the words rather scornfully. 'And it was all hushed up.'

'The murder? Will you tell me what happened?' I pleaded.

'I can tell you what I know. But it isn't much.'

Jane poured me a cup of tea and pushed it towards me. 'The family acquired a young ward years ago. Elizabeth Jones. She was the orphan of some poor relations who'd passed away. They took her in. She was the prettiest child, but the sort that knows it, if you know what I mean? Both the boys were of that impressionable age. Both fell madly in love with her. That worried the parents. She had no money, you see. None at all. They weren't having their precious sons marrying a penniless nobody.

'I don't rightly know what happened next. There was gossip below stairs. Of secret betrothals and the like. All I know is that she was sent away suddenly. But then four years or so later, she reappeared with a child. Knocked on the front door, she did, demanding to see the earl and his wife. Well, you can imagine the scene and I daresay you can imagine the gossip in the house among the servants.'

'I can,' I said, having overheard snatches in my own home. I tried to imagine a similar scene in my parents' house, but as I had no brothers, I failed. 'So what happened next?'

'She declared the little girl was their grand-daughter.'

'Will's child?'

'No one heard that. At first we all assumed it was James's. Many of the maids knew what he was like, you see . . . ' she broke off in confusion, blushing. 'I'm sorry, I didn't mean . . . '

'It's quite all right,' I assured her. 'I'm not really very surprised.'

I was lying. I'd always idealized James. I'd thought he was the perfect husband, of whom my father had cruelly deprived me by losing our money. Perhaps I had been mistaken. How well had I known him after all? A few balls, a couple of dinners and formal morning calls; I realized now that would have given me only a knowledge of his company manners, not of his backstairs habits. Perhaps he was every bit as vile as the man I *had* married.

'When Elizabeth was leaving,' said Jane, taking up the story again, 'she tripped on the stairs. Both she and her infant were killed by the fall. At least that was what we were told at the time.'

'My God,' I breathed, horrified. 'But it wasn't true?'

'I don't know. I don't know to this day. But a few days later, Master William fled. Just before they arrived to arrest him for murder.'

I gasped. 'He pushed them? No, surely not!'

'That's what they said. There was a witness, you see. A man who claimed to have been with Elizabeth. A relative of hers that it seems no one had known of until then. He went to the magistrates.'

I shook my head confused. 'So you left?'

'Yes. Master William asked me to come here. To look after the child.'

'I thought you said the child had died?'

'I said we were told she had. It wasn't true. Her mother died in the fall, she didn't.'

'This doesn't make any sense,' I cried, completely bewildered. 'If Will was a murderer, why did he go to trouble and expense to look after the child? And if he did, surely it must be his child, not his brother's? Why did you trust him?'

'I was unhappy in that house. Master William had always been kind to me, even when he was just a child. When he offered me a cottage and a job of raising a child, I jumped at the chance. I've never asked him what happened that day. If he did it, he's sorry for it, for he's taken good care of us ever since.'

My hands were shaking. I gripped them together on the table in front of me. 'So you think the child is his? And that he did do the murder?' I asked, dreading the reply.

'I don't know. He was so young at that time. Barely more than a schoolboy. But I've always thought he might have done it.'

I leaned my head forward on my hands and groaned. That wasn't what I'd hoped to hear. I'd come all this way, sure that if this cottage held any answers at all, it would be to clear Will's name, not to sully it. I thought about him; his fair hair caught back in a black ribband; his piercing blue eyes laughing at some joke. It couldn't be right.

'You're quite wrong, Auntie Jane,' said a small, clear voice behind me. I jumped and looked round. A little girl stood at the foot of the stairs. She was dressed simply and plainly in a grey gown and a blue pinafore. Her fair hair was neatly plaited, and she couldn't have been more than about eight years old.

'Beth!' cried Jane, flustered. 'What are you doing here listening? I sent you for a walk!'

Beth shook her head. 'I didn't go. I thought perhaps this lady was bringing a message from Will. He told me he'd send a message.'

'It's very wrong to eavesdrop,' said Jane angrily. I could tell she was upset about the things the little girl must have overheard. But I was intrigued.

'Why did you say your Auntie Jane was mistaken?' I asked her. I pushed my empty tea cup aside and leaned forward to look at her. She met my eyes with an open gaze. She had the same blue eyes and fair hair as both Will and James. It was easy to believe that she was daughter to one of them.

'Because I remember that night,' she said.

'Beth! You've never said so before!' exclaimed Jane, obviously astonished.

'I told Will.'

'And what did he say?'

'He said "You're quite right. But mum for that, little Beth", and ruffled my hair. Then he gave me a hug. And he promised he'd always take care of us.'

'Then perhaps you should keep quiet as he said,' said Jane nervously.

Beth ignored her and looked straight at me. 'It wasn't Will that pushed Mama down the stairs,' she told me. 'It was the other man. Will's brother. At least, perhaps he didn't mean to push her down the stairs. I can't quite remember that bit. It was all so loud and confusing and I was crying by then. But Mama was holding onto me with one hand and to the man with the other. She was crying and saying things to him.'

'Like what?' Jane asked.

'Grown-up matters. I was too little then to understand. I only knew she was upset and crying and that upset me. She made him angry, I think.'

'And what happened then?' I asked curiously. I was amazed by the girl's self assurance.

'He pushed her. And she fell down. Down those hard stairs. I fell on top of her, but it still hurt me a lot. I can remember. It was the worst night of my whole life.'

'And Will said that you remembered correctly, did he?' I asked her. Beth nodded.

'He did,' she said. 'And he told me not to tell anyone, but he was really my uncle. Is he coming to see me again soon?'

CHAPTER TWENTY-NINE

✳

The spring had resolved into summer and there were leaves on all the trees. I woke in the stuffiness of a warm night, feeling stifled in the tiny bedchamber under the eaves. Beside me, my sister was fast asleep. From across the landing, I could hear my father's rumbling snores. That was the worst of a cottage. You couldn't get away from each other, even in sleep. I looked at my sister slumbering, her face peaceful. We had talked a great deal in the last few weeks. I understood much about her now that I hadn't understood before.

The room was hot and stuffy and I was restless. That must have been what had woken me. I couldn't go back to sleep in this heat. In fact I couldn't even lie still. As I sat up in bed and threw back my covers, I felt something out of place among the linen bedding; something rough against my skin. I grasped it and lifted it to the moonlight. It was a short length of thin rope knotted into a clove hitch around a small stick. I stared at it in bewilderment. How had this got here?

It was such a poignant reminder of my time at sea that I felt my heart contract. I scrambled to my feet and went to the window, wondering if it had been thrown into my room that way.

Leaning out of the tiny cottage window, I could smell the roses in the garden below, their scent magnified by the cool night air. A full moon shone overhead. There was no sign of anyone, but the rope hadn't appeared from nowhere.

I threw a light wrap around my shoulders and crept quietly down the stairs, determined to see if anyone was there. I told myself there would be no one, but my heart whispered that it could be Will and wouldn't listen to my attempts to silence the seed of hope.

We had no live-in servants in this small cottage; only a maid who came to us during the day, so there was no one to see or hear me lift the latch of the kitchen door and creep out into the summer night.

The grass was cool and damp on my hot feet and the air was still. I looked around the garden, but could see no one. I sat down on our rustic bench in its arbour of honeysuckle with a sigh, wishing . . . well, I wasn't sure what I wished. If only I had heard some news, any news at all from my friends of *The Invisible*. But there hadn't been a word in the two months since I'd left the coast. We'd moved on several times, looking for somewhere pleasant and yet small and cheap enough that we could support ourselves on what little money we had left without getting into debt. I thought we were settled now, but how was anyone to trace me to send news? I clutched the knot tightly in my hand.

There was a rustle in the greenery beside me and I nearly jumped out of my skin. I squeaked and cowered on the bench.

'Shh! Isabelle, it's only me!' whispered a shadowy figure. 'I threw the knot through your window to wake you!'

I peered at the speaker, but whoever it was stood between me and the moon and all I could make out was a silhouette with wild black hair. The person sat down beside me, pulled off a wig and the moon fell full on his face.

'Will!' I cried in excitement.

At once he clapped a hand over my mouth. 'Isabelle, for heaven's sake, don't you know better than to be so loud?' he whispered in my ear.

I laughed and cried together, pulling his hand from my mouth and holding it tight. 'I thought I'd never see you again!' I said.

'I wasn't sure you'd want to,' he replied. 'I wasn't sure if I should even try and find you. Now that you know what I'm accused of.'

He looked away, his posture defensive, coiled as though ready to spring away and go if I uttered angry or hurtful words. Instead I pressed his hand which I was still holding in both of mine.

'Will, I know the truth,' I said. 'It wasn't you that killed her, was it?'

Will turned towards me and stared at me in the darkness, as though he was trying to read my expression.

'Was it an accident?' I asked tentatively. 'When your brother pushed her?'

Will gripped my hands painfully hard. 'How do you know this?'

'I went to see Jane and Beth in Harman's Cross. Don't be angry, Will! I was desperate to know the truth and you'd gone. I still don't understand it all. I just know you didn't do that dreadful deed you're accused of!'

Will released me and jumped to his feet. For a dreadful moment, I thought he was so angry that he was going to leave. But he didn't. He paced the little lawn a couple of times and then came back to me and sat in silence staring at his hands.

'I think it was an accident,' he said at last. 'I've always tried to think so. But he was so angry. You'd think he'd never loved her, to hear him speak to her as he did!'

'Maybe he didn't?' I suggested timidly.

'I thought we both did. She was only ever interested in him, of course. He was the eldest, the heir, the most dashing of us. I was too young and too shy. But what he did was unforgivable. He promised to marry her; got her with child. I never would have . . . oh God!'

Will covered his face with his hands and rocked back and forth.

'But your parents wouldn't allow the marriage?'

'No, of course they wouldn't. My father had huge gambling debts; the estates were mortgaged. It was essential that my brother made a good marriage. So she was sent away; given an allowance if she promised to stay away. I didn't know then that she was expecting a child. They must have known though.

'By the time she returned, four years later, my brother was on the eve of marrying an heiress. That's why she came back. She was furious and said it was her he should be marrying. He called her terrible names and so did my father. They fought and then . . . Oh, poor Eliza.'

'And poor Beth!' I added softly. 'Why did she wait so long? Why not ask him to marry her before?'

Will shrugged. 'I don't know. Perhaps she thought, at first, that the settlement my father made on her to stay away was generous. But perhaps later she grew greedy or bitter. Truly, I don't know, Isabelle. But you are right: Beth has suffered greatly. I don't feel I can ever sufficiently make amends to her for what my family did between them. And after . . . they were going to send Beth to the orphanage: to abandon her there in poverty and lovelessness. That's why I took her away. I couldn't bear it. I persuaded Jane to care for her; found a cottage.'

'That was well done,' I said warmly.

'It was essential. But when I returned, it was to find I was accused of murder. A witness none of us knew had gone to the magistrates and sworn he saw Elizabeth being deliberately pushed down the stairs. James stood accused, but to save him, my parents said it was me. The fact that I'd disappeared made me look doubly guilty.'

'They accused you to save him?' I asked, appalled. 'How could they do that to you?'

Will bared his teeth in a bitter smile. 'Oh, James was the heir, the eldest son. The apple of their eye. And besides he was on the brink of this wonderful marriage. The marriage that would save my father from his self-inflicted debts. Of course they sacrificed me.'

I could hear the hurt in his voice. He had felt betrayed and no wonder. 'Money,' I said bitterly. 'It ruins everything. So what did you do?'

'My father gave me five hundred pounds and organized me a safe passage to France,' said Will. 'He told me I had to save the family. I had to stay out of the country to save my brother, our family house, and name. I accepted my role, left almost all the money with Jane and I went. I found work. I've stayed away from them ever since; the first years I was in France, later I joined *The Invisible*. I knew Holbrook, you see. He was my father's steward but later inherited a property of his own. I ran into him in France. He knew my story and offered me work as his agent. I see Beth occasionally, as you know. That was the appeal of the contraband trade. It brought me to England regularly.'

I swallowed hard. 'So that's why you said, all those weeks ago, that I was not the first to sacrifice myself for my family?'

'That's right. Parents have been sacrificing themselves for their children since time began. You and I have done it the other way around, have we not?'

'Except I didn't go through with it,' I said. 'I ran away.'

'Yes. Isabelle, I thought . . . I thought that it was because of James that you'd tried to kill yourself. It made me feel so dreadful. That there was no end to the misery that my wretched family had caused to others.'

There was suppressed anguish in his voice. I laid my hand soothingly over his clenched fist. 'I'm sorry. I did try to tell you. Several times. Only there was more to my story that I was denying even to myself. I was refusing to think about it. I'd shut it all behind locked, bolted doors in my mind.'

'Hence the nightmares?'

I nodded. 'Yes, the nightmares, the sleeplessness, the horror of my husband.'

'Isabelle, it must have been such a shock. First my brother rejecting you. And then that. Your chosen husband unfaithful to you. You must despise men and marriage.'

I hesitated, looking away. I had told him so much. I needed to tell him the last bit. The part I hadn't been able to say in front of the court.

I drew a deep breath. 'I didn't love him,' I said. 'Not the least bit. I still considered myself in love with your brother. I married him purely for my family's sake. What overset me was not his faithlessness. Though that was hard to swallow on the actual wedding day. It was *who* he was with, Will.'

Will clasped my hand in his. 'Tell me,' he said.

I felt a lump in my throat and tears in my eyes. I tried to speak, but couldn't. Will waited quietly for me to master my emotions.

'It was my little sister,' I managed to say at last. Tears spilled down my cheeks, but my voice freed up and now I'd begun, the whole story came tumbling out: 'We'd often fought, Mary and I. So when I saw them, I thought . . . I thought she'd always hated me and now she was stealing my husband. And he preferred her to me. I thought they were laughing at me behind my back. He saw me. He knew I knew. But he just laughed. And then he took me away to his dark gloomy house, miles from anywhere—truly, Will, you never would have guessed from it that he was a man of such wealth! He expected me to be his wife; to go through a wedding night with him just as though nothing had happened. Will, I just *couldn't*. It was so horrific. When he left me to get undressed, I fled. But I had nowhere to go. No one to go to.'

Will lifted my hand to his lips. When my tears continued to fall, he put his arms around me and pulled me against him. I cried into his coat for a few minutes, until he released me and gave me his pocket-handkerchief. Mopping up my tears, I sniffed and found my hands were shaking.

'But she wasn't laughing at you, was she?' Will asked gently.

'Oh no. We've talked since I returned. I don't know how I could have blamed *her*. She was only thirteen. What did she know of the world? He persuaded her into that room and then threatened her. She had to do what he said and not tell, or it would be the worse for me. Poor Mary! She was trying to help me. And instead she ruined both of us.'

'Good God,' said Will. 'I've been about the world and heard and seen a great deal. But that is villainy indeed. And from a man I've been working for! My poor Isabelle.' He paused, looking at me. 'You consider yourself ruined, do you?'

'A whole winter alone aboard a ship full of smugglers?' I gave a watery laugh. 'Yes. In the eyes of the world, I'm utterly ruined. I don't care, though,' I shrugged. 'I had the time of my life. And I'm no longer married.'

'That I did hear,' said Will, his voice more cheerful. His eyes gleamed in the moonlight. 'So what do you do with yourself instead?'

'Oh, I lead the most ordinary of lives,' I said with a slight sigh. 'It's all terribly respectable, of course, though less elegant and sophisticated than formerly. I sew and I darn; I'm learning to bake. I take long walks every afternoon. And I read to improve my mind.'

Will regarded me gravely for a moment. 'Are you teasing me?' he asked.

'No, I'm quite serious.'

'How do you stand it?'

'I confess I have to make a considerable effort. It is good to be with my family, of course. But even that can be too much of a good thing some days.'

'And do you have any suitors in this thrilling new life?'

'You jest! I told you, I'm disgraced. No decent man would have me!'

Will caught his breath as though he were going to speak. He got up and paced the garden again. Then he came and stood in front of me.

'Isabelle, I took a solemn vow with myself not to say this to you,' he said. I held my breath, wondering what was coming next. It wasn't at all what I expected: 'How would you feel about a spell of privateering?'

'Privateering?' I repeated blankly.

Will nodded, sat back down beside me and grasped both my hands in his. There was mischief in his eyes now. 'The crew all got off the charges,' he said. 'As we hoped they would. We've got the money we all saved up the last two winters doing extra runs and being thrifty and we've bought our own ship. The skipper has called in some favours and got a licence to sail as a privateer for several months. We leave Weymouth in a few days.'

I felt excitement rush through me, making my fingers and toes tingle with anticipation. 'But aren't privateers . . . ?'

'Pirates? Yes. They are pirates with a government licence. It'll be dangerous. But the possible rewards are good.'

I didn't care about profits. I cared about going to sea once more, about excitement and being with my friends. And above all being with Will. 'Just give me five minutes,' I said to Will.

He laughed, but caught my wrist as I got up to run towards the house. 'Are you sure about this?' he asked. 'I didn't think I ought to ask you. I have no right to disrupt your life like this.'

'What life?' I asked mischievously. 'Will, I'm absolutely certain,' I said.

He shook his head with a rueful smile. 'You mad girl,' he said. 'I've missed you so much. Would you really trust me?'

I smiled down at him. 'It turns out I was betrothed to a murderer, married to a smuggling ringleader and spent the winter aboard a smuggling vessel. So really, it seems quite fitting for me to run away with a pirate next.'

Will laughed and pressed a package into my hand. 'I owe you this,' he said. 'It was my excuse to come and see you one last time. Don't forget to leave your parents a note.'

Some ten minutes later I was in the garden once more, dressed in a simple gown, as I no longer owned any boys' clothes; a small bag packed with a few essential items. On the kitchen table, I'd left a note and the package of money for my family. I'd counted the notes. There were two hundred pounds in it. Unable to believe my eyes, I'd taken twenty and left the rest to make them more comfortable.

Will was sitting on the garden wall, swinging his legs and waiting for me. My heart skipped a beat at the sight of him.

'Ready for another adventure?' he said as he pulled me up beside him. We both jumped down into the lane beyond the wall.

'More than ready,' I assured him. 'If you hadn't turned up soon, I'd been thinking I was going to have to run away to join a travelling fair or some such thing.'

Will laughed and pulled me close once more, his arm around my waist. My heart beat fast, but I wasn't afraid. I looked up and met his eyes. Will stroked my cheek, looking down at me. 'You have no idea what a relief it is to have told you everything. And to have heard your tale.'

'I'm glad. Me too.'

'I'm not sure I'm a man of honour, you know,' said Will. 'In fact I think I'm a dishonoured one, whether I did anything to deserve it or not. I'm on the run. I'll probably be on the run all my life. I've broken all sorts of laws in my smuggling career. Are you sure you want to throw your lot in with mine?'

'I was never more sure of anything,' I told him, my words heartfelt. I felt a rush of love for him as he stood close to me in the darkness of the lane. Will caught his breath as he stood looking down into my eyes. Then he slowly bent his head and touched his warm lips to mine.

I let go of my bag so that I could wrap my arms around him and kiss him back, tasting his sweet breath, losing myself in my smuggler's kiss. Will tightened his arms around me, holding me close against his chest, and kissed me fiercely.

When we broke apart, I was breathless and happier than I ever remembered being in my life.

'Then it's a deal,' Will said. It took me a moment to remember what we'd been talking about. I must have looked puzzled for a moment, because Will laughed joyfully and lifted me right off my feet in a bear hug.

'Let's go,' he said, releasing me at last. 'It's a long walk from Gloucester to Dorset.'

'Walk?' I cried horrified. 'You're not serious?'

Will threw back his head and laughed again. 'You're still the easiest person in the world to tease, I see.' He took my hand and started to walk. 'No we won't go all the way on foot. There's a carrier's cart going as far as Bristol with a load of lime. We can get a lift with them.'

'My, you *do* know how to treat a lady, don't you?' I said with a grin. I didn't really believe he was planning to travel all the way to Bristol in a manure cart. But then, with Will, I could never be quite sure about anything.

Marie-Louise Jensen (née Chalcraft) was born in Henley-on-Thames of an English father and a Danish mother. Her early years were plagued by teachers telling her to stop reading and stop writing stories and do long division instead. Marie-Louise studied Scandinavian and German with literature at the UEA and has lived in both Denmark and Germany. After teaching English at a German university for four years, Marie-Louise returned to England to care for her children full-time. She completed an MA in Writing for Young People at the Bath Spa University in 2005.

Her books have been shortlisted for many awards including the Waterstones Children's Book Prize and the Branford Boase Award.

Marie-Louise lives in Bath with her two sons.

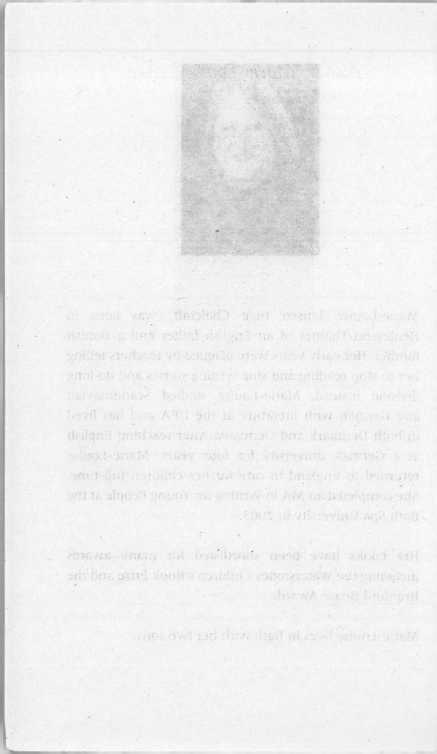

Also by Marie-Louise Jensen

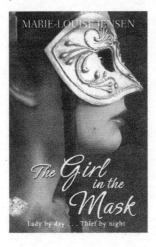

'Stand and Deliver! Hand over your valuables if you value your life!'

Sophia's duty is clear: look pretty, behave well, and find a husband as soon as possible. But Sophia hates the social whirl of balls and masquerades—so under the cover of darkness, she secretly swaps her ball gowns for breeches, and turns to highway robbery.

When one man begins to take a keen interest in her, Sophia must keep her distance—or risk him unmasking her secret life…

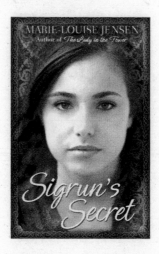

'Their garments are black as night. They carry torches in their hands, darkness and anger in their hearts. They are coming.'

When a dark family secret is exposed, Sigrun's peaceful life is shattered. Forced to pay for her parents' misdeeds, she finds herself exiled from all she knows—and from the boy she loves—for three long years.

Yet more secrets lie ahead; not least the power Sigrun finds awakening in herself, seemingly passed to her from a mysterious amulet. Can she use her new-found gift to save herself and those around her from the dangers they face? And will true love wait until her return?